Broken Nose picked Sara up and put her over his shoulder. Her hair tickled his back and he could feel the warmth of her buttocks near his face. He put her up on Mister's back and got up behind her so that she could lean against his chest as they rode on. The pain had subsided, but Sara felt weak. She rested without resistance against Broken Nose's body, but she still clutched the Bible.

She closed her eyes and felt the man's forearms close to her, railings that kept her from falling to either side as he held the reins.

"What is going to happen to me?"

CRAZY WOMAN

Kate Horsley

IVY BOOKS • NEW YORK

Ivy Books
Published by Ballantine Books
Copyright © 1992 by Kate Horsley

ISBN 0–8041–1232–0

This edition published by arrangement with La Alameda Press

Manufactured in the United States of America

First Ballantine Books Edition: April 1994

10 9 8 7 6 5 4 3 2 1

ACKNOWLEDGMENTS

Thanks to my sister Melinda Skinner and my friend Tim Cockey for their editing help; to Scott Atole and his grandfather who provided Jicarilla Apache translations; to J.B. whose support put this book in your hands; to my son Aaron who always inspires me; and to Michael Reed, typographer, editor, and overall great guy.

This book is dedicated to Alice H. Parker,
wherever she may be.

I

Out in the yard, in the light of the three-quarter moon, a beast lumbered from the barn toward the house. It stumbled, dragging one arm so that the long fingers almost touched the ground. It mumbled and grunted. It spoke to something cradled in the crook of its arm. The face of the creature's daughter, Sara Franklin, showed palely in the attic window. Sara looked down and saw the hair on the beast's head gone wild around a bald spot.

"You are not really my father," she whispered. Her long fingers rubbed the smooth, oily wood of the windowsill while she remained on her knees, staring down at the man who soon lurched out of view and into the kitchen. She heard the door open and the low thuds of his making his way to the bedroom to lie beside her mother.

Sara heard his voice, low and growling in the room beneath hers. She heard the old bed crack under his weight. She smelled his liquored breath come up through the floorboards, but she couldn't hear her mother. Sara never heard her mother's voice come up through the floorboards because sometimes the mother said nothing, or she spoke very softly.

Adele, the little sister, lay in the bed Sara was supposed to be in. Adele was asleep and breathing loudly.

1

Even in sleep she had a smirk on her face as though taunting some younger child in her dreams. The object of her torment in waking life, Timothy, slept in a little rope bed on the other side of the room, behind a thin and stained bedspread hung on a line that separated his side of the attic room from the girls' side. It was a drafty attic, full of three children's loneliness and their viciously guarded dreams. The angled roof was right at their heads, too close to let Sara, the oldest, stand to her full height. She had thoughts of busting through it and stomping off down to the cow stream where she could live an enchanted life with leaves in her hair. She stood up, bending her head against the beams. She looked down at Adele before getting into bed beside her.

Sara was going away soon. There was no avoiding that fact now, and she wasn't going to the woods to live as an enchanted being. She was going away from the beast, and maybe there would be some other kind of enchantment in another place. Maybe she'd find a man who could transform her, who could enchant her. She prayed every night that God would bring this man to her soon, and she promised many things to God in return because He was not a fool who gave things away for nothing, or to those who didn't deserve them.

Sara was the most religious of the Franklins, yet she did not rub elbows with the folks at the First Presbyterian Church. Those grey-skirted, black-suited, unpretentious folk wanted only the drama of green beans in their lives. But Sara had a drama about her that went way beyond green beans, way beyond Roanoke and the First Presbyterian Church. Some people said she was arrogant, that she put on airs the way she held her prayer book in her folded arms and walked ahead of her family into church. Others said that she was lazy and strange because her father complained often that she wandered about in the woods, daydreaming. He laughed about how he often caught her talking to herself by the stream. People sometimes stared at Sara.

Her hair, a storm of black curls, occasionally had dried bits of leaves in it. And her dark eyes, so dark people couldn't distinguish her pupils, seemed to plead with everyone they looked at. That look of hers jangled her father's nerves, though she never threw it his way. He told her, and just about anybody who'd listen, that he was going to put her in an asylum one of these days. It was a notion he repeated often. When Sara was seventeen, Mr. Franklin got drunk and tied her hands behind her back then put her in the back of the wagon. He told her he was finally going to do it. Sara had learned not to cry in front of her father; it made his eyes sparkle. But she couldn't help it then, and what was worse, she got sharp stomach pains. All her fears seemed to be coming true. And her mother just kept folding the laundry and said, softly, "Now, Joseph, the girl doesn't know you're playing with her."

Indeed, Sara did not know. She knew something more true than that, that her mother would still tell her that her father was a good man when she came to visit at the asylum.

Besides telling his daughter that she was crazy, Mr. Franklin told her that she was funny looking and that no boy would want anything to do with her. He had proof that he was right in that Sara had no suitors. The boys of Roanoke didn't like that look of Sara's, though plenty of them watched her from behind. They liked the way her skirt fell from her small waist and moved like a pendulum when she walked.

There had been a boy who met her gaze and more, but he paid a price for his spunk. The boy was Daniel, a second cousin who had come through Roanoke on the

way to college and took a few days to go hunting with
Mr. Franklin. The two men had been at the jug during
their quest for turkey and came home swaying. Daniel
found Sara in the barn pulling eggs from the nests of
the chickens who roosted there. She was eighteen at the
time, and she looked like pagan mischief. Her hair was
as wild as a briar. When Daniel came into the barn,
leaning his head to one side so his long, corn silk bangs
fell away from his eyes, Sara stood straight and gave
him her stare. It looked little-girlish and hungry at the
same time. The liquor in him told Daniel that he could
handle the danger and take advantage of the girlishness.
He walked up and grabbed her by the waist. Then he
bent down and kissed her hard on the mouth. What
scared the boy was that Sara kissed back. Though she'd
never had a boy's lips on hers before, Sara seemed to
know from strong instinct how to apply herself. She announced to herself that the passion the boy had in him
was profound stuff and had only been unlocked by her
presence. The unspoken power between them must be
God, she thought. Her lips were so warm and rich that
Daniel's blood heated up and gave him a powerful dizziness. It got into his head that the girl meant to kill
him. He broke free and careened into the house. Sara
refused to come to the table for dinner that night, complaining of sickness. She heard her father tell Daniel,
"That girl ain't right in the head." And Sara, crying so
hard she was afraid that they might hear her downstairs,
bit the pillow. "He's right, you shameful thing," she
hissed at herself. Her teeth were gritted, shut on the pillow. "There is something wrong with you, Sara Franklin, and you're going to be punished for it."

Sara went to dances where other girls let boys kiss
them, and they got husbands out of it. The music was
fine, good fiddle music. Her schoolteacher, a woman

Sara liked because she didn't seem to care much about what people thought of her—Miss McCarthy—played a good fiddle that made everyone dance until they were red in the face. When Sara listened to that music she thought of the woods; she could imagine Miss McCarthy's raucous tunes flying through the low-lying fog from one misty hill to another, making mischief all the way up into the mountains. When a boy tapped her shoulder to ask her to dance, Sara looked like she'd been woken up and seemed sad to see where she really was.

Once she said to a boy, "Let's go outside and listen to the music from the woods." The boy thought his time had come, that he was going to have the best story of all to tell—about Sara Franklin who put on airs, Sara Franklin who was small and wild-looking with a waist a farm boy could grab full around with two hands. He had an erection before they'd cleared the door of the barn.

But in the woods Sara had a quick, deadly reaction to the boy's sweaty hand. It was as much to the pleasure she got from that hand as to the boy himself that she reacted. She was going to have nothing to do with unclean passion. It felt good to have someone like her breasts to the point of having to close his eyes to keep from passing out; and it was sickeningly wonderful to feel the heat of his hand through the homespun material of her dress. But Sara had learned her lesson with Daniel and so pinned this boy's hand to the ground and smashed it with a rock. While the boy screamed in pain and examined his hand for broken bones, Sara told him that she wanted to be left alone to hear the music by herself and pray. She helped him to his feet and assured him that she would pray for him. The next Sunday she saw him sitting two pews in front of her with his hand wrapped in bandages. He married a girl one month later, a skinny girl named Rachel who didn't seem to have the strength to smash a man's hand. There were lots of marriages like that going on.

As these marriages took place, Sara pretended not to be lonely. She explained to herself that it would be the rare man who would understand the communion she was after. As she lay next to Adele, aware of the bear snoring in the room below her, Sara tried to imagine this man who would love her. And when that fantasy went as far as she was willing to take it, Sara thought about being a teacher, about being like Miss McCarthy who didn't care what people thought of her.

She wanted to share her soul. She wanted somehow to fly, like music, or like enchantment and romance. She wanted to fly, and the thought of this kind of freedom always made her breasts ache. And she tried to satisfy that ache by concurrently imagining a man's warm hands on her breasts and a clutter of schoolchildren pressed against them. She made no commitment to either image. She was restless. Sara thought that wonderful, unimagined things could happen to her in Connecticut, where she was going to a teachers college. But she was scared, too, because she knew that in Roanoke at least she could dream. Roanoke was a good place for dreaming, if you didn't show it by having leaves in your hair.

The plan about the teachers college in Connecticut came after Sara had what the women in the church called a "hysterical episode." She told the preacher that her father had done something troubling. She told him that ever since she was a child he had her take off all her clothes in front of him so he could "see how she'd growed."

"He'd sit me in his lap and put his hands on me," she

said as though discussing some point in the scriptures with the preacher. "I didn't mind so much about this. My father don't . . . I mean, doesn't pay much attention to me except for when we're alone together and he wants to look at me. But, I've been thinking, having studied the Bible like I've been doing . . . I've been thinking that there's something bad in what he's doing. So I told him that I won't be taking my clothes off in front of him anymore, because I'm a woman now. He says it's a sin for a girl not to mind her father. And I know that the Bible says that, but it says other things, too. So I thought you might tell me, reverend, what I should do?"

Sara was usually a quiet girl, and this tirade took the preacher completely off guard. He stammered and finally told Sara that she had said some shameful things. He told her that the devil had made her think about unspeakably disgusting acts. And he told Sara's mother.

Mrs. Franklin had been educated by her father, who believed in the emancipation of men and women of all races through knowledge. His was a liberal household with all kinds of free-thinking incubating in it. Mrs. Franklin loved her father, but she hated being different. So she jumped at the chance to marry a man as ordinary as Joseph Franklin, a man who clearly needed her as a steadying influence. Still, her education had taught her many things and given her a sense of art and beauty that even Mr. Franklin couldn't mess up. She found Sara to be the condensed version of all that she'd given up—the thirst for ideas and beauty, the want of answers to big questions. And Mrs. Franklin encouraged Sara's sparkle in many secret ways. She insisted that Sara go all the way through school. And then the mother pressed flowers in her girl's schoolbooks so that Sara found them there as surprises: tiny violets with dots of yellow in them; ordinary ragweed that looked special when pressed in a book; and every now and then a rose, probably taken from Widow Marrimot's garden. And Mrs. Franklin told Sara stories when they walked together to get the cows or feed the chickens. These stories always had the smell of magic on them, and Sara excelled in making up ones of her own. But perhaps, Mrs. Franklin thought, they had given the girl a taste for drama that had made Sara get hysterical, as the ladies in the church put it. This outburst of Sara's, this shameful loss of control and decorum was the worst thing that had ever happened to Mrs. Franklin since her father died—Sara telling horrible stories about things no one should ever see or even think about.

The pastor arranged for a very confidential meeting between himself, Mrs. Franklin, and the three widow ladies of the church who really ran things. They told Mrs. Franklin not to worry, that they had been reading books lately about just such attacks of hysteria in young girls. That what the girl needed was a vocation. One of them suggested that Sara be sent to the Presbyterian Teachers College in Connecticut, and the group merrily agreed that it was a wonderful idea. Perfect!

"But, I just don't know," Mrs. Franklin said, wiping her eyes. She had not wanted to cry in front of these silly widows whom she had always treated in a kind but patronizing way. But the whole ordeal was too much. Her mind had played such tricks on her that she had even considered that her daughter might have been telling some weird truth. She wept, listening to the three ladies who softly whispered, "Poor dear."

"Mr. Franklin must not hear of this, and I do not think that he will feel financially capable of sending the girl to a teachers college."

The women told her not to think of it, that the church

funds could be used; for, after all, the college was Presbyterian and did train missionaries, and hadn't they been giving money to that college anyway? One of the widows promised to look in their contribution records but was sure they had indeed sent money to the Presbyterian Teachers College at least once.

Mr. Franklin was drunk as usual when his wife softly told him about what she'd arranged. Sara pretended to be asleep but heard her father seeping up through the floorboards like a demon.

He bellowed to his wife, "You want to make me look bad. I don't know why I've been cursed with a wife and family what shows no respect. After all the work I do, breakin' my back for you and them children, you run all over the country tellin' folks I can't make enough ta take care of my own family. You're tryin' ta do me wrong, Emily, and I ain't gonna lie down and take it."

The mother said something in a low voice. Sara lay down on the floor to try to hear her mother's words.

"I break my back for you and this damned family and still you treat me like a snake," he said.

And then, "How can I go to sleep when you have made it so the whole town will think me low? You want to ruin me! You already ruined the girl with all that schoolin'. That's why she has no husband. Your damn family and their airs about education. You always did think you was better'n me, Emily, and I'd jes' like ta see how far your education'd get you without a husband ta break his back."

Sara shut her eyes and prayed. And she curled up in the bed beside Adele wondering if her mother did not want to be rid of her, too. She asked God why she had been made unfit for a normal life.

When Sara left for the teachers college, none of the boys who'd tried to feel her breasts were at the train platform to see her off. Her father stayed at the farm, waiting for the farrier to come and reshoe the work horse. Adele was there, though, twisting her upper torso, swaying back and forth in a kind of teasing impatience. She was impatient for Sara to be gone so she could have her mother all to herself. Timothy was silent. He'd always been quiet, except for making funny noises that came out of his fantasies about soldiers and wicked magicians. He talked just enough to answer questions and to show that he was *not* an imbecile. He loved Sara because she didn't ask him many questions and because she taught him how to read and was the only one whom he didn't have to keep reassuring that he wasn't stupid. He held on to Sara's hand because he was afraid of her going and didn't know why. He was almost as silent in his own head as he was outside of it, so he didn't even tell himself why he was scared of his father's not having Sara around anymore to take up his attention. Sara bent down and said to him, "See that man over there? Doesn't he look like a goat?" The boy put out his hand pretending to offer the man a clump of grass. Mrs. Franklin looked down and smiled at him, though she didn't know what he was doing. Adele had spied two boys her own age throwing rocks at the track; she was swishing her skirts around to get their attention.

The train station was an exciting place. There were people dressed in Sunday clothes waiting to be taken to places they'd never seen. The air smelled like engine grease and men's sweat. All the noises were impatient and big—the sound of the steam coming out of the train and of the porter telling people to get on board. Most people were smiling, seemed to be unable to keep from smiling, but Sara felt sick. She wanted to hold on to her mother and not let go. She wanted to plead to stay home. She didn't know about the world. She'd dreamed worldly dreams, about going away from Roanoke, even about becoming a teacher or a missionary. She'd always imagined herself in some grand religious adventure; but, now that the adventure was as present as the worn boards of the train platform, she was not so sure anymore. Perhaps she'd been foolish and arrogant to imagine herself capable of adventure. There might be bad things; and now she'd be alone. She had always relied on her mother to keep her safe. And if horrible things happened anyway, even with her mother there, what would happen without her?

Sara looked down at Timothy who was making popping sounds with his lower lip and watching his own foot draw an invisible line on the boards. She didn't want him to see how scared she was. Her stomach hurt and she was afraid that she was going to have diarrhea in front of all the smiling people. There were big circles of sweat under her arms on the grey linen of her Sunday dress; she kept the shawl around her shoulders so no one could see the stains. She was trying to look like a casual young woman of nineteen who was about to do something normal and worthwhile. But her heart beating, the sweating, and the pain in her stomach made her feel horrifyingly abnormal and unable to do what other people could do easily. Why was there such a huge difference between who she was in her own head and who she was in the world with other people? Adele kept whining about getting some candy and Timothy was starting to hum—as though trying to drown out the enormous panic overcoming their sister.

"You look hot," her mother said. "Why don't you take the shawl off?"

Sara snapped, "I don't want to take it off."

She looked away to find the man who looked like a

goat and pick out some detail about him to share with Timothy, but everyone else had boarded the train.

"Well, it's time for you to get on board, dear. Sit next to someone nice." Mrs. Franklin pushed her gloves down between her fingers and added cheerfully, "What fun you'll have."

Sara didn't move or say anything, so Mrs. Franklin hugged her daughter hastily and then gently pushed her away.

"We'll miss you," the mother said, looking down at Timothy.

"Mother," Sara said, starting to weep, "I don't want to go. Please let me go home."

"Don't be silly," Mrs. Franklin said, beginning to look a little pale herself. "Go on and get on the train. It'll be fine. Go on now, or it'll leave without you."

"I feel ill," Sara said.

And now Mrs. Franklin's smile sank and she almost hissed, "Get on the train, Sara. You'll feel fine once you've sat down. Now don't be so silly."

Once Sara was on the train, tears came into Mrs. Franklin's eyes. Although Adele yanked on her skirts and Timothy was singing to himself, Mrs. Franklin stayed on the platform. She wanted to give courage and the ability to take some joy out of life. She wanted somehow to tell Sara that this was her chance, that she would miss her, but this was her chance. Maybe now things would change for everyone and everything would be fine and people would stop being so difficult.

Inside the train Sara, numb and aching, saw her mother waving to her, her eyes full of tears. Now her mother was standing on the platform, paying no attention to Adele and Timothy, as though she were the one who wanted to hold on to Sara and not let her go. Sara stopped crying because she realized that her mother loved her and that it was no use trying to go back home. A spell had been put on the world, as mysterious as her mother's strange affection that could not be seen except through train windows.

II

In the train window Sara could see both herself and the passing landscape. As it got darker outside, her solemn face became clearer and the night became a black river rushing behind it. Sara saw her eyes whisked away from everything familiar.

A woman sat down beside her. Sara didn't stop staring at her own reflection though her new companion tried to make conversation. She was an old lady who kept patting the silver ringlets around her crepe paper face. This woman smelled heavily of rose water which reminded Sara of roses pressed between the pages of her school reader. The crinkled old lady said something about the train, about where she was going and about her niece who'd just given birth and needed assistance. Sara nodded, only moving her eyes as far as her own lap before she looked again at the window. The woman fell off to sleep good-naturedly without taking offense at Sara's taciturn behavior.

The train got to the station in Barnsfield after midnight. Sara could see no one waiting for her. She asked the ticket seller, whose breath smelled like whiskey, "How do I get to the teachers college?" He licked his thin lips as though oiling them up before he spoke and then just pointed.

Sara picked up her bag and went off in the direction

14

he pointed, toward a group of grey buildings that looked like a jail or convent. She rang a bell at the door of the office and conjured up a large, middle-aged woman who seemed not to have been asleep. The woman was in good humor.

"My, it's so late," she said patting Sara on the back. "Come in, come in. My, that train gets later and later."

"I'm Sara Franklin."

"Good, good, yes. Please excuse my attire. I was in bed reading scripture."

She shut the door and Sara stood in the middle of a big, old front hall that had double doors on either side of it and a massive stairway at its far end.

"You're here early," the woman said. "Most of the girls don't come for a day or two. But your room's ready and you'll have it all to yourself for a while."

The hall had a large dark red rug on the floor and several gold-framed portraits of ministers on the walls. There was a grandfather clock that ticked richly and gave Sara the feeling of time itself being old and weary.

"I am very tired," Sara said, "and yet I don't know that I can sleep."

"Is this your first time away from home?" the woman asked her.

"Yes," Sara answered, and she felt weepy again.

"Well, you'll do fine here. The girls are good Christian souls and there'll be enough of God's work to do to keep your mind occupied."

Sara yawned.

"Oh, my," the woman said. "Let me get the keys and let you into your room. Sara Franklin is it?" She got a big ring of keys and led Sara upstairs, holding a kerosene lamp to light their way. The stairs were wide on the first floor and creaked deeply. The lamp called out giant shadows from the furniture and bannister. Then the stairway narrowed and the woman led Sara to the third floor. Her shadow stretched back behind Sara and up the wall as she looked at the numbers on the doors and then stopped before one that was marked in black paint, "38." The door wasn't locked, and the woman made some noises about fetching the keys for nothing. When she opened the door Sara had the impression that the room was embarrassed. It seemed to have been caught naked and shabby. It was small, with two iron cots in it, a dresser and a desk. It smelled like dry, dusty wood.

"The sheets are on the end of the bed there. You'll get your choice of beds, you being here first." The woman stayed in the room as Sara put down her bag and began to make up the bed.

"It's awfully quiet," Sara remarked.

"Well, there's hardly anyone here, and it's the middle of the night. If you open the window there you'll get a breeze. At this time of night you can hear the river."

Before she left, the woman remembered to introduce herself, "I'm Miss Tyler, and you're to come to me if there's any problem. I see to it the rules are kept, no talking after ten o'clock, no food or bad language. There's a list of rules just inside the closet door."

Sara wanted to take her by the arm and ask if she could stay downstairs with her, where she slept and read scripture. It was so far away up in that little room on the third floor.

"Get a good night's sleep, and remember that there'll be other girls coming along tomorrow to keep you company. If you need a light there's a candle and some matches in the top drawer of the dresser."

The woman left and Sara sat on the end of the bed in the dark thinking of what she would write in a letter to her mother. She would tell Timothy about the river and tell her mother what a nice woman Miss Tyler was.

The other girls did arrive, a variety of shy and religiously fervent young ladies from middle- and upper-class families. Sara's roommate was a pale, thin girl from upstate New York named Helen. She was quiet and excessively fond of sentimental things. She kept many mementos of her family, including a picture of her mother and father that she put under her pillow. Helen hung up a sampler of the Lord's Prayer that her mother had cross-stitched for her. She liked to take Sara's arm when they went to breakfast in the barely lit hours of the morning. Sara would have found in her a good friend except for the fact that Helen had no genuine interest in intellectual matters, and it was Sara's intention to immerse herself in nothing but intellectual matters. Even her relationship to God was to be unemotional and disciplined.

The school was a morality play to Sara, whose real life back in Roanoke had too many untidy complexities. The other young ladies at the college put on public personalities based on simple truths. A woman should be ladylike, a Christian should be morally certain, and a student should work hard. The private side of these hard-working, moral ladies appealed less to Sara. They gathered in their rooms to gossip and giggle. They complained about the rules and talked about men. Sara didn't want to waste time on these pedestrian matters. Sara believed she had no time for anything less than intellectual obsession and profound dreams. She had determined that her overwhelming emotions concerning her departure at the Roanoke train station were the painful result of too much indulgence in childish feelings.

As a result of this conviction, Sara was thought to be, by everyone but Miss Tyler and Helen, a cold fish, and an oddly intense one at that. The other students remarked that her appearance was outstanding and perhaps too exotic for a Presbyterian, especially her eyes that still gave off the hint of a power that controlled the soul behind them. Despite Sara's primness, there was a sensuality about her that almost gave off an odor when she passed. This disturbed the ladies of the Presbyterian Teachers College who predicted that Sara would either collapse of some nervous disorder or be seduced by another, less dignified sect, such as the Methodists.

As a matter of fact, Reverend Willoughby, one of the more intimidating teachers at the college, found Sara quite disturbing. The first thing that Reverend Willoughby noticed about her was her hair. It disturbed him deeply. Sara sat in the third row during his lecture series, "The Tribulations of the Christian Soldier." Her storm of curls brought to his mind the swirling black cloud that God visited upon Sodom and Gomorrah before pulverizing those sinful towns. He didn't dare dwell upon the dark eyes and plump lips. Better to fast and strike himself with his own belt than let Satan crawl into him through Sara's eyes.

As for Sara, she gazed fixedly at the reverend's hands. They were large with long fingers and light angelic hair on them. They slipped powerfully over the edge of the lectern as Reverend Willoughby made his points on the temptations a missionary faced in the field. And when he grabbed the air with one of those hands, as though to take the world by the collar and shake Christ's morality into it, Sara held her own throat.

At night when Sara made Helen think that she was asleep, she thought about Reverend Willoughby. She imagined him gazing into her eyes while his hands held her upper arms. She imagined him quoting a passage from the Bible and then slowly kissing her lips. She imagined him taking her to his bed. Then she turned roughly in her sheets and started her fantasy from the beginning. During the days, Sara anticipated the reverend around every corner. And she stared at him during his lectures until he was forced to look back, and one side of his mouth twitched upward.

As the course progressed, the reverend and Sara developed into two celestial objects circling each other from a distance, pulled ever toward and away from one another by an invisible force. This geometry was not lost on Sara's classmates who tittered about it when Sara was not with them at meals.

Once Reverend Willoughby appeared from around a corner. He was coming down the steps of the main building as Sara and Helen came around on the path that led to the river. Sara leaned against Helen slightly as the reverend nodded and stopped to chat. He clasped his hands behind his back.

"Well, Miss Franklin," he said, making no effort to acknowledge Helen, "you've been to the river?"

"Yes, Reverend Willoughby," Sara said, standing away from Helen now to distance herself from frivolity. "I gather much strength from nature."

"Yes, it's a fine day. But one must be careful of nature's weakness." He looked up at the blue sky.

Sara dared to speak.

"Sometimes God's presence is as sweet as a sparrow and sometimes as terrible as a raging river. I've seen cows during birth; and, though the birthing is horrible, the new calf seems such a miracle."

Both Helen and Reverend Willoughby looked at Sara with some curiosity and disgust. But Sara smiled knowingly and looked down at her feet in humility.

"Yes," the reverend said absent-mindedly. "You are a good student, Sara. Keep working hard and don't let your mind wander. Perhaps I could give you some books that would keep you from unsafe thoughts."

"Oh, yes, books," Sara said breathlessly.

After class the next day Reverend Willoughby said, "And oh, Miss Franklin, I have some books for you."

The other ladies made faces at one another and left the two alone in the lecture hall. Sara and the reverend stood close together as the man's large hand slid over the pages of some theological tome.

As a patronizing gesture and in order to keep himself from publicly chastising Miss Franklin, Reverend Willoughby presented Sara with a silver hair clasp one day after church. He remarked sternly that she was to bind her hair up so that she did not give the impression of being subject to nature's passions. A smattering of tiny sweat beads bloomed on his upper lip as he spoke to Sara.

Reverend Willoughby announced to the class one day that he would no longer be teaching at the Presbyterian Teachers College, but was about to embark on a mission. Following the footsteps of his mentor, Reverend Barkstone of the First Presbyterian Church of New Haven, Reverend Willoughby was going into the wilderness to administer to the souls of the remote territory of New Mexico. Many coyly lashed eyes turned to Sara.

After the lecture, Reverend Willoughby asked to escort Sara to the dining hall by way of the little walkway that went to the river. Sara could barely see for her excitement.

It was a warm day, and there was a little breeze that caused some of Sara's hair to climb around her face. Reverend Willoughby stood with his hands clasped behind his back and his face toward the river. Sara kept pulling the hair away from her face and made a few comments about the season. It was late March; spring had warmed early. There were already crocuses blooming in the yard outside the main office of the school— and Narcissus's flower, the flower of self-love and its cruel but beautiful consequences.

"Miss Tyler does such a wonderful job of keeping things nice," Sara said. She immediately felt that the statement was way below her capacity for insight, but she could not think above the beating of her heart.

"You have been a good student, Miss Franklin," Reverend Willoughby said. "There is a spirit in you that would suit the field. Some girls seem too weak in constitution to take on a task such as the missionary life."

Sara lifted her head and looked, as he did, toward the river. She was not really seeing it. She was seeing a ripping away of the drop cloth that covered her magnificent potential. She glimpsed the fine fabric of her soul finally being admired, being felt between the expert fingers of a man of God.

The reverend was speaking about his mentor, Reverend Barkstone, and about New Mexico.

"There is no civilization to speak of in the territories, and there are Indians and Catholics to be dealt with."

"I am sure you will be a great benefit to their lives, Reverend Willoughby," Sara said.

"I would like you to accompany me on this mission, Miss Franklin," he said and his big forehead turned red. He had the fair coloring of the Danes, reddish blond hair that was retreating from his head exposing pale freckles and easily sunburned skin.

Sara pretended to be confused. "Do you mean to take a group of ladies from the college?" Finally, she looked into his face, for she wanted to be sure she understood him clearly.

"No, you are the only one I am asking. And I thought it best that we become husband and wife. In that way we could work closely together. It is common for the wife of a missionary to act as his assistant. But I must ask you to be sure that you are up to such a task."

Sara bloomed inside. All at once she saw her mother's beaming approval, her father's chagrin, and the reverend's wonderful hands all over her body. She blushed.

"I will write to your father as it is proper to do," Reverend Willoughby said.

Sara giggled, not caring that she had disdained others who did that. She giggled to think of her father receiving a letter from a man so far above him in deportment and articulation. And then the reverend indicated with a small twist of his upper body that it was time to walk back to the school. Sara waited for him to kiss her, to take advantage of their engagement and come closer. But instead Reverend Willoughby turned toward the college and waited for her to fall in line beside him. He kept his hands clasped behind his back and talked about the excellence and virtue of Reverend Barkstone, who would graciously see that they were well taken care of and occupied once they arrived in New Mexico.

Sara was so joyous that night that she ate everything on her plate and could not have told anyone if it had been chicken or fish that she had eaten. She said more to Helen that night than she'd said all year. She would have talked to the gardener, anyone, but Helen was thrilled to be made confidante by the roommate she had always adored.

"Oh, he is so good. I cannot believe that he wants to marry me," Sara said, almost squealing. "What will Mother think! Oh, she will be so happy. And Father—he will feel oh so fortunate and approving. Oh, I cannot believe that Reverend Willoughby . . . Helen, he is so kind and strong and gentle, he would not even kiss me for fear I would be degraded or frightened. Can you imagine? He is so considerate. He has a strong will, Helen, and his fondness for me is of the highest form. And his hands. . . ."

The letter that Reverend Willoughby sent to Sara's father politely requested Mr. Franklin's approval of the union and frankly outlined Reverend Willoughby's intention of taking his new wife to the wilderness of New Mexico. There, he explained, Reverend Barkstone had begun work in civilizing the savages and papists. He also explained that the wedding must take place before the school year was over seeing as how they had to embark on the journey westward by the end of April at the latest. His plans were to marry Sara on the fifth of April, leave for a brief visit to Roanoke that same evening and then begin the westward trek after Sara had had a few days to visit with her mother.

Mr. Franklin replied:

dear reverend willoughby

i do not foresee any better use of sara than as a ministers wife she has no tolerance for farm work nor sewin much i do not figure why you would want to go to mexico when theres plenty of heathens right here in virginia

joseph franklin

At the wedding Helen cried. Seven of Sara's classmates and Miss Tyler attended. In their severe, dark dresses the women looked like a line of tarnished bells set down upon a table, unrung. Sara wore her finest black dress with the daring addition of imitation black pearl buttons. Her mother sent her a silver brooch to wear since Mr. Franklin had insisted that he and "the missus" not travel all the way to Connecticut. It would have been impractical to spend the money and disrupt

the farm's routine merely for a twenty-minute ceremony.

Reverend Willoughby had wanted the wedding held
in Connecticut so that an old teacher of his, Reverend
Coughlin, could perform the ceremony. Besides, after
reading Mr. Franklin's letter he intended to regard his
wife as an orphan. Reverend Coughlin had very bad lar-
ynx deterioration due to old age and a lifetime's over-
use of scriptural proclamation. The vows he led the
couple in were barely audible. After Reverend Coughlin
wheezed that they were man and wife, Reverend and
Mrs. Willoughby kissed for the first time. Sara's lips
lingered in the air alone after a chaste peck. Helen then
threw her arms around the bride, weeping violently. The
force of her affection jerked Sara's head so that her hair
clasp snapped open and let forth a froth of black curls.
Reverend Willoughby instructed his wife to collect her
tresses in another room while the rest of the assembly
went on to enjoy the tea and cake so kindly provided by
the Presbyterian Teachers College. His tone seemed
cold to Sara, and so she spent the moments she had
alone weeping. As she gathered up her hair she wept
like someone vomiting, unable to stop bringing up what
was in her gut. She became aware of how much it
pained her that her mother was not there at her moment
of glory to speak to her in those familiar, encouraging
tones. As her shaking hands snapped the clasp shut, she
spoke aloud to herself as her mother might have: "You
are now the wife of a man of the cloth. You must behave so that you will deserve the respect that you will
receive."

The motherly reminder could not obscure the lus-
cious implications of the word *wife*—the intimate
warmth to come that was now sanctified by church and
state.

Reverend and Mrs. Willoughby spent their wedding night in a small inn off the southern highway. The room was dusty but grander than any other Sara had been in. Reverend Willoughby lit the candle on the bedstand, throwing into sudden light a fine maple bed laden with comforters. Husband and wife stood statuelike for several seconds until the reverend went behind the screen to prepare himself for bed. He emerged transformed into a rather large version of an elf in winter. He had woolen long johns on and a woolen shirt that came to his weakening knees. The cap on his head had a point on it which drooped down beside his absurdly serious face. Upon seeing her husband so transformed Sara let a little laugh pop from her mouth. But the reverend's disdainful glare quickly settled the night's mood into something less mirthful. Sara slunk behind the screen to take her turn at preparing for bed.

The reverend was lying on the bed like a plank when Sara came forth in her long gown. Devoid of high collar, full skirt and hair clasp, she caused the man to squeeze his eyes shut and fiercely pinch the skin between his eyes. A moan vibrated his Adam's apple. As beautiful and soft as an angel, Sara sank into the bed and lay as stiffly as her brand-new husband. The reverend blew out the light. The last thing Sara saw was his large hand held behind the flame. In the stifling darkness they heard the floor creak in another room. Sara breathed deeply, unable to bear the unconsummated proximity of her husband. She turned and lay her head on the reverend's shoulder. He allowed his fingers to get tangled in her hair and held Sara close to him. He mumbled something about the devil in Sara's ear. Then he bounced off the mattress and onto his wife.

"You must be punished for this," he told her breathlessly.

He mashed himself down onto her, pressing something hard and unfamiliar against her belly. She wondered what he had brought into bed with him.

"You must be punished for this," he said more hoarsely.

Sara dared not speak. She did not know what she was supposed to do, but having seen animals mate she was almost certain that she would have to take off her bloomers before any serious copulation could occur. Struggling against the reverend's sweating, becapped frame, Sara tried to raise her gown and push down the bloomers. But her movement sent the reverend over the edge. Calling out loudly, "You must be punished for this," he let go his sperm all over Sara's clothing.

The cold liquid seeped through to Sara's skin while Reverend Willoughby fell from her to his own side of the bed. This made it possible for Sara to remove her bloomers. She surreptitiously dropped them on the floor and lay on her back eagerly awaiting her husband's second assault. But Reverend Willoughby, not being a snorer, had quietly gone off to sleep, or was at least pretending to be asleep. Sara dared to reach out for his most appealing hand and got no response. She sat up, peered hard at his face until she could see through the dimness that his eyes were shut tight. Bewildered, she lay back and managed to squeeze a few hours of sleep out of the rest of the night.

They chatted congenially the next morning, the reverend instructing Sara on a number of things, including how to pack her bag. Once upon the road in their wagon, Sara thought more clearly about the previous night's adventure. She finally reasoned that the initial awkwardness would drop away, leaving room for the pleasures she knew could be wrested from her husband's marvelous hands. She linked her arm through his and lovingly watched the reverend steer the horses. It was to her as though he could hitch lions to a coach and drive them to the moon.

That night, at an inn in northern Virginia, Sara stepped from behind the dressing screen to find her hero on his knees beside the bed. He was praying and indicated to Sara with a movement of his head that she, too, was to go down on her knees. She did, placing her elbows on the mattress and folding her hands reverently in front of her tightly closed eyes.

Reverend Willoughby then spoke to the Lord on behalf of himself and his wife. "Our father," he began, "we are embarking upon a holy mission and pray that you help us find the strength to be worthy Christian soldiers. Help us hold off Satan who tempts us to stray from our path. We know we must give our heart and soul and body to your work, oh Lord, and ask that you help us remain chaste. Help us to resist the sin which caused Adam and Eve to be cast out of Paradise. . . ."

At this point, Sara's eyes popped open, for she realized exactly what her husband was requesting God to do. A little whine escaped her throat, and her husband stopped and glared at her.

"What are you saying, dear?" she whispered as though making sure that God couldn't hear the interruption.

The reverend did not answer her directly, but addressed the Lord, saying, "And Holy Father, help us to remember that our children are the wretches of the world who are not yet in the fold of our saviour Jesus Christ. We must put aside our own selfish, sinful whims and give ourselves to the saving of those souls who have not yet tasted the fruits of the resurrection."

Sara was lost in some frantic thinking when the reverend repeated "Amen" loud enough for her to pick up the cue.

"Amen," she said meekly.

Reverend Willoughby rose up, got into bed with his back turned toward Sara, and pretended to go to sleep. Sara remained on her knees, at first with no particular purpose, but then she found her own prayer.

"Oh, God," she mouthed silently, "I am a wretched beast, Satan's servant." She did not know where to go from there, so she wept a little and then crawled into bed beside the reverend.

"Sara," the reverend said as clear as day, "ours will truly be a holy marriage, dedicated to God's work."

"I fear I am a terrible person and you should not have married me," Sara said pitifully.

"You will grow wiser," her husband assured her. "And I will be your tutor. When we are in Santa Fe the most honorable Reverend Barkstone will guide us in our work. There was never a more Christian man, Sara. He will keep our minds and bodies filled with the Lord's work. He took me under his wing when I was young and ignorant as you are now. You will have two of God's staunchest soldiers to support and teach you."

"You are a good man, Reverend Willoughby," Sara said, "the finest man I have ever known. I just hope that I can be a deserving companion."

The reverend patted her hand and then turned more decidedly from her and into sleep. Sara curled herself around the pillow and said the Lord's Prayer over and over until she fell asleep.

III

Mr. Franklin saw two Reverend Willoughbys sitting at the table. He forced them to draw together to form the one solid flesh so he could address the man eye to eye. Mr. Franklin's chores had taken him to the still that afternoon where he celebrated a brief escape from Reverend Willoughby's stern and arrogant silences. Mrs. Franklin smelled her husband's mood before he was in the door, but preferring to hope for the best rather than force it to happen, she just pressed her thumbs into the lump of dough before her and resumed an expression of stubborn obliviousness.

"Studyin' the good book, reveren'?" Mr. Franklin asked loudly, standing behind and over his son-in-law.

"There is always time for God's word," the reverend answered without turning around to meet his host's wavering but forceful gaze.

"God works in mysterious ways," Mr. Franklin said leaning close enough to the reverend so that his breath was stronger than God's word. Reverend Willoughby looked up, incredulous that human stench could be so toxic. A cardinal soared in and out of sight in the doorway behind Mr. Franklin. It was a brilliant red male whose flamboyance irritated the reverend more than foul breath. He returned his attention to the gospel according to John.

Mr. Franklin sneered and then went into the back bedroom. He fell upon the mattress and mumbled, "Yessir, God works in mysterious ways."

Sara came in with a basket of eggs. The reverend did not look up at her, but pinched the skin between his eyes as had become his habit whenever his wife first came into view. Mr. Franklin's snores resonated in the next room. Mother and daughter exchanged a glance that said many years' worth of shared observation and warning.

"Go tell Timothy and Adele to wash up for supper," Mrs. Franklin said to her eldest. She had been awkward around her daughter since she had come home as a married woman, married to a clergyman. She had thought it best to be more distant than usual to let the marriage set without being disturbed, like bread that needed to be left alone to rise.

Sara put the eggs down and said to her husband, "Would you like to come with me, dear? We could stroll down by the stream."

"I am preparing for Sunday's sermon, Sara," he said with a show of patience despite the frivolity which assaulted him constantly.

Mother and daughter exchanged another glance. This time the mother quickly looked away, for she saw that old pleading in her daughter's eyes.

Timothy was lying in one of the empty cow stalls, asleep. Adele was in the loft with two old dolls pretending to teach them spelling. She was a childish sixteen-year-old girl who still preferred dolls who could be controlled to real life which could not.

"Have you fed the chickens, Adele?" Sara called up, causing Timothy to waken suddenly.

"Yes," Adele answered curtly. One of the dolls leapt off the loft and fell onto a pile of hay.

Timothy's hand slipped into Sara's. His curls held on to bits of straw.

"Father has been at the still," Sara said.

Adele came down the ladder slowly and then sauntered out of the barn leaving her two students behind to stare at the beams in the barn's ceiling.

At dinner the family ate succotash and roast pork. Mr. Franklin broke the silence to ask Reverend Willoughby what he intended to speak about on Sunday. His son-in-law answered, "Strength of character in Christians, sir." And that was the only thing that was said until Sara told her mother to stay seated while she and Adele cleaned the table.

Reverend Willoughby had been honored by the First Presbyterian Church of Roanoke by being asked to deliver the sermon that Sunday. A visiting preacher, no less than the man who had delivered Sara from "old maidenhood," was someone to be respected. It is good, several of the Ladies Auxiliary maintained, to have an outsider shake up the congregation every now and then. Oh, it wasn't that Reverend Thomas with his shoe-polished hair was not satisfactory. Oh, no, they assured him, clucking their tongues. It was just that, well, it would be a Christian thing to do to show the Willoughbys that they were welcomed and respected for the work which they intended to do.

The congregation, which usually settled down for an inconspicuous snooze during Reverend Thomas's gentle sermons, sat straight up in their pews when Reverend Willoughby strode up to the pulpit. They had just finished singing "A Mighty Fortress Is Our God," and Reverend Willoughby seemed to prove it. Right away they knew that he was not going to let them off as easily as Reverend Thomas did. He looked well stoked with faith and conviction. He seemed to heat up the

church which still had some of March's chill in it
though April was twelve days old.

Sara watched her husband's lips part slightly. She
knew the mannerism and knew he would wait before
speaking, as though he was modifying his words so that
mortals could understand them. Sara knew that he
would place his large hands on the front edge of the
pulpit and lean forward.

Reverend Willoughby's hands grasped the front edge
of the pulpit. Sara looked down at her lap. The shuffling
and coughing of the congregation ceased. Not even a
three-year-old spoke. Then Reverend Willoughby
started, his voice crashing down on the congregation
and filling the church.

"Friends," he began, "today's scripture was about a
man who had much to complain on, a man whose life
was torn asunder by God in order that his faith be
tested."

Reverend Willoughby went on to wonder how many
Presbyterians from Roanoke could keep the faith as Job
had. He wondered if any man in that church could still
worship the lord after his farm failed, his wife and children died, and his plow horse came down with hoof-
and-mouth disease. And when he was able to smell the
shame smoldering in their bosoms, Reverend Willoughby came down upon the simple folk of the First Presbyterian Church of Roanoke like a hawk on a hare.

"How can you hope to have the strength of Job when
you have not the strength to bear up under the smallest
tribulation? Do you not curse God when your plow
sticks against a rock? Do you not use His name in vain
when a wheel falls from your wagon? And you commit
the sins of the flesh, rebelling against God's authority.
God does not want the weak in spirit."

At this point, half the congregation shifted simultaneously in their seats. Sara's palms sweated inside her gloves.

Reverend Willoughby's right hand formed into a fist and lay on the edge of the pulpit. His eyes swept menacingly over the congregation throwing each creature it passed over into shadow. His gaze stopped when it got to Sara. She looked up.

"There is no room for the weak in God's army," he declared.

Sara did not loosen her fix upon the reverend's eyes. Something fierce compelled her to meet his stare as though it was a force to be overcome. Her eyes narrowed. The congregation shifted. Reverend Willoughby leaned forward. He clenched his fist more tightly. Sara's hands curled into fists. Her breath came faster. Neither she nor the reverend would look away. Finally, Reverend Willoughby jerked his head back as though dislodging it from a narrow hole and exclaimed, "Hymn 245."

The congregation sprang to its feet. The organist slapped his hands upon the first chord. Sara held a trembling hand against her throat and slowly rose to join in singing "Onward Christian Soldiers."

IV

⁄⁄⁄⁄

Light clouds striped the blue sky like the trains of many brides. The wagons plodded onward in a long line. The Willoughbys' wagon was last. Reverend Willoughby guided the two horses, a black mare named Mrs. and a brown gelding named Mister. Sara's head kept falling against her husband's shoulder. She had not slept well in Independence. It was a raucous town full of the restlessness of transients and those who took advantage of transients. Independence, Missouri, was the last stop before the frontier, the place where wagon trains assembled and stores sold provisions at high prices that people had no choice but to pay. It was where wheelwrights and horse traders made a good living. Some men spent all night talking to each other in the saloons, feeding each other stories about what riches and freedom they'd find out west. Meanwhile, wives wept in boardinghouse rooms or lay awake in the backs of wagons among goods for the trek. Some men got drunk and met prostitutes in the little sheds set up in the alley behind the saloons. Some were too excited to sleep, others were too cautious. People who'd sold everything they'd owned to go west got their money stolen or tricked away from them in Independence. There were gamblers there who made a man think he could beat them and then took him down to his wife's jewelry.

Some of these men, the ones who lost everything, ended up being citizens of Missouri and never getting any farther west. No one slept well in Independence.

And if anyone was to get cold feet about the whole adventure, he had his last chance to back out in Independence. During the two nights that Sara and the reverend were there, two women, black domestic slaves, snuck off in the night from the wagons of a Colonel Carter Bradford and his family who were on their way to Fort Union. But the Bradfords soon found replacements, for there were women in Independence ready to hire on as servants for the free ride out west or to get away from some trouble they were in with the law or just to find some means of living without resorting to the prostitution cribs in the back alleys. In Independence, wives, some seven months pregnant, begged their husbands for the last time to give up the notion to go to the wilderness. But no one listened to those wives.

No matter how scared or tired or sick or remorseful one was, the wagon train didn't wait. Once on it, one had to see the adventure through. Sara stayed quiet. Reverend Willoughby had warned her that all kinds of rabble traveled on wagon trains and that one should stay aloof. He thought he'd given himself and his wife some protection from the rabble by choosing that last place in line, but what he'd really given them was the dust of the twenty wagons ahead of them.

"At least we don't have to mix with any of the others," he said to Sara. "One never knows what kind of person one might meet among so many strangers. Why just now in the store I met a man who had every bit of money taken from him by a man who said he'd deliver two good horses and then ran off and wasn't seen again."

Sara sighed and squeezed her husband's arm. The

wagon jangled violently over a particularly rocky patch of road. The trunks and furniture in the wagon slammed against one another.

"The chairs," Sara cried, referring to the only nice things they had with them, a set of dining room chairs that had belonged to her mother's family.

"They'll be fine, Sara. I tied them in well." The reverend patted her hand without letting go of the reins.

"Now you must get used to the elements and trust in God. We have a long journey. I suggest you use the time to study your soul and pray."

Sara started a prayer, but her mind wandered back to the last time she had seen her parents. Adele had swaggered into the barn where Sara was idly stroking one of the cows and remembering all the things she had done and imagined growing up on that farm. She was thinking about her dreams, when she went down to the cow stream and pretended that it was her home and she had a husband and five children. She had imagined that they were able to make a home out of the trees and the moss, that the moss was their carpet and the ceiling was always as beautiful and light as the leaves in spring. She had pretended that in her home the ceiling turned dark at night and sparkled with stars and that magically neither rain nor cold harmed them. There were no secrets, no unsaid things in that enchanted, fairy home with invisible walls, and only those who loved Sara knew how to find it. When she was remembering these dreams and treasuring them a little sadly Adele watched her and then came into the barn tearing up a piece of straw with a careless destructiveness. The younger sister was anxious to have her elder sibling gone again. Being the only girl and the oldest at home suited her. She had gotten used to a certain amount of authority and attention since Sara had gone off to college. She had always felt overwhelmed by Sara who was smart and the subject of a great deal of conversation between her father and mother, and who intervened when Adele tried to play tricks on Timothy. Adele thought of her elder sister as arrogant and only tolerable when she was pitiable as an old maid.

"Father wants to talk to you," she had said in a sing-song kind of taunt to Sara, a tone of voice she only used when they were alone so her reputation as the sweet little sister was not soiled.

Mr. Franklin sat at the kitchen table as he spoke to Sara, who stayed standing behind one of the chairs. Mrs. Franklin was outside hanging the wash up on the line, getting tangled in the sheets when the wind blew.

"You're married now," Mr. Franklin began. Sara nodded sheepishly, pride flushing her face. She was embarrassed to stand before her father as a woman with a husband. Sara knew why he had asked to see her, because in his own awkward way he would admit his respect for her after so many years of abuse. Now was the time, Sara thought, when he would present her with some token of his crippled affection. No doubt he would give her a dowry of sorts, some money to help them, for the Willoughbys had put everything they had into the wagon and horses and provisions they needed for the westward journey. And Mr. Franklin knew this.

"Yer mother says we ought to do somethin', sech as give a pres'nt. She says you can have them chairs a' hers we been keepin' in the big shed. We ain't gonna use 'em anyway. But still yer lucky ta get 'em. I could sell 'em for a good piece a' cash."

Sara nodded. "Thank you," she said, thinking surely this couldn't be all.

"But I don't care nothin' about that. I got somethin' else ta say to you, girl.

"Now that you got a husband—and he ain't the sturdiest thing I ever seen . . . I figure he had no choice but ta be a preacher 'cause he sure don't have the strenth ta do any real work as I can see. I don't give a wart how much a man knows the Bible if he can't put money in his pocket he can't take care of nothin', let alone a wife."

Sara clutched the back of the chair and leaned toward it.

Mr. Franklin lifted his hand and rhythmically sliced the air with it to emphasize his points.

"But you got his name now, girl. I ain't got no more responsibility for you. I done my job with you. I ain't obliged to do no more. I got a wife of my own ta feed and two children left. I just want you ta understand that you'd best make do with this reverend of yorn 'cause you can't come crawlin' back here." He narrowed his eyes and waited.

Sara's eyes had grown big and wide. She looked down at the table where there was always some residue of flour. She imagined that her mother would be making bread on that table tomorrow and the next day and the day after that and it would be as if she'd never been there. Tears filled up her eyes.

"Do you understand, girl?" the father said. He leaned forward folding his hands on the table in a mockery of patience.

"Yes," Sara said.

Mr. Franklin stood up and came to his daughter. There was a strange grin on his face and he bent his knees awkwardly. Sara thought for a moment that he was going to kiss her cheek, then she felt his hand grab a hunk of her skirt and pinch through to her bottom. He held her flesh and shook it as he squeezed so hard that Sara cried out. Mr. Franklin laughed.

"I'll wager the man's gettin' somethin' outta you, girl."

He let go of her and walked out.

Sara stood in the same spot for ten minutes, until her mother came in with the empty laundry basket. The elder woman was smiling and cheerful.

"Did your father tell you about the chairs?" she asked.

But Sara did not answer.

"Your father was so happy to be able to give them to you," Mrs. Franklin said, ignoring her daughter's trance.

Sara slowly moved her eyes upward to look, incredulously, at her mother's face. Did she really believe that that man was happy to give her the chairs? Did she really believe he was a good and kind man? But, no, because the mother could not meet her daughter's eyes.

And Sara wondered what would happen if she said, "He told me I was no longer welcome here, that I have no home, and he pinched my bottom and left a bruise as he has done so many times that you know nothing of." But she was afraid, and determined to put it all behind her and find some other route to her mother's heart, through being a wife, through religious service. If she told the truth, the ugly things and the pain they caused her, her mother might turn away from Sara in disgust, in horror. Perhaps her mother would say, "You are just weak, Sara Williams Franklin Willoughby, for not enduring. You are just weak."

Sara lied to Reverend Willoughby. She told him that her father had given her, in addition to the chairs, forty dollars to be kept for a rainy day.

While Sara thought about her parents, Reverend Willoughby began to chat about this and that. It seemed that everyone on the wagon train but Sara was lively and chatting, excited by the adventure ahead of them, determined to forget the sorrow of leaving so much behind. Reverend Willoughby was talking about Reverend Barkstone in Santa Fe, about how much the man had done for him when he first went into seminary. He told Sara for the hundredth time what he'd written in a letter to Barkstone, how he'd told him when they were coming and what they were prepared to do once set up with a modest home and a small salary from whatever Barkstone could carve off of his congregation's tithes.

But Sara still wandered about her parents' farm. Sometimes she drifted off to sleep with the wagon bouncing her; sometimes she heard her husband's low voice beside her. And finally she saw herself standing between the barn and the house looking at the back of her mother and filled with overwhelming need and love. She gazed almost in awe at her mother's slightly stooped back and the dark hair pinned at the nape of her neck, the grey dress she always wore. Sara ran to her to be embraced, but when the figure turned around it was not her mother, but Adele, scornful Adele. And then she saw her mother's back again, by the pond, and she ran there. But this time it was her father, his eyes swollen and reptilian with drunkenness. Again, in the distance, there, her mother. And her need to be held by her mother increased with each failure to reach her, until she was stumbling and weeping, and still finding Adele or her father where she thought she'd found her mother. Then she realized that she was dreaming and tried to call out to someone to rescue her from this cruel scene. In her dream she tried to call so loudly that someone in the real world would hear her and wake her up. Then she felt herself being shook, and she believed that her mother was shaking her awake. She opened her eyes, letting go of a little moan that escaped from the screams of her nightmare. Reverend Willoughby was still chat-

ting, this time about the riffraff of Independence—
specifically, the whores.

"They are the basest form of life. They are the
damned and the damning. They are going to hell and
they don't care who they take with them." Reverend
Willoughby had to talk loudly above the rattling of the
wagon. Sara listened; she had been fascinated by the
whores. Some of them looked tired and sick. Some of
them coughed up blood and spit it into the street. Some
of them looked like little girls who wouldn't live another night. But one or two of the whores in Independence had a sparkle in their eyes that matched the
shimmer of their crimson dresses. They painted their
cheeks and lips and they didn't seem to care what people thought of them, just like Miss McCarthy, Sara's old
schoolteacher who played the fiddle in Roanoke. These
whores laughed together and knew that they were
pretty. They made jokes about people who passed by.
Two blonde-haired beauties had shown their legs to
Reverend Willoughby as he passed. One of them had
said, "Man does not live by bread alone, reverend," and
then they had laughed. Reverend Willoughby's face had
turned the deep red of shame and rage. He lectured Sara
on the undisputed fact that any woman who liked to fornicate had been chewed up and spit out by the Devil
himself.

This is the subject on which the reverend was pounding as they slowly rattled over grass, dust and rocks.
The wagon bumped over a big rock, nearly knocking
Sara off the hard little seat. She looked up at her husband's face that was now softened and muted by a thin
layer of brown dust. Brown dust had powdered his
black trousers and jacket, his shoes, his hair, everything.
Sara looked at her own hands and saw the same gritty
layer of trail dust. She could taste it in her mouth and

feel it in her nose. It occurred to her as a tremor that she was completely alone, like a dusty porcelain doll left on a table in a house where everyone had died.

V

Children loved the wagon trains. Men had to pretend they did because they were the ones who had gotten their families into the miserable adventure to begin with. Some women liked the adventure; most regretted it with all their hearts. All the manners and deportment they'd learned at their mothers' skirts didn't add up to a mote of dust on the trail. Every propriety they believed in got washed away by flooding rains or burnt up by the blazing prairie sun. The hems of the women's skirts wore perpetual rings of caked mud, and the noses that poked out of their bonnets turned rosy red.

And whereas the physical indignities were bad, the mental strain was terrible. Particularly disturbing to the women were the graves of people who'd been buried alongside the trail. They were mostly miniature tombs made of little piles of rocks and wooden crosses, conspicuous lumps in the tall grasses—children's graves with the name of an infant or toddler crudely scratched into the wood. The crosses were almost always awry. Occasionally there was a fence around the little grave; like the stones, these were to keep out the wolves that might ravage the dead child. Indians didn't bother the graves. They knew better than whites not to dig up people's kin just for some curio or piece of gold. The women who passed by these pitiful monuments could not keep from imagining their own children left in graves in the middle of nowhere, graves that they might never be able to find again.

If anyone had pretended that the journey was not death defying, the dead proved it to be so. And some women almost went mad over them, methodically recording in their journals each grave they saw: some days eight or nine, some days just two or three. And they stayed awake in the night and listened to their own children breathe and gently cough out the trail dust in their little throats. Mothers constantly felt the backs of their children's necks to see if the cholera fever had grabbed on yet. Two or three women had to begin the journey with a baby on the way. It didn't matter when their time came; the wagon train had to leave in spring so it could pass over the mountains before the first deep snow.

The woman in the wagon in front of Sara's had four children, and she didn't seem to be much older than Sara. Having been warned by Reverend Willoughby not to fraternize with anyone but him, Sara kept her distance. From afar, she watched the woman and imagined her to be a tough soul, though physically petite. She didn't wear a bonnet like the other women, and she walked with the children beside and behind the wagon, carrying a baby to whom she sang cheerful songs. A boy of about four sat on the back of the wagon, often pretending to shoot Reverend Willoughby who sternly pretended not to notice but mumbled to his wife that even children could be eternally damned if they didn't watch out. When she caught him at the game, the boy's mother told him to stop and then smiled at the Willoughbys as though to say, "What can be done?" A six-year-old girl mostly sat beside her father on the front seat, but sometimes Sara saw her dusty face in the shadows of the back of the wagon. A beanpole of an eight-year-old girl, with a long braid down her back, walked beside her mother, holding on to her skirts.

The woman often smiled at Sara. Once she called out, "I've got some extry coffee made here I'm gonna pour on out. You want some beforn I do?"

Sara just shook her head and went on putting her own breakfast dishes in an open crate on the back of the wagon.

Though she didn't talk much, Sara began to know the others on the wagon train well. When they stopped in the evening, the women went to get water and talked about their day's troubles. There were, even on that small wagon train, distinctions between classes. Most of the women knew how to behave like upper-class ladies, but had the worn hands and weary faces of the unprivileged. This majority disdained both those beneath and those above their station. Some of these middle-class women even had servants, poorly paid or unpaid governesses and domestics. But only two families owned slaves that fetched and hauled while their mistresses sat in crisp fashion under parasols. It was important to end up the journey as one began—with pale, smooth skin.

The woman who was in the wagon in front of Sara's had rough ways that the other women rejected. She didn't wear a bonnet, for one thing. It was just such carelessness, the righteous ones proclaimed, that would threaten the establishment of a Christian society in the wilderness. And didn't Sara think so? She was, after all, a preacher's wife. And with such an identity, Sara was never completely encircled by the other women. She had their distant respect, and not much more, which was just fine with Reverend Willoughby who continued to instruct Sara on the necessity of keeping her distance.

Sara did speak often to one boy, a fourteen-year-old

son of the oldest couple on the train. There were widowed grandpas and grandmas with their children and grandchildren, but this couple was alone with their one boy. The father often spoke loudly of his wanting his son to have a chance to make a good life for himself in the West. He wanted to give his son a head start in the miracle of free land and unknown riches. The boy's name was Sampson and he had a little black dog named Musket. Musket followed Sampson around as the boy offered to get wood or carry water for the childless and servantless, or for women who had only little ones. He was a good soul but a little careless, so that most people thanked him but said that they were doing all right. Sara talked to him about little Musket whom Sampson had trained to do a few tricks. The dog could jump high from his back legs. Sampson spent most of his time walking beside the wagon master's horse, talking to the man about this and that while Musket trotted behind.

The first time Sara spoke to the woman from the wagon in front of hers was about Sampson.

It had been raining for three days straight. There was nothing in the whole wagon train that wasn't damp. The going had been slow, with wheels sinking into the mud and horses getting their hooves stuck. On the day the rain finally stopped, the wagon train came to Great Bend Crossing where it had to ford the Arkansas River. The rains had swollen the river to a raging brown thickness. The men talked over the situation and then boldly sent the wagons forth, worried about the time they'd already lost going slow through the rains.

Sampson, who had been waiting for just such an adventure, got down from his parents' wagon to pull the balking horses along. His was only the third wagon to cross; all the others were on either bank with people beside them watching each crossing with growing doubts about the sanity of attempting it. The boy was up to his chest in water, and was pulling on the reins of one of the horses. He was laughing because Musket kept barking at him and bouncing up and down on the seat trying to get up the nerve to jump in after his boy. Then the boy must have slipped. His hand dropped the reins and in seconds he was swept down the river. His arm stayed up, his hand grabbing at nothing. His mother stood up and tried to jump in after her boy, but her husband held her down. The people on the shore could hear her weak screaming above the water's roar. The boy's head was now just a dot in the distance. Anyone who tried to jump in was held back by the reasonable ones who knew that rescue attempts just meant more dead in a river like that.

When everyone had crossed the river the wagon train waited on the other side for several hours until Sampson's father had found his boy's dead body caught on a felled tree downstream. He brought him back to be buried. It was his and his wife's only child, he kept saying. The dog was still barking.

Reverend Willoughby managed the ceremony. The people found comfort in his stern composure. He seemed so sure that God still figured in their lives. Yet the grave looked strange, a single, organized hump in all the random weed, grass and rock a few yards from the river. The father kept asking the wagon master if he was sure the grave was above floodline.

People moaned and wept all through the night. Sara clung to her husband, lying so close that when she spoke her lips moved on his cheek.

"Could we not have a child of our own?" she dared to whisper.

"Don't speak of such things, Sara," the reverend scolded.

"Surely we are as pitiful as Sampson's poor parents. Isn't it God's plan for men and women to bear children?"

"We are meant for better things. We are not animals, Sara."

"But would an animal love its children as those two loved their son? Why did God do such a cruel thing as to kill that boy?"

"You must not question these things. God works in mysterious ways."

And the reverend squirmed away from his wife's grip and turned his back to her.

Sara could not sleep. She wanted her husband to touch her, caress her, make her forget about the boy's death. Her skin was hot and her muscles tight. She got up and went outside. The stars shone crisply, as though the rain had washed them clean. Sara went away from the wagon and sank down on her knees.

"Oh, God, why am I filled with so much longing and fear? Why am I so weak? I am not fit for this mission. I am so alone, Lord. I am so alone. I know that I am wicked and weak. . . ."

Then she fell on her side, wishing that her husband would come pick her up and lay her gently on their bed and kiss her. And at the same time she hated herself for wishing such a thing. She grabbed her own flesh, pinched the skin on her upper arm. She squeezed hard murmuring to herself, "I will pinch you until you bruise, you wicked creature." She pinched until the pain burned hot, until the skin throbbed when she let go.

And then she noticed another presence standing beside her and above her. It seemed a looming dark figure, so near that Sara could have touched it. She sat up quickly, her mind completely emptied of thoughts and flooded with terror. For a second she heard nothing but the dog still barking in the distance. Sara thought of Mary's being visited by an angel and told that she was going to bear the son of God.

"It's a hard thing to take," a woman's voice said, and then added, "the boy's death."

Sara's mind adjusted itself to this earthly utterance and she tried to say something but found her throat unready. She cleared it and then said, "Yes."

The shadow folded up and then was squatting next to Sara. It was the woman from the wagon in front of hers. Sara's face flushed deeply. Had the woman heard her crying and tearing at her own flesh? What must she think of her lying out in the grasses in her nightdress?

"My name's Hattie," the woman said. "Your husband did a mighty fine job at the buryin'."

"Thank you," Sara said.

Hattie sat down on the ground beside Sara and pulled her skirt tightly over her knees. She threw her head back to look at the night sky.

"I ain't never seen stars like that," she whispered. "It's a mighty beautiful sight."

Sara looked up, too.

Hattie spoke again.

"Yeah, I lost two myself. They were just babies, stillborn. Still it's hard ta take. You lost any children?"

Sara looked down.

"I haven't had any children," she said quietly.

Hattie sighed. "They're a blessing and a curse all at once."

Sara turned and stared at the woman. She studied and studied her, fascinated that beside her sat a woman who had fornicated with her husband many times. Her eyes moved down her companion's body to the waist where she saw a bundle of yellow prairie flowers stuck in the top of the skirt.

"Those are pretty flowers," she said.

"Oh, yeah," Hattie said, touching them. "Edmund gave 'em to me, tryin' ta cheer me up. Edmund's my husband."

"My husband's name is Edmund, too," Sara marveled.

Hattie shrugged.

"Yeah," she said, "there's a lotta Edmunds in the world, I guess."

The two women sat for a while in silence, Sara mulling over the variety of Edmunds there must be in the world.

"I wish that dog'd stop that barkin'," Hattie said. "Spooks me ta hear him goin' on and on, like he's tryin' to rouse that boy to his senses."

"I wonder why God would do such a thing as to let a poor boy like that drown, his parents' only child, too," Sara said, looking back up at the stars.

"I don't know as I think much of God," Hattie said. Sara winced and waited for one of the stars to shoot down and burn them both to crispy ash. "But I sure do admire some of the things He thinks up, like them stars and the sun goin' down and turnin' the grass all gold. There's things we seen that nobody in North Carolina ever gonna see. Where you from?"

Sara was staring at Hattie again, and Hattie laughed.

"You got the most powerful stare I ever seen," Hattie said and Sara looked away. "Your eyes look like two black pearls shinin' in the moonlight. I don't mean no insult. They're right fine lookin' eyes, but they do dig into a person." Then she asked, "You got any cornmeal? I got a powerful lot of beans that we are all gittin' mighty tired of. I was thinkin' I could swap you some if you got any cornmeal."

"We don't have any cornmeal," Sara said. "We've got flour, but Reverend Willoughby doesn't like beans."

"I don't blame him," Hattie said. "Ain't nothin' more disturbin' than a family of six sleepin' in the back of a little ole wagon after eatin' nothin' but beans all day."

She stretched up to her feet and said, "Well, I guess I'd best be goin' back before Edmund comes lookin' for me. You all right?"

"I'll walk back with you," Sara said standing.

They strolled, both with their arms crossed over their chests.

Before they parted, Hattie said, "You never told me yer name."

"Sara."

"That's a better name than Hattie."

Reverend Willoughby was asleep when Sara got into bed beside him.

The dead boy's dog had finally stopped his barking. Musket was lying watchfully with his muzzle on his paws and his eyes opened and worried.

VI

🖋️

The wheels turned and bumped. Sara was used to tensing the muscles of her legs to keep her seat. She was too exhausted to fight the conditions of the journey anymore—the dusty mouth, the gritty skin, the tight muscles, the disorientation when everything familiar is left behind and life is just moving. Life is noting every nuance of dirt and prairie grass and rain clouds. Life is noting smoke in the distance, a movement in a line of trees—signs of other beings, of people-like creatures who seem to be part of the dirt and grass and bark. When Sara first saw the Indians, she wanted to walk up and touch them. She stood transfixed watching a Cheyenne woman waiting, smileless but calm, on a beautiful, spotted horse, while two dark men with bone armor on their chests talked to the wagon master. The men dismounted and unwrapped a parcel of dried meat. The woman appeared disinterested in the wagon train and its foreign creatures. Sara stared so hard at her, this woman who rode a horse like a man and didn't seem to care what the ladies of the wagon train might have to say about it, that the Indian turned her head slightly and looked back at Sara. For a moment their eyes locked, like pieces of a puzzle that fit together. The woman nodded and Sara blushed. She had the giddy sensation that she'd been acknowledged by royalty. Then the

Cheyenne rode off, their horses' hooves kicking up a screen of dust.

Many days later, the Willoughbys' wagon came down on Santa Fe after a treacherous turnoff from the main trail. As they rattled through the dry hills, polka-dotted by piñon bushes, Sara waited to see this town, this supposed oasis of order and refinement at the end of the long journey. And so she stared incredulously at the mud geometries below that were the town of Santa Fe.

"That is Santa Fe?" she asked the reverend. Her husband did not answer, having fallen into the habit of remaining silent when an answer might reveal ignorance or, worse, anxiety.

"It's all mud," Sara said in a high voice. "Even the houses are made of mud."

Scrubby hills surrounded the cluster of adobe structures that made the plaza. The old Catholic church reminded Reverend Willoughby of who owned the souls in that place. They passed it by, their wagon creaking and bumping down the little lane that led to the plaza.

All Reverend Willoughby could think of was seeing Reverend Barkstone and finally resting in the older man's guidance and support.

"If it were not for Reverend Barkstone I would urge you to move on," Sara said.

Sweat beads formed on the ill-shaven upper lip of Reverend Willoughby. Without looking at his wife he said, "Sara, you have adopted crude ways on this journey. You have begun to talk entirely too much. I fear it is your fraternizing with that woman that has ruined you."

Sara hung her head and looked at her hands. She didn't want to think of Hattie.

"I am covered with dust," she said, thinking of the impression she would make on a better minister's wife.

"I want you to remember your upbringing when we enter Reverend Barkstone's house," Willoughby lectured. "Stay quiet and make him glad that he has taken us under his wing."

He stopped the wagon in the square and looked around. A group of Indian women sat under an arcade surrounded by basketry and blankets. They wore cotton shirts and shawls, not the earthy-looking stuff worn by the Cheyenne. And the faces of these women were round and their eyes glistened with some secret merriment. They had dignity, but they also saw the humor in life; for life had a lot of irony in it. They looked at the Willoughby wagon with their shawls held up over their mouths and their eyes shining as they spoke to one another. A mule was tethered to a post in front of a gunsmith's shop. Two swarthy men walked toward the wagon, arguing with one another about something. Each had a blanket thrown over his shoulder. A woman's free laughter rolled out from behind one of the walls.

"Excuse me, sirs," Reverend Willoughby called out as the two men passed. Interrupted in their heated discussion they both looked up and noticed the wagon for the first time.

"Hí-jo-la!" one of the men called out, noticing the vehicle's distinct lean to one side.

"Sirs," Reverend Willoughby said. He squinted against the bright blue of the sky that seemed to drown him and his voice. "I wonder if you could be so good as to tell me where Reverend Barkstone lives?"

"No hablo ingles," one of them said. He shrugged his shoulders amicably. His friend had moved to the horses and said something which made them both look at the swayed back of the mare and laugh.

"My God," Reverend Willoughby said under his breath, "these men do not even speak English!"

Sara looked around her, and then from tiredness she shook her head and laughed, not bothering to move a stray hair off of her lip.

"Barkstone," Willoughby said loudly as though talking to deaf people. "I am looking for Reverend Barkstone."

The two men spoke to one another shrugging and shaking their heads. "Parsom? Parsom?"

"Bark-stone," Reverend Willoughby screamed, *"Bark-stone!"*

One of the men grabbed his companion's arm and said, "El gringo habla del esposo de Maria Cabeza de Baca, el gordo, Señor Barkstone."

"Yes, yes, Barkstone," Willoughby said angrily.

The two men pointed to a door on the plaza and then nodded their heads. They pushed their big hats away from their foreheads to watch the confusion of creaks and bumping go into motion and rattle past.

The horses wearily hauled the wagon a little farther. They'd been many hundreds of miles; what were another few feet?

"We will have to attend to the wagon after we have presented ourselves," Reverend Willoughby said as he helped his wife down.

Sara's legs wobbled as she took the first few steps behind her husband.

Willoughby knocked on the door. He was giddy, breathless. "Well, here we are, Sara. This is our destination. God has brought us safely to Reverend Barkstone's door."

Sara thought about eating food that didn't have dust in it. She thought of taking a real bath.

The door opened and a stout, black-haired woman stood there, grinning widely and nodding. Sara saw a similarity between her and the women on the plaza. But this woman wore a maid's black dress with a white, starched apron over it. She carried herself as though the clothing was part of a good joke that she played along with.

"Hello, I am Reverend Willoughby. Reverend Barkstone is expecting me."

The woman grinned and nodded but did not move.

"I have come to see Reverend Barkstone," Reverend Willoughby said more loudly.

"Sí, Reverend Barkstone," the woman said jovially.

"My God, she doesn't speak English either," Reverend Willoughby said to his wife. "What kind of place is this?"

The house was dark behind the woman. The Willoughbys could hear the slow ticking of a clock. The air of the house smelled cool.

"Let us in, good woman. The reverend is expecting us," Willoughby said pushing past the servant who still smiled. Sara followed him, looking down.

A rolling soprano laugh came from behind one of the doors in the dark hall. It was the same laughter they'd heard from outside. The round woman came up behind the Willoughbys and opened the door.

"I smell meat cooking," Sara said closing her eyes.

But Reverend Willoughby had passed into the little parlor. Sara heard a man's voice. "Edmund, Edmund, Edmund! What a surprise!" Sara looked up and took in the surroundings which were shockingly opulent.

Despite the house being adobe, it looked like an interior right out of Boston's finer section. There was heavy wooden furniture, dark and well oiled. There were portraits in gilt frames, and needle-point chairs with matching settee. A small Louis XIV desk relevéd daintily in one corner, and an equally delicate baby grand piano was in the corner opposite it. Sara never imagined a Presbyterian's house to reek so of wealth.

Reverend Willoughby, however, stared only at Reverend Barkstone. His whole deportment was unexpected, different from the image Reverend Willoughby carried so preciously in his heart. For one thing, since his days in New England Reverend Barkstone had become much rounder, like a balloon caricature of himself. His face looked like the personification of the sun in children's books. The man gleamed as though the grease of many meaty meals oiled his skin. And the most shocking accessory of all was the glass of brandy in Reverend Barkstone's hand. This was not the crisp-yet-kindly man in whose presence Reverend Willoughby had trembled, whose self-confidence and rote knowledge of the Bible had inspired Reverend Willoughby to read the New Testament three times in two days.

Reverend Willoughby, upon being invited to seat himself, sank speechlessly into a fatly upholstered leather chair. Sara remained standing, afraid of leaving a patch of dust if she sat anywhere.

"What brings you out here, Edmund? I never pictured you as the pioneer hero! My God, what a journey you must have been through. You must tell me about it."

Rather than listen to what Reverend Barkstone was saying, Sara became aware of a very elegant female presence in the room. The delicate dark woman was sitting like a porcelain doll in a small, needle-point chair by the window. Her hair was slick and as black as crow's feathers, her black eyes polished like onyx. Small, heart-shaped lips pressed shut, and even as she looked up and nodded graciously at Sara, laughter still sparkled in the woman's eyes. She wore deep brown skirts trimmed in black lace. The smell of rose water hung about this woman.

Barkstone smiled at her. "This is my wife, Maria Cabeza de Baca Barkstone. Her family has a very long history here. They once owned a great deal of land. She is a true aristocrat—royalty, wouldn't you say, dear?"

Señora Barkstone smiled and said, "Do not bore these good people with the history of my family." Then her small hand reached out and gently pulled Sara into the chair next to hers. Sara's face felt hot with shame over the appearance her dusty dress made next to her host's elegant fashion. But in the manner of the truly gracious, Maria found something to admire in her ragged guest.

"Your hair clasp is very beautiful, Señora Willoughby."

Sara looked down and toward her husband and Reverend Barkstone so as not to have to engage in conversation. It was then she noticed that her husband's face was the color of ashes. Sara thought to go to him, but she saw a fixation in his eyes that she dared not interrupt. Reverend Barkstone was still standing, looking down on Willoughby while he chatted about this and that.

"You'll have to see my horses while you're here," he said. Then noting that Sara's attention was on him, he added, "We even have a side saddle that I'm sure Maria will be glad to let you try out, Mrs. Willoughby."

A picture of the Cheyenne woman, sitting erect and disdainful up on her spotted horse, came into Sara's mind.

"Thank you," she said.

"So, Edmund, you must be exhausted," Reverend Barkstone boomed. "What are your plans?"

Sara looked at Reverend Willoughby. She was thinking, "What does he mean, what are our plans?"

Reverend Willoughby said something, but his throat seemed to have closed on him so he had to clear it and begin again in a rather tiny voice.

"Didn't you get my letter, Reverend Barkstone?"

"Letter? Oh, the mail's a terrible thing out here, Edmund. I . . ."

"Yes, Wallace," Maria chimed in, "I remember that you did receive a letter some time ago from a colleague. I believe you mentioned the Willoughbys' name."

Sara heard a little challenge in Maria's tone.

"As my letter said," Reverend Willoughby began, "you remember . . . I believe I mentioned that the Presbyterian Church . . . that some of the clergy . . . I am looking forward to the work you suggested needed my . . . the Lord. . . ."

"Well, it's good to see you, Edmund. I had no idea you'd embark on that treacherous journey. How well I remember the trek." Reverend Barkstone sweated a lot and was particularly hot under the collar at that moment.

"Goodness, it does get warm here," he said taking out a handkerchief and wiping his mouth.

"I am ready to do the Lord's work," Reverend Willoughby mumbled as though to himself.

"Where will you be staying, Edmund?"

The Willoughbys shared a glance.

Maria said quietly, "I have a new baby. I would not want him to keep you awake all night as he does to us."

"Reverend Willoughby?" Sara called out, but she did not know what to say.

Finally Reverend Barkstone, whose face was streaming with sweat so that he looked like he was a big rock in a stream, straightened himself and took charge of the situation. Maria looked down at her pointed little hands.

"Look here, Edmund. I had no idea you would take

on a trip out west. It's a hard life here." He took a sip
of brandy. "The papists have these people by the neck.
There's hardly a handful of Presbyterians, and most of
them are ministers. I don't even have a church,
Edmund. I just had no idea you'd actually, well, you'd
just come out here."

Reverend Willoughby looked at the rug.

"Look here, Edmund," Barkstone tried again, "we
can put you up here until you get on your feet. . . ."

"What about your work? Couldn't you use some assistance with your work?" Willoughby asked and he
twisted his hands around and around until Sara had to
look away.

Barkstone looked to his wife who said, "Reverend
Barkstone has his hands full, I'm afraid, with matters
outside the church. He came into many responsibilities
when he married me. There is a great deal of land, you
see."

"God has rewarded him," Willoughby said loudly to
his wife. This put a pall on the conversation. No one
knew what to say after that.

"Wallace," Maria said gently, "why could we not let
them stay for a few days in the chicken house?" She
turned to Sara and said, "Don't worry. There are no
chickens there. There is a small bed. Soon we will need
it for the workers who come, but for a few days. . . ."

Neither Sara nor Reverend Willoughby was able to
say anything in their defense. Exhausted, stunned, they
let the Barkstones discuss the arrangement in front of
them.

Later, in the small darkness of the chickenless
chicken house, Reverend Willoughby and Sara lay on a
cot and stared at the ceiling that was only a few inches
from their eyes. Little white feathers floated in the air
around them.

Every few minutes Sara wept.

"We are homeless in a strange, horrible place, Reverend Willoughby," she sobbed. "I am so tired. I am so very tired, and yet we must move on. What on earth are we to do? We're all alone with no food, no kin to help us."

"The Lord will show us the way."

"Oh, Mother," Sara wept. "I should never have left. What am I to do?" She turned her head to her husband and said, "I am afraid, Reverend Willoughby. I am too weak for this hardship. What are we going to do?"

"You are a grown woman now, Sara, not a little girl on the farm. You must control your passionate nature and try not to burden me."

Sara pictured her parents' house and was shocked by the intimacy with which she knew it, even in her imagination. She knew the exact color and pattern of the boards on the porch and their texture in various kinds of weather. She ached to be so familiar and comfortable with something again.

"The Lord will show us the way," her husband repeated, "and at least we have the money your father gave us.

"You must show me that you are a grown woman," he added, and he reached out his hand to pat her arm. But the touch made Sara even sicker with fear of the world and its strangeness and cruelty.

She turned on her side and lay in a ball, crying.

"Please, God, please do something," she prayed in her head. In the quiet of her prayer she could hear Maria Cabeza de Baca Barkstone's laughter roll around in the halls of the house.

VII

A few days later, Sara got a letter from her mother. The very paper of it seemed like a miracle, and that her mother's handwriting was on it—from months and thousands of miles and many variations in landscape ago—made Sara afraid to open the envelope. She was afraid that what was in it would deteriorate like the corpse in some enchanted, long-sealed tomb. The mother wrote of news of the family as though this would be enough for Sara. And yet also in it was a pressed ragweed flower that came, the mother said, from a spot by the road where Sara had once found a turtle that bit her. Mrs. Franklin's writing was more formal than her speech, and so the letter seemed cold to Sara. Adele was doing very well in school. Sara looked up from the letter for a moment, sighing.

As was true of all the letters Sara received from her mother while at the teachers college, this one spoke of a father who was a character from the mother's day-dreams. She freely attributed sentiments to Mr. Franklin that the man did not have. She wrote, "Your father misses you and thinks of you often and prays for your safety." The only time Mr. Franklin got down on his knees was to retrieve the cork from the second jug of moonshine he was drinking. And his sincerest desire was that his eldest daughter, indeed all his children, take good care of themselves and leave him well alone. These less noble sentiments were clearly known to the children, so the mother's letters only confused Sara and tormented her with the image of the kind of father she had never had. She was ashamed that she was not Christian enough to see the good qualities in the man who commanded her mother's coveted attention. But Sara thought that she could never be so good and strong as her mother.

Like her mother, Sara did the laundry, washing three months of grit off of her and her husband's clothes and linens. The slightly yellowed sheets and petticoats, dark skirts and britches flapped in the wind on a rope strung up between the chicken house and the kitchen at the Barkstones' hacienda. She had had help putting up the clothesline from the stout, half-breed servant, Consuela, who had opened the door when the Willoughbys first arrived. Though the two women did not know the meaning of each other's words, they understood the almost universal language of domesticity. Sara had looked up at the sky at dusk just as they had hung up the last pair of bloomers, heavy with rinse water. Forgetting that Consuela did not speak English she had exclaimed, "Look at the mountains! Why they are pink! It is as though the sunset covered all the world here." And then she added, ashamed she had not begun with it, "Praise the Lord."

The maid followed Sara's eyes, nodded and grinned, saying, "La Sangre de Cristo."

For a moment a thought came into Sara's mind that she would run away into the mountains and live by herself like a holy hermit immersed in the rich, deep sky.

Reverend Willoughby had gone away for a few days. After spending an afternoon in Barkstone's study with his mentor, Willoughby had emerged as though baptized in the older man's sweat. Apparently the two men had prayed a good deal and discussed the matter of Willoughby's prospects in New Mexico. Barkstone beat Willoughby into a lather over the idea of administering to some outpost somewhere, either to Indians or to soldiers at one of the forts. Willoughby, gasping for breath, had explained to his wife that he was going to travel alone to Fort Union and see if the chaplain there needed any assistance, or wanted to relinquish his duties to a new man.

Sara had been able to put her husband off about the forty dollars her father was supposed to have given her. Now that Willoughby was gone, she intended to present her dilemma to Reverend Barkstone and beg him to lend her the money without her husband's knowing of it. This was a plan that seemed far more sensible than running off to the mountains.

Barkstone had not been unfriendly to her. Indeed, he had personally given her the letter from her mother as soon as it arrived, and he patted her arm and said, "I know this must be hard for you, dear, being so far from your family." And he added, leaving his hand on her arm as though he was blessing her, "And if you need to unburden your soul to anyone, my door is open."

The thing that burdened Sara's soul the most was lack of money. Soon, according to Señora Barkstone, the migrant workers would take the Willoughbys' place in the chicken house. And then what? The wagon moaned for repairs; there were bugs in the little flour left in their supplies.

Barkstone was no longer a functioning man of the cloth, but Sara concluded that his wealth and his genteel wife were manifestations of God's approval. How like a father he was, after all, to Reverend Willoughby! Who could blame him for enjoying his blessings and becoming a fat man?

Many men, tall Anglos with twitching eyes and smiling lips, passed through Barkstone's home. They were men who'd been disdained in the East but who had become important and rich in New Mexico because of their keen ability to feed off a defeated culture. They had used the victors' new laws, American laws that the Hispanics had not had a chance to digest, to take land away from families who'd tended that land for hundreds of years. Clever men with waxed moustaches, they knew the tricks of taking away other men's goods and then setting up stores to sell their goods back to them at a nice profit.

Maria quietly supplied these men with ashtrays for their cigars. She served them drinks and ignored their leering at her breasts that bulged for her half-Anglo baby. Often, when she left them alone to wait for her husband, she heard their laughter and she spit into a dark corner of the hall. But in public, like her father, Maria accepted the dismantling of her people's authority in that land with passive contempt and dignity.

When Sara asked to speak to Reverend Barkstone, Maria showed not the slightest interest in the purpose of her request. When she had decided to marry Barkstone and ensure her family's place in the new breed of kings, Maria had made a secret chamber in her heart for all her opinions. She quietly regarded Sara as an underling to whom she should be kind. As for Reverend Willoughby, Maria had never seen so little sensuality in a man. But then, her own husband had strange notions of what a man and woman did in bed. Still, the white woman showed no backbone, no disdain toward her man's foolish ways as Maria did.

Barkstone was alone in his study. He had suddenly

frozen just after standing to do something. He no longer remembered what he had intended to do. He stared out the window, suddenly struck by a memory of himself in New England. He was thinking of a girl who had come to him weeping, a young woman with red hair fixed in plaits wrapped around her head. She had been a cleaning woman for one of his parishioners and had discovered her master in bed with a young boy. It was at that moment that Reverend Barkstone had seen whole new vistas in the landscape of his life. He had convinced the girl, and himself as well, that to exorcise the demons in the house she must have sex with a member of the clergy once a week on her day off. The girl came every Thursday. It was remarkable to Reverend Barkstone what a refreshingly liberating experience it was for a man to be in charge of a woman's soul, especially when the woman was of the serving class. Surely he enjoyed his wife, but poor Reverend Barkstone missed those Thursday afternoons when the first order of business was to spank the girl's naked buttocks, a ritual he had once suggested to Maria only to get his face slapped.

He was in the midst of that memory when Maria tapped on his study door and then opened it to let Sara in. Sara was as meek as a servant girl. She took tiny little steps and hung her head. Never had Reverend Barkstone seen her so charming. She looked, indeed, like she expected a spanking.

"I was just taking a quiet moment," Reverend Barkstone said, taking Sara's hand and leading her to a seat in front of his desk. He stayed standing, very close to her.

"What do you think of it here, Sara?" he asked.

"It is . . . strange, but in many ways very beautiful," Sara said. "You have a very beautiful home and family.

God has been good to you." She looked at her fingers and counted them.

"Surely, it is hard for a young woman such as yourself to be so far away from those you love, and with your husband away. . . ."

"We are very grateful for your kindness, Reverend Barkstone." Beginning to weep, Sara could not say any more.

Reverend Barkstone felt his groin ache and handed her a handkerchief that was still damp with his perspiration.

"I am afraid, Reverend Barkstone, that I must ask more of you," Sara whimpered, "for you see, we are in a bad state concerning funds, having thought . . . well, it is not your fault, I am afraid that my husband . . . well, it is not his fault. No one is really to blame, I suppose . . . I am sure God's will. . . ."

Reverend Barkstone had many people come to him about money matters. It bored him. He did not have to listen closely if money was all the woman wanted. He looked carefully at Sara's shoulders and walked auspiciously around her chair to look at the back of her neck. It was here that Reverend Barkstone felt a strain on his breathing, and he began to sweat more profusely than usual. Since he had given Sara his only handkerchief, he let the moisture collect and roll down his head and neck.

"We must buy things for the wagon," Sara said. She had made herself stop weeping, thinking that the reverend had gone behind her in order not to see her discomforting display of emotion. But she entwined her fingers together and was twisting them, making them writhe like a nest of baby snakes. "In order to do God's work. . . ."

"You know, dear," Reverend Barkstone said, alarming Sara with his noisy breathing, "even in the wilderness, one must take care to stay clean. There is dirt on your neck here." He wiped beneath her hair with his palm.

Deep shame overcame Sara.

"Reverend Barkstone," Sara whispered, "I know I am a lowly, wretched creature. . . ."

"Yes," Barkstone breathed, for it was just such a phrase, he now recalled, that he had asked the servant girl to say. He closed his palm on Sara's slender neck. "Well, child, now. . . ."

"Please, forgive me," Sara said, "but, you see, my husband believes that I have some money which I, in truth, do not have."

"I am a rich man," Reverend Barkstone said. And it made him feel less fat.

When he came around to face Sara, he was trembling. The redness and wetness of his face alarmed Sara so much that she stood up.

"You must be spanked," Reverend Barkstone said.

"I must be what?" Sara asked.

"Spanked," Reverend Barkstone said hoarsely. "I am a rich man."

He pressed Sara back into the chair and kneeled like an elephant lowering itself to be ridden.

"Perhaps if we pray together," Sara suggested.

Reverend Barkstone's hand circled around Sara's ankle.

"If we prayed . . ." she said loudly.

"If your husband knew that you lied to him, Sara," Reverend Barkstone wheezed. His hand moved up her skirt to her calf, which he squeezed as though to hold on and not fall over. "It is a sin to lie to your husband."

"Our Father, who art in heaven," Sara began, and she

saw her roommate's sampler hanging on the wall of her room at the teachers college.

Reverend Barkstone thrust his other hand under her skirts so that he now had her by both thighs. The fold of skin that bulged over his collar was red and wet.

"My husband," Sara muttered.

Reverend Barkstone tried to move Sara's thighs apart, but she pressed them with all her strength.

"You are a man of God, Reverend Barkstone," she gasped.

Barkstone was now emitting steam. He undid the buttons on his pants and pulled out something that Sara had never seen before, except on dogs and horses. It seemed horribly naked, like something skinned.

"Oh, dear Saviour," she said. And she could not move. Reverend Barkstone tore at her bloomers. Sara looked up at the ceiling.

"Tell me you are wretched, a wretched sinner," Barkstone said sweetly, breathlessly, "and I will give you the money."

Sara was studying the ceiling in painstaking detail. There were three large beams in it. She felt her bloomers gather around her ankles, and she began to count the knots in all the beams. Then she felt something like a club push against her pubic hair. There were eighteen knots altogether, she told herself, and now how many boards made up the upstairs flooring that rested on the beams?

Reverend Barkstone was trying like blazes to push into Sara, but was having a hard time of it. He got part way in and then came across a tightness that reminded him of his wedding night with his wife. He lost his erection.

With irritation, Reverend Barkstone let go of his limp penis and it got lost again beneath his belly. He stood up and buttoned up his pants. Sara slowly bent over and brought her bloomers up. She said nothing.

"Well, my dear," Reverend Barkstone said, "you realize that I have no obligation." His voice was stern and righteous.

"Yes," Sara said. "No obligation."

Barkstone drew open a drawer and took out a leather pouch with paper money and receipts in it. He jotted down something on a piece of paper and then handed Sara three dollars without looking at her.

Sara clutched the money in her fist and stood up.

As she walked out Reverend Barkstone said, "I don't want to have to tell your husband that you lied to him, Sara."

Sara nodded and went on out to the chicken house where she lay down on the bed and did not move until Consuela, noting that the sun was setting and the Anglo woman had not eaten, brought her a bowl of cornmeal and milk.

When it was dark, Sara took a candle and went into the back of the sad, creaking wagon. She squeezed past all the trunks. She tore her hands pulling at the cord that held her mother's dining room chairs. She took a little gun off a nail thinking to shoot at the cord and break it. Then she laughed at herself for being so crazy. There was a sewing kit in the wagon that had some scissors in it. She cut the cord, scolding herself for hurting her hands when she hadn't needed to.

Then Sara sat on one of the dining room chairs that had once been in her grandfather's fine house, when her mother was a little girl and hadn't yet met Joseph Franklin. The candle sputtered and went out. Sara stayed there in the dark, stroking the smooth silk of the seat next to hers and softly singing, "Jimmy crack corn and I don't care."

VIII

Many Visions had a bad dream. He dreamed that he saw a woman with a head made of black storm clouds come into the settlement and knock him down. He lay flat on his back and the women were laughing at him. The monster female bent low over him as though to eat him with her swirling black mouth. When he woke up from this nightmare, Many Visions spit something out of his mouth and came to realize it was some of his own coarse hair.

He usually told his dreams to a gathering of leaders, men like Most Important Man, who told the people when it was time to move on and where they would move, and Three Fingers who owned the sweat lodge ceremony. But that morning Many Visions said nothing about dreaming. Instead, he sat just outside his dwelling and repaired one of his pollen bags so that everyone could see he had important work to do.

Toward noon, Little Bird, Most Important Man's youngest wife, ran up to Many Visions, pulling a woman named Long Skirt by the hand. A woman did not visit a man, especially a man like Many Visions, without a chaperone, a witness.

"Di-ii' haɫka—I have seen an omen," she said breathlessly, looking at her feet as it was impolite to look into a man's face. She held on to Long Skirt's

71

hand, but the other woman kept twisting to face the opposite direction.

Many Visions had a gas pain in his lower stomach. It was part of a paranoia that lingered from his dream. He stood up to stretch out his middle and to let a fart seep out unnoticed.

"When I was getting water," Little Bird said, "a hawk came down with its talons bared. They were out like this." Little Bird let go of Long Skirt's hand and put down the pitch-covered water basket that she carried under her arm. Then she stood in front of Many Visions with her hands up like claws ready to strike. They stood that way, facing one another with the woman in an attack pose, like a mountain lion. But her eyes were big and innocent, still held downward though her hands were almost touching Many Visions' cheeks.

"Yes, I understand," Many Visions said to release her.

Little Bird picked up her water basket again and said, "Since the hawk is your spirit guide I thought I should tell you. It dove for something in the tall grasses by the arroyo. I could not see what it was after. But when the hawk flew up again it had nothing. It flew up into the air, screeched angrily and circled four times before flying southward."

Many Visions stared at the mole on the left peak of Little Bird's upper lip. He always had an urge to suck on the mole as though it was a source of nurturing, like a mother's dark nipple. Then the medicine man looked up to the sky. It was difficult, sometimes, for him to make his mind stay on one thing. He suddenly had the impression that the sky was such a deep blue that one would drown in it if the world was turned upside down.

"It is an omen of drought," he said.

Little Bird's mouth hung open.

"But," she finally said, "we have had drought since the middle of the growing season. Why would such a vision be sent to us now?"

"It is bad to question those wiser than you," Many Visions said. "I don't wish to speak of it. It is not good to speak of these things. If you fall sick from seeing this, you come and I will do something to cure you."

He shooed the woman away.

Little Bird went into her dwelling, a humped tent made of branches and skins. Most Important Man's first wife, Walks Like A Buffalo, was inside, asleep. It scared Little Bird to see so many good women sleep during the day. It was the hunger that made them lazy. There was little food to prepare, and little energy to find more. The drought had shriveled up the world until it was rumored that the coyotes were eating their own tails.

The men could not sit still or sleep. Most Important Man and some of the other old men had gone off on a mission. The gossip was that they went to the army post to ask for provisions. Walks Like A Buffalo didn't like this idea at all. She had spoken aloud to herself in her home when her husband was there, saying, "To beg like weak dogs . . . I'd rather starve than take their white dust to eat. They will give us more sickness, that is all. When we ask for something to eat from the soldiers, we end up with our own blood in our mouths."

But a little boy, a brown spirit of only three years, had grown weak from hunger and died of something putrid that ran from his nose and ears like mud. His mother was called Laughs A Lot and she had loved the feel of her warm child. She liked her boy's face near hers where she could teach it her smile. She liked the smell of her boy's hair and had given him a secret name when he died so that no one could shame her for speaking to the dead. She called him Boy With Sweet Smelling Hair and she spoke to him. Maybe she had loved him too much and that's why he was taken. Maybe she was holding on to the dead too long and would cause trouble with ghosts.

Other women loved their children too much; other children got very weak and full of bad medicine. Their mothers spoke to Walks Like A Buffalo about the need for someone—though they carefully mentioned no name—to do something. As was intended, Walks Like A Buffalo spoke out loud to herself one day when Most Important Man was in their dwelling, spoke about how somebody better do something fast before their people died and became food for buzzards.

Most Important Man then consulted Many Visions. Looking out toward the western mesas as though what he had to say was inconsequential, Most Important Man asked, "How would a leader end a famine?"

"He must fast and refrain from sexual intercourse," Many Visions said. He sounded authoritative, but he always felt as small as a rodent with Most Important Man who had a bigger, more solid body, and tattered but flowing hair.

"It is not so difficult to fast during a famine."

"Give whatever food you have as a sacrifice to the spirit world," Many Visions said. "I will take what you give and make a proper offering of it. It is good to prove your strength and courage."

After one day of fasting and listening to Walks Like A Buffalo speaking aloud to herself, Most Important Man got his brothers to ride with him on this sacred mission. They took all the horses so that the young men had nothing to ride.

But the young men had their strong feet and the restlessness of youth that made them angry and violent.

Hunger made them angrier. Boys grown too old to stay near their mothers chipped the ends of their arrows and scraped them on rocks until they were as sharp as needles. Then they stared out at the yellow earth against the blue sky because there was nothing to hunt. The older ones, those who were of marrying age, crouched together and scowled at the world. Their anger was the only dignity they had left, and sometimes they wanted to kill each other.

The core group of the young men, the angriest and most frightening, were three friends—Small Face, Eats Fish, and Broken Nose. These three walked together through the camp with their chests out. Women giggled when they passed; old women clucked their tongues. The old men watched them carefully.

Small Face talked the most of the three. He argued about anything. He was suspicious that many people tried to insult him in various ways, that old ladies left their grinding stones in his way, or dogs scratched themselves in front of him just to mock him, to insult him. Then he would rant on and on about this or that—whites, women, children, old men, lame horses, wormy dried meat. He felt good when he was angry. He kicked dogs and showed his mother very little respect. She had given him his face on which the eyes and nose and mouth were all crowded in the middle. Small Face wanted to go to war, to mutilate white people because they rode their horses with the arrogance of gods. Small Face's sister, Talks To Deer, had been taken by white soldiers two winters before the drought. She came back with a white man's baby in her belly. The girl hung her head and no one spoke to her. All her friends had gotten husbands while she was away, and they did not want her in their homes. If a man was to speak to her he lost his own friends for a day.

When Talks To Deer went into labor she went down to a stagnant pool and lay in it. The baby was born face-down in the slimy water and that is where Talks To Deer left it with the afterbirth. She only lived for three days after that. A fever took her over, and she sweated and moaned until Many Visions gave up trying to save her.

"She is in a great fire," Many Visions had said, "a great fire. It is the fire of fornication with witches. My spirit guide tells me that the fire must take her or it will spread."

Talks To Deer's family never regained their status. People always greeted them with a little pity and it was this pity that always stank in Small Face's nostrils. Everything smelled to him because of this piece of stench in his own nose. He beat his wife, Long Hair, even though she cooked well and gave him three children in three years.

Now Small Face saw a good opportunity for violence against whites. There was famine and several deaths. And the old men had left on some mission that he was sure would insult and humiliate the people.

"Chinii adade'—They are dogs who eat their own shit," Small Face said of the elders. He and his two friends were crouching in the dust near a clump of scrub oak where they went to piss and talk. "I say we go on a great raid, a thing like a war. I say we take food where we find it."

"We will be shot," Eats Fish said. "We don't have bullets for our guns."

"We'll get bullets," Small Face spit at him. "You are a dog with his tail between his legs. I know because I have seen you with your wife."

Eats Fish, who was taller than Small Face, stood up to show himself off. He had gotten his name because he never had the proper disgust for fish eating. Children could be excused for roasting trout by the river. But as a young man, Eats Fish still had a taste for the slimy, white flesh. His wife refused to cook fish. She blushed when other women asked her if her husband's light skin got its soft, oily look from all those years of fish eating.

"You dogs," Small Face muttered. "You want to sit and starve like dogs."

Broken Nose listened and felt his knees ache. He fell back to a sitting position and said, "I am ready to go. There is nothing here."

"You have no wife," Eats Fish said, and as soon as he said it he regretted it.

"Your wife is fat," Small Face said. "I do not let women keep me like a dog."

"If we are going to do this," Broken Nose said, "let's leave tonight. There is no reason to wait."

"You are always speaking boldly and with no respect for others," Small Face said. "Who are you to command your friends?"

Broken Nose was the tallest of the three friends and the broadest in the chest. His full lips and high cheekbones prompted the old women to say he was as pretty as a girl. But he had a broken nose. The jokers in the tribe said that he'd gotten kicked in the nose by a doe that he was trying to have sex with. Men did not like the way Broken Nose looked at their wives. He did not avert his eyes when another man's woman passed him. He spoke to women about matters that did not concern them.

"It is rude the way you stare," his mother told him time and again. "One day you will stare for the last time and your eyes will be taken out of your head by someone's husband. Or you will call a man by his name to his face and he will cut you like meat." And she said over and over again, "I do not know how I came to have a son who does not act decently."

Broken Nose's mother even went to her friends for advice. "What does one do with a boy whose soul is between his legs?" she lamented. And soon the whole tribe knew the boy as lustful and undisciplined. But what could one say about a boy who'd fallen into the hands of the Hopis?

And it was rumored that sometimes, when a woman wanted a man who liked sex too much, she went off behind the rocks with Broken Nose. A man named Two Horses cut off one of his wife's fingers when he caught her looking back at Broken Nose one day. The woman took her things and went back to her mother's home where she swore she had never touched Broken Nose except that he came to her in her dreams where she could not defend herself against him.

Famine had only made the gossip nastier and more serious, so that Broken Nose feared that one of the stories about him would cause trouble soon. It was a good time for going off on a raid. He stood up and stretched. His beads and amulets rattled when he moved; they rattled softly like good power.

"You like women too much," Small Face said to him. "You are like a dog in heat who can think of nothing else."

"We should go to the south where the herders are," Broken Nose said. "We can get some sheep from the Mexicans."

"What about the pueblo? What about the Osuna people?" Eats Fish said. "They have been left alone for a long time. It will surprise them to see us."

"And we can slit the throat of the priest who holds those dogs by their balls," Small Face said.

Broken Nose walked away. He got tired of Small

Face and his references to dogs. But Small Face was the most entertaining person he knew; even in famine he could be counted on to put on a good show of violence and rage. Even now, as he walked away, Broken Nose could hear Small Face insult Eats Fish's wife. The two men rolled around in the dust like boys. Broken Nose left them to wash his hair and sharpen up his knives on the rock by the arroyo. It was a good rock that he often thanked for giving him a place to hide behind when the women were bathing. He thanked the rock for letting him watch Little Bird rub her breasts and pull little bits of leaf from the hair between her legs. Or sometimes it was just as good to sit up on a dirt hill and look out at the desert. His Hopi mother had taught him to see into the mind of the world by looking at the desert, by sensing what it wanted and why it existed, how it could be seduced into sustaining a man. What was it she had said to him when he fell and cut himself, or got a cactus thorn in his finger and cried as though he was dying? She had held him on her lap and said, "Look, look, Corn Boy"—he was called Corn Boy because he'd been found just born in the corn fields—and his Hopi mother loved him like her own. She used to hold him on her lap with his face all dusty except for the wet lines that his tears made. She faced him toward the desert with its many mysterious colors and big rocks and mesas and said, "Look, little Corn Boy, you have scraped your leg but the world is still beautiful."

IX

When the Spaniards came to New Mexico, came glittering up from the south, Coyote watched from behind the rocks. He snickered behind his paw figuring what a mess was going to be made and what entertainment he was going to get watching things happen. He especially kept his yellow eyes pinned on the men who moved along like black clouds, the ones with crosses hanging from their necks, heavy crosses that reflected the sun into Coyote's eyes.

"These are the dangerous ones," Coyote guessed.

The soldiers came with their hands on their weapons and with fantasies of gold, visions of loot hidden in the humble baskets and jugs of flat-faced Indians. But the priests held their hands out for the more destructive profit of bringing new souls to Mother Church.

The sight of these black crows gave Coyote gas and a desire to spread the news. So he ran ahead of the conquistadores, ran farting up the Rio Grande to warn the people not to be fooled by the threat of swords. To tell them to keep their eyes on the crosses, to play along with the men who wore them. "Go into their strange kivas," he said. "Play like idiots and laugh behind your hands like me. This way you'll stay out of trouble. You fight these white eyes and they won't only kill you;

they'll also raise up your dead ancestors just so they can kill them too."

This is what Coyote ran up the Rio Grande howling. Some people thought he was joking and paid him no mind. Some got mad at the idea of people going after their dead grandfathers and prepared to slit throats. Others listened well to Coyote's advice and practiced nodding and grinning while they made safe hiding places for their masks and pollen bags and stories. The children hid the stories in the mazes of their ears where soon little drips of baptismal water would tickle them.

When Coyote got to Osuna Pueblo he was tuckered out and couldn't even get enough breath to speak. The people let him rest and listen to their gossip. He curled up right in the middle of the pueblo, in a clearing of dust that was the same color as the houses. There he slept and defecated. There he got up to walk four times around and then fall again to sleep.

Finally Coyote was rested enough and he told the Osuna people about the priests.

"Will they run us off the land?" they asked.

"No," Coyote said showing his pointy little teeth.

"Will they take all our corn?" they asked.

"No."

"Will they take our children away from us?"

"Well, not exactly. Not yet. And not if you do as I say."

When the first priest came to Osuna Pueblo, Coyote ran off, heading once more up the Rio Grande.

The Osuna people giggled when they saw the priest. He had a long face with big jowls and a long body with a small round belly that stuck out from inside the black robe. If the Osuna people had known what a monkey looked like they would have thought that the priest looked like a hairless monkey. Through a boy who could speak both Spanish and Indian, the priest told the Osuna people to call him "padre." He told them about a woman who had sex with a ghost and had a son. He told them about Jesus who got himself nailed to two pieces of wood shaped like the thing the priest had around his neck.

"Does he bring rain?" the people asked.

The priest told the story of Noah and the flood.

"Too much rain," the Osuna people thought but they didn't say anything.

"Does he cure disease?"

The priest told them about bringing Lazarus to life, and in their hearts the Osuna people thought this pretty disgusting. Who wants to see one's uncle walking around after a few days of decay?

But the Osuna people nodded and grinned and the priest, feeling his oats, announced that he needed a church.

One of the elders said, "Oh, I know the perfect place."

Now some of the people thought this old woman was going to give away their ceremonial place, a circle behind the houses where the spirits came as dancers, a clearing on a ledge that dropped way down and the view spread all the way to the southern edge of the world. The people held their breath waiting to see if the old woman had been stupid enough to be mesmerized by the business about the kingdom of heaven.

"There is a sacred place," the old woman said, "a perfect place for your worshipping house, a place where all the Osuna people will gladly worship Jesus and Mary and all the others you've told us about."

The priest almost burst his cassock over his skill at winning souls; he could smell his impending sainthood baking in the Vatican ovens. The old woman led him over to the spot where Coyote had spent several days sleeping, where there was a mess of Coyote hair, and turds that looked like an orange clump of chewed-up berries.

"Here is where you should build this kiva of yours," the old woman said.

"What is this?" the priest said pointing to the coyote droppings and balls of dusty fur.

"Oh," said the old woman. "Animal shit is sacred to Osuna people. It fertilizes our spirits."

Many hands went up over many mouths, and eyes glistened.

The priest nodded his head and smiled benevolently at the silly beliefs of his new flock. And he began to plan his church that would be built on coyote shit.

And so a Spanish chapel got built in the middle of Osuna Pueblo and it's still there. It's the same orange color as all the houses, but it separates itself from them with its arcs, with its tallness, with steps, and with a wall that goes all the way around it.

By the time the Willoughbys got to Osuna Pueblo, about three hundred years' worth of priests had smiled benevolently in the illusion that they had the Osuna people's souls tucked in their sleeves. The church building itself had become so cocky that it leaned to one side like a hoodlum. It wasn't Coyote who watched the Willoughbys' wagon limp into view, but the church. It narrowed its eyes and didn't take the intrusion as a joke. The current priest had a broad face and a barrel chest. Clasping his hands over his ribs he strolled out to meet the Willoughbys and to ask them what they wanted. He could tell by the contraption they were in that they didn't have much of an institution behind them. One of the wheels on the wagon was about to fall off. The man on the wagon's seat appeared nervous and defensive as though he had an itch somewhere that he didn't dare scratch in front of anyone. But the woman was scary.

Sara was sitting straight up on the seat with all the pride of the insane. She looked hard in front of her. Her hands lay palms up in her lap; occasionally a finger twitched like the wing of a dying bird. Her hair jumped around her face in mischievous strands that had gotten free of the pretty silver hair clasp that had been put in askew. The priest kept his eyes on her though it was the man who addressed him.

"Good day, sir," Reverend Willoughby said. "I am Reverend Willoughby."

The priest knew a little English; he knew the word *reverend.*

"We are here in God's name," Willoughby continued.

"Sí, sí, entiendo, señor," the priest squinted as he looked up, for it was afternoon and the sky was nothing but blue. "Pero, hable español, por favor."

Reverend Willoughby looked at his wife who did not look at him but said, "He wants you to speak Spanish."

"I don't speak Spanish . . . español," the reverend said.

The priest shrugged and said, "You want what?"

"I want to speak with whoever is in charge here. I want to speak to the chief, an authority of some kind."

The priest shrugged again, "No entiendo, señor."

"What is wrong with these people?" Willoughby muttered.

"The gospel, the truth," he yelled down at the priest.

"Ah, sí, señor. En Osuna, *yo* hablo 'the gospel.' " The priest unclasped his hands and pointed to himself.

"Of course this man will not relinquish the hold he has over these poor souls," Reverend Willoughby said to his wife.

"Osuna es católico." The priest spread his arms out

and twisted his upper body to encompass the houses behind him. "Todo el mundo—católico, señor."

Sara surprised them by speaking.

"We need food," she said as quietly as a breeze. "We
are almost out of food." She opened her mouth and
pointed into it.

The priest smiled and stepped back.

"You ask, you ask the people, señora, pero no hay
mucho." He pointed to the earth. "La tierra tiene sed."

Sara jumped down from the wagon. She touched the
horses as she came around them and headed straight for
the first doorway.

"Sara!" Reverend Willoughby called out. Then he
said, "You must pardon my wife. She is very tired." He
jumped off and followed her. When he took her arm she
shook him off and kept walking. The priest watched
them, standing still with his hands refolded over his
cassock.

"Sara, you must not beg."

"We are almost out of food," Sara said. She stopped
in front of the thick rectangular opening of the first
house.

"But we have money. It is not wise to continue like
this. Let us use the money your father gave us, before
begging from savages . . . from Catholics."

Sara turned her mottled face to her husband. "There
is no money," she said.

Willoughby felt acid collect on the lining of his stomach.

"Forty dollars," he said.

"There is no forty dollars," Sara said, and then she
could not help but laugh. She was mainly laughing at
the beads of sweat on her husband's high, smooth brow.

"Sara," Willoughby said, grabbing his wife's collaps-
ible shoulders, "what have you done with the money?"

"There never was any money. We have no food. We have no money."

"What are you saying?" Willoughby felt the sun boil his skin underneath his frail hair. Never in his life had he been so physically uncomfortable and forlorn.

"I am saying, there never was any money. We have no food. We have no money."

"You have gone mad," Willoughby moaned.

Sara turned to the house.

"Hello?" she called out.

A big woman who'd been waiting to be summoned came out smiling without showing her teeth.

"We need food," Sara said.

Willoughby bent his head and moaned.

The woman shrugged. Sara opened her mouth and pointed inside it.

"Toda la comida es para mi familia. No tengo mucho." Then she repeated, "Para mi familia," and turned away.

Meanwhile, Reverend Willoughby had gone running back to the wagon which the priest had left.

From inside the next house an old man whose skin had hardened into wrinkles spoke English to Sara.

"Ask the padre, señora. He will help you." And he turned away.

Reverend Willoughby came running back, stumbling and stopping to pick up something that fell out of his arms. He reached Sara just as she got to the third house.

"Give them these, Sara," he wheezed, handing her one of the Bibles he had with him.

In some of the homes people squatted in the dimness and didn't even bother to come and meet the woman to see what she wanted. One woman let Sara have a drink of water. They all took the Bibles and nodded. When all the Bibles were gone, Willoughby dragged himself back to the wagon.

Sara walked back slowly. She shaded her eyes with her hand and looked at the sky, not at anything in particular. She was weary from everything, and they had had to travel again because of Reverend Willoughby's anxiousness to prove himself. They had passed through Albuquerque ten days ago. It was a horrible place, muddier and more ramshackle than Santa Fe. There were more Anglos there, and so the architecture included stumbling imitations of eastern homes and long wooden structures with no tree or bush to decorate them. The man who clerked at the store there had warned them that the Osuna people kept to themselves and didn't like strangers.

"They're ignorant," the reverend had said. "They've been told how to think by the papists. They just need to be treated like children, with discipline and patience. They will see the error of their ways."

"A lotta buildin' goin' on here," the man had said, seeing Sara's ragged look. "You might wanta pick up some kinda job for a while, get a little cash in your pocket."

"I am a man of God, sir," Reverend Willoughby said. And as he took his wife out of the store she heard the clerk laugh and say to a man who was leaning on the counter, "Man of the cloth got a stomach jes' like ever'one else, don't he, Abe?"

Now Sara walked back to the wagon, feeling the eyes of the Osuna people on her. These people were wondering if she'd figure out how to survive, wondering why Anglos and priests were cursed to wander around on the earth with no grandfathers and grandmothers, sisters or brothers.

"What are you looking for?" Sara asked her husband

when she found him tearing apart the back of the wagon.

"The money," he said. "The forty dollars."

"I told you, there is no money." More of her hair had come out of her hair clasp, and her cheeks were red.

Reverend Willoughby got a knife off of the low wall of the wagon where it hung beside the small pistol. He went for the chairs, shimmying between the mattress and trunks.

"What are you doing?" Sara asked.

"If it is sewn in the chairs that he gave you. . . ."

"He didn't give me the chairs."

"If you hid the money in them. . . ." He ripped the fabric, the green silky weave splitting easily.

"Edmund!" Sara screamed. "Oh, Edmund, no! It is all I have! They were my mother's . . . oh, dear God, Edmund, please. . . ." Her numbness fled, and she began to weep terribly, wildly. She bit her knuckles while she watched the straw pop up out of the seats.

"You have gone quite mad," the reverend said calmly.

"I will show you what my father gave me," Sara howled.

"Damn you, woman, be quiet, or that priest will hear," Willoughby hissed.

"Good God, woman, you are truly mad. Satan has you most certainly."

He finished with the chairs. Sara sank down below view, on the ground behind the wagon. She wept until she imagined that tiny rows of corn might grow where her tears had ended the drought.

"My father," Sara mumbled, sucking her knuckles, "he did not give me money, and he did not give me those chairs."

Reverend Willoughby stood above her. Tufts of his

thin hair were sticking out every which way, and his
eyes were perfectly round.

"You have gone mad," he said.

Sara got up, sucking in air convulsively, trying to
control herself.

"Reverend Willoughby," she said, trying hard to be
calm, "I want to tell you about my father and about
Reverend Barkstone. They have violated me. You must
know this. You must finally know this. Now that I have
no chairs. . . ."

The reverend stepped back from his wife and narrowed his eyes. "In the name of God, woman, you are
insane. You are demon possessed, and I will not listen
to you!"

And he went some ways away from the wagon to
pray to God for guidance in dealing with his tremen-
dous burdens. When he had come back from Fort Union
to the Barkstones, he'd sensed that his wife was crack-
ing. But it wasn't the kind of thing he wanted to believe. Now he could not ignore her. God knows what
she might say, and in front of the priest. Thank God she
didn't know español. He went off by himself, to a little
hill full of juniper and sandy gravel, and found a place
out of the sun beneath an overhanging rock. He narrowed his eyes, looking at the endless sight of browns
and the jagged, distant purples.

"I had a dream," Sara told the ground. "I had a
strange dream. I dreamt that a dog that looked like a
ragged, hunched-over fox was barking and barking outside my window. And when I looked out I knew that he
meant for me to follow him, and yet I could see in his
eyes that he was up to some mischief. Still, I followed,
and I came to a hole in the ground and went into it, and
I saw the dog's face looking down at me, laughing. And
he said, 'You must go down there, Sara. You must go

down there.' And I went down there and felt that many, many people were hidden in the shadows, and I knew that they were not going to hurt me. They were all around me, almost like part of the earth itself they were so well hidden. Yet I knew they were there and I knew that I needed them, and I guessed that the strange dog was an angel."

As she told the earth this dream, the priest came to tell the Willoughbys that they must move on or he would have to move them himself. But when he came around to the back of the wagon and saw the woman, he stopped. He thought she was retching because she was on the ground, propped up by her arms with her head hanging down and her mouth aimed toward the earth. Then he realized that she was speaking and that there was no one else around. He crossed himself and went back to the church.

X

A sheepherder, a short Hispanic man with one milky eye, stopped in on the padre of Osuna Pueblo to confess his sins. He had few sins, so he talked mostly about the trials of sheepherding. In Spanish he said, "And the drought makes everything that much worse. The Apaches are on the prowl again. Just the other day three of them stood up on the ridge above my herd and gave me a lot of trouble."

The man was obviously upset. The priest made sympathetic noises.

"And one had a mean voice and spoke Spanish," the poor herder continued rubbing his thighs with the palms of his hands. "He called out, 'Fatten them up for us, lard head.' I swear to you, padre, it was the longest day of my life. I don't have a gun."

The herder went on to explain that he had then lost one ewe to the raiders, but that he was grateful that the thugs hadn't bothered his wife and eight children.

The priest blessed the man and sent him on his way, and then his mind was diverted by the arrival of the Willoughbys. Given a choice of threats, the priest would rather have had a band of Apaches than one Protestant.

Reverend Willoughby didn't concern himself with Apaches at all. He was, just as the priest feared, preparing to startle the souls of Osuna Pueblo into Presbyterianism. He was preparing a gripping sermon to be given in the priest's cocky little chapel. It would be a Protestant sermon, a Presbyterian sermon. Never mind that it, like the Bibles he had handed out, was to be in English and no one in Osuna Pueblo spoke English fluently except one old man who was a trader and never went to any services in the church.

Reverend Willoughby's pupils shrank into sharp little points of black as they darted over the frail tissue of the scriptures. Mrs. Willoughby lay in the wagon with her dead dining room chairs. She lay very still, for she'd come to the conclusion that if she moved she'd bring attention to herself, and whenever God took notice of her something terrible happened.

Sara had been shushing the voices in her head in an attempt to find a way to satisfy God. God was silent; it was a punishing silence that wasn't going to end until Sara transformed herself into something decent, something worthy of God's love.

She heard her husband snap a page of the Bible as he paced outside.

A thought came up in her mind, a thought about Reverend Willoughby's hands as she had seen them at the teachers college, curled over the lectern. She talked over it, saying anything to keep away from that thought.

"Find a home," she mumbled, "a Christian home. I am weak. I know that I am weak."

Willoughby heard his wife muttering to herself again, and he rubbed the back of his neck.

"Please, oh please," he heard her moan, and then he heard the weeping that had been going on at intervals since the day before when he had slashed the chairs and found no money.

When Willoughby was ready to go to the church he called to Sara, "Come along. I am going to gather these poor people together and give them the true word of God. I suggest that you be present at this miracle."

Sara turned on her side, and she knew that this was the only movement she was capable of. She now had the side of the wagon to stare at.

"Sara, I am speaking to you. My wife should stand beside me. I want you to stop this fit of yours and come with me."

Sara tried to imagine herself getting up and going outside the wagon. And she felt sure that in the bald light all her flaws would be horribly exposed. She patted her hair, and it felt wilder than ever to her.

"I am sick," she said, not getting up from the bed. She suddenly realized that her life could be immensely simplified if she became an invalid like her Aunt Betsy on her mother's side who always lay in bed with a little lace cap on. She never had to do anything, and no one would have dreamed of asking her to go to the desert in a broken-down wagon.

"You have no fever," the reverend answered.

"I don't feel well," she said and as an afterthought added, "Perhaps I am . . . in a frail condition." Pregnancy, it was always whispered, had been the first phase of Aunt Betsy's demise.

Reverend Willoughby walked off to the chapel alone.

Sara listened to the crunching of his Christian shoes on the dust and rock. Some minutes after this crunching faded, she heard the blunt clanging of the church bell.

Sara bit hard into the flesh on the side of her hand.

She said, "I want to go home."

Sara tried to picture a home. She saw her mother, but she could not think of any place, not even the farm in Roanoke. She made up a warm room in her mind and put her mother there. Sara did not belong in the house where her sister and brother and mother seemed to belong, where the father defined them with his miserable drunkenness. Sara didn't know who she was there, and yet some naughty, rebellious demon in her refused to belong. As a little girl she had made up stories about where she belonged. She made them up down by the cow stream where her shoes got red mud on them, or up in the barn loft where she watched the goats nuzzle each other below, or in her bed at night where the stories ended up between her thighs. In the stories someone loved Sara, a man with large hands. This man watched her, always watched over her, and touched her as though he knew and loved her well. He read the Bible and they went to church together. It hurt to think of those stories while imagining Reverend Willoughby pacing in the Osuna church.

In the back of the wagon, Sara imagined burying her head in her mother's skirts, burrowing so deeply that the image became obscene and violent.

"Everything is coming apart," Sara cried. "I don't understand, God. What do you want of me? I know I have been lazy and weak. Please take care of me. I'll be good. I'll be good."

Her hand stroked her own shoulder and arm and then it passed over her breasts and down along her thigh. Then she began weeping again and rocked, rubbing her shoulder over and over. Sometimes she muttered, "Poor Reverend Willoughby."

This went on until she heard a faint crunching of footsteps. She sat up wild-eyed and flew her shaking fingers around her head until she had all her hair in the silver clasp again. Then Willoughby's panting, red face popped into view in the opening in the back of the wagon.

"Get ready to go," he said, "we're going now."

He disappeared and Sara heard him banging and shuffling around.

"Sara," he called back, "come up here now. You had better sit up here with me."

Sara slowly got out of the wagon and stood on the ground blinking against the setting sun. Although the sun had been hot all day, it now lost its force and the coldness of early fall drifted in like fog with the twilight. Sara dreaded another cold night camping out in the wagon. She had a bad headache. She shaded her eyes and looked up at her husband.

"Get up here!" Willoughby called out and he looked terrible, red and frightened.

Sara got up beside him and sat down. She stared at his face and thought, "It is up to me now, with God's help. My husband needs me. I must be strong. God will show me a sign soon."

The wagon creaked and reluctantly hobbled out of Osuna Pueblo. Willoughby was yelling, "Hiya! Hiya!" to the horses who paid no attention to him and walked very slowly. Sara looked behind to see if anyone was chasing them, but there was no one.

"God help us. God give us the strength to go on with no food and a wagon that needs repairs," Sara prayed.

And then suddenly she turned to her husband and announced, "I am the child of God, coming home as the prodigal son."

Willoughby looked at his wife as though she'd turned into a lizard. He was shivering in his sweat-dampened black suit that was wearing out at the elbows. He turned back to the horses, which had sped up to a lope.

"I did nothing to deserve this, Lord," he said.

"Hey! Hey!" a high voice called out. Sara leaned out to look behind. A young boy was catching up to them.

He held a basket. Three other children, one a small little girl, ran after him.

"Stop," Sara said to her husband.

"Get the gun," Willoughby said.

Sara protested, "They're just children." But Reverend Willoughby yelled, "Hiya!" and shook the reins. He believed that his impetus was the only sane and righteous thing in the world. The horses still didn't care. The wagon was wobbling so badly that the boy was able to catch up and run alongside.

"Para la señora," he said, breathing hard and grinning shyly. He handed Sara the basket and then stopped, leaving himself behind.

The basket had a lump of blue corn bread in it.

"Look," Reverend Willoughby said, "those demons have given us moldy bread."

"It is not mold, reverend," Sara said while simultaneously thanking the Lord for this little miracle. "That is the color of the corn. This is a sign from God. We will not perish!"

"No thanks to those godless savages," Reverend Willoughby said, annoyed that he needed to relieve himself but didn't dare stop the wagon.

Reverend Willoughby did not tell his wife, whose mind was obviously already overburdened, about the occasion of his heroism in the Osuna chapel. He did not tell her that the priest was at that moment scratching out a letter to the governor requesting an indictment against a Reverend Edmund Willoughby for trespassing on church property and assaulting a priest.

When he'd heard the church bell ringing, the padre knew good and well who was ringing it. The Osuna people wondered why the bell was ringing at an odd time of day when no one had died. After five minutes of the ringing, a couple of men went to find out what was up. Some women and children followed. Those who wandered in saw a wild man dressed in a tattered black suit, bellowing in English, words that sounded like rocks falling on a roof. Some knew English enough to recognize words like *God* and *Hell* and *Jesus*. They watched the man grow redfaced. They watched the thin hair over his forehead drip sweat. The padre swished in and passed through the people. Reverend Willoughby slapped the Bible he had in his hand. The padre watched; he clenched his teeth so that the muscles of his jaw twitched.

"El loco no habla español," he said laughing, but there was no mirth in his laugh, and it made people cover their mouths and giggle.

"Vamos," the padre said to a young man who often did repairs on the church and worked in the padre's garden. Then the two went up to Reverend Willoughby who was entreating the people, in English, to let Jesus into their lives.

"Habla de Jesús," the young Osuna man said to the padre.

"Sí, pero es loco. No es católico."

"This is no your church, señor," the padre said to Willoughby.

"A church belongs to God, and to those who speak God's truth," Willoughby said in a voice loud enough to be heard in Albuquerque.

"I speak to you, señor, that you are against the law. I ask for you to leave."

"I follow God's laws."

"You will leave my church, señor," the padre said.

The people smiled at them and the children stopped running back and forth in the pews. Two elderly women shook their heads in pity for the loco whose wife had been reduced to begging.

"God has sent me to save these people." When Willoughby said this, some of his spittle sprayed onto the padre's oily face, which was a little bit below his own.

The padre's white, soft hand closed around Willoughby's wrist. Reverend Willoughby held his free hand up with the Bible waving in it as though it was his enemy's head on a stick.

"This is God's word," he called out. "Listen not to the papists. I bring you God's true word."

"Ayúdame, hijo," the priest said and the Osuna man took the reverend's upper arm.

"You keep them in ignorance," Willoughby said as he was being dragged down the short aisle to the doorway. People parted.

"Go to your own people," the padre said.

He helped drag Willoughby out past the souls that no one owned. Willoughby stumbled into the dust, and a thin elderly woman stopped to offer her hand to raise him up. He would not be touched. He got to his knees and started to pray out loud, but the priest pulled him up to his feet and walked him out of the churchyard. The young Osuna man walked away, unwilling to play any more of a part in this loss of dignity.

When the two men were a good distance away from the church the padre said, "I will tell the governor to put you in jail, señor." His eyes flashed. "You have made a very bad day for me, señor, and I no want to have bad days. Entiende?"

Willoughby wouldn't look anywhere but heavenward, and he said, "Yea, though I walk through the valley of the shadow of death . . ."

The padre put his finger on the reverend's jumping Adam's apple.

"I will slit your little neck if you no leave, señor."

And so the reverend had stridden off to his wagon and his weeping wife.

As they rode in the desert, the wagon thumped badly. Sara sat stiffly erect, smiling against the headache that put pictures of her doing violence into her head. The dark and cold hurried in from the east, so that soon Reverend Willoughby was shivering and steering the horses into piñon bushes.

"This is a strange place," Sara said.

Reverend Willoughby turned and looked at her as though he might go get the gun and shoot her in the head. Sara looked away and clasped her fingers together.

"The devil is a strange thing," she said, looking out toward the desert. "He is clever, and I'm beginning to see the ways in which he works. I am, reverend, and you will see that God means for us to do great things in His name. This place is so strange."

"It has been forsaken," Reverend Willoughby said. "It is the way the Garden of Eden looked after Adam's fall. No water, no trees."

"Oh, but there are trees," Sara said. "They are just squat and twisted."

"Like demons trying to come up through the ground."

This silenced Sara. She moved closer to Willoughby and clutched his arm.

"I am afraid, Reverend Willoughby," she said. "I think they are here because of me. I think they want to convince me to do something terrible." She began to weep again, and the reverend jerked his elbow and moved her off of him.

"I demand that you stop this weeping, Sara," he said. "I regret that I ever brought you out here. You must pull yourself together."

Sara said as quietly and calmly as possible, "Reverend Willoughby, my head hurts terribly. I have never in my life had such a pain in my head. It is as though even now demons were fighting in my soul. I think that I cannot go on, Reverend Willoughby. I think that I want to go home or I will die."

"And what will we say when we return? What will we do?" Reverend Willoughby hissed and snapped the reins.

And Sara could not help but weep again, and she grabbed her husband's arm. "Could we not just live normally, as normal man and wife and have children and such? I know that I would be a good mother, Reverend Willoughby. Oh, I can think of many things I could do, if we had a home and I could tend it, wash and cook and arrange furniture." She thought of the chairs that Willoughby had slashed and let go of his arm. Sniffling, she looked away and her mind raced with pain and voices and pictures.

Then the wagon, as if exhausted by the activity in Sara's mind, banged down on one side. The left front wheel had finally decided to take off and was rolling into the twilight. The horses kept dragging the wagon. There was a terrible, scraping noise. Unseen branches snapped. Reverend Willoughby yelled at the animals, "Whoa! Whoa! Whoa!" Then it dawned on them that something was amiss and that they had a good excuse to stop. When the whole contraption was finally still, the Willoughbys sat in the middle of a vast flatness. Huge mesas, motionless black gods standing guard at the gates of the cosmos, did not notice the small and pitiful disturbance.

"I suppose we are stopping here," Sara said, and instead of weeping she looked at her husband and laughed.

XI

At night in the desert the stars form sparkling streams in the sky. The air feels cold and clarifies the huge blocks of darkness made by the mesas. In all that emptiness it is amazing how many animals and spirits hide and make sounds that seem to come right out of the air: a coyote's yipping, an owl's call, a crunching of something—perhaps a footstep, perhaps bones being crushed. An outsider cannot hide: there are no big trees to scurry to, the rocks can't conceal all sides of a person. As Sara stared around her, unable to see anything familiar, she thought that either this was a place that showed God's hugeness and omnipotence or it was a place that showed His absence.

The Willoughbys had managed to build a smoky but warming fire out of piñon and scrub oak. They boiled two cups of the little water they had left and made tea to drink with the blue corn cake given to them by the boy at Osuna Pueblo. Sara stared at her husband and, stubbornly, Willoughby did not once glance into her eyes. He refused to be a dupe in her relentless drama.

True enough, Sara had been welcoming a growing party of voices that vied for authority in her head. At the moment, she was listening to a debate between Job and the man who used to sell subscriptions to magazines at the farm. Job went on and on about enduring and believing in the abstraction of God's will. The magazine subscription man pitched the joys of earthly delights which involved pictures of men and women in department store underwear.

"We must admit defeat," Edmund said to Sara. "I was not meant to administer to savages. That task must be left to rougher men, to men who don't have my intellect but have coarser ways that these people can understand. I don't see how Reverend Barkstone endures. Oh, it is horrible to think of the ways Satan has taken these people into his clutches."

"Yes," his wife said, and she blinked rapidly to try to drive a picture of Reverend Barkstone in department store underwear out of her head.

"I am afraid, Edmund," Sara whispered. "I am afraid that Satan is taking over my soul. I am so tired."

Willoughby clenched his jaw several times and then said, "I am weary of your selfishness, Sara. Can you only think of yourself?"

Sara looked wildly into the fire, horrified by her failure to be good. She wondered if she could please her husband by putting her hand in the little flame that tickled the air. Then she found some spark of hope for herself.

"I have always wanted children," she said. "I always wanted to take care of them and protect them."

"You are a child yourself, Sara. I shudder to think how careless a mother you would be. Why, you'd most likely forget to feed them." He stood up and said down to her, "And you should count yourself lucky that you don't have to endure the horrors most wives have to endure with their husbands and child begetting."

Sara began to weep from confusion.

"By God, Sara," the reverend said in something daringly close to swearing, "sometimes I think your being raised on a farm has exposed you to the basest kinds of things. Your parents should have sent you off to school instead of letting you learn from the barnyard. The things you must have seen!" He clasped his hands and touched his forehead with them.

"What am I to do with you, Sara?"

"Your hair needs cutting, Edmund," Sara suggested.

In the small dot of firelight their camp made in the desert—a light that made the blackness outside of it that much blacker and that illuminated only pieces of wagon, pieces of horse, pieces of ground—Sara worked on Reverend Willoughby's hair. He sat on a stool, and she stood above him managing a fat wooden comb and a pair of shears. The smell of his fetid hair oil spoiled her love of his head. Still, she held up grimy pieces of his thin hair and snipped with devoted concentration. A pair of coyotes wanting attention from the big universe let forth some plaintive howls. Crunching noises came and went. Sometimes one of the horses stamped the ground. The little fire chewed on its wood and spit out sparks in loud pops. From a great distance the camp was a circle of light in which a man sat and a woman stood very still—like a float in a religious pageant.

When one of the crunching noises got close, Sara looked up. She saw on the other side of the light the dim outline of three persons. At first she thought that they were women who had stepped out of the underwear advertisements in *Godey's Lady's Book* because they had long, flowing hair and something like bloomers on. But soon she noticed the streaks of dirt on their faces and the naked hard flesh of their chests. They muttered to each other, two of them grinning widely. One of these two had a squinched-up face that reminded Sara of a gargoyle, a demon.

Sara stopped with the shears ready to cut and a strand of her husband's hair sliding from between her fingers.

"Sara," Reverend Willoughby said, "I am thinking that perhaps you should enter a rest home when we return. I am not capable of doing my work and seeing to you as well. I realize that you have been through some terrible ordeals here. Sara? Sara, are you listening to me?"

Sara whispered, "I refuse to have dealings with you," speaking to the devil she saw grinning at her from the blackness outside their light.

Reverend Willoughby shook his head and said, "A normal woman would not speak to her husband in such a way. And it illustrates what I am saying, Sara—that you are not a healthy woman."

"No, reverend," Sara whispered, "I was not speaking to you."

"It is no matter, Sara," the reverend sighed. "I have come to the conclusion that you are not in your right mind. I suppose I am partly to blame for this, having made a poor decision in asking you to accompany me. I have failed, Sara. If I had known what a burden you would become. . . . I could have succeeded on my own."

Sara didn't move. She heard what her husband was saying and wondered if she should pretend that she didn't see what she was staring straight at. She remembered when her father had tied her wrists behind her back and put her in the wagon to be taken to the insane asylum. She was ecstatically grateful when the demon with the squinched face loudly kicked a puff of dirt into their camp so that the reverend swung around and saw him grinning. This man stepped forward, casually, and the others followed. They sauntered into the firelight.

"Hey, señor y señora," Small Face said, showing off his Spanish. "Buenas noches."

Reverend Willoughby jumped to his feet, letting the tablecloth he'd had around his shoulders slide to the ground. Sara could not think. Her head was filled with a nasty whispering that said, "Here they are, Sara. They've come for you, Sara." They were dark people, broken off of the night, like the people in her dream who were made of dirt, pieces of the earth who hid, waiting for her in a hole in the ground. When one of them moved, he rattled softly; to Sara's ear he sounded like a baby's rattle.

"How far away from home we are," she said to her husband, and then, like the tablecloth, she slid down and landed on her knees, still holding the scissors and the comb. Small Face said something in Apache to Eats Fish and they both laughed. Broken Nose surveyed what was to be seen, looking for food and guns.

"What is this?" Reverend Willoughby said, bending his chin into his neck until it almost disappeared. "What do you want?"

"No habla español, señor?" Small Face asked.

Sara began to say the Lord's Prayer very loudly. Willoughby spun around and slapped her so hard that she fell over on the ground. This caused even Broken Nose to laugh. Small Face and Eats Fish were almost doubled over.

"Be quiet, Sara," Willoughby hissed. "These are savages. Just keep quiet and let me deal with them."

Sara left the scissors and comb on the ground and got back to her knees.

The three men broke apart, strolling about the little camp. Sara smelled meat and grease on them and felt powerfully hungry.

Broken Nose stopped in front of Reverend

Willoughby. He looked him over, narrowing his eyes, and said, "Give us some food."

His English surprised Willoughby so much, pleased him so much that he almost grabbed Broken Nose's hand to shake it. For a silly moment the reverend wondered if Broken Nose weren't some Yale man engaging him in a prank.

Small Face and Eats Fish looked at Broken Nose who now had power over what happened because he knew some English.

Sara had begun to let portions of the Lord's Prayer slip out again.

"For God's sake, Sara, shut up!" Reverend Willoughby cried.

This amused Small Face who started whooping and shouting "Shut up!" in English.

Sara and Broken Nose exchanged a glance. They looked right into each other's eyes, and Sara heard her voices go silent. With his own people, Broken Nose would have disdained a woman who was rude enough to stare into a person's face. He looked away, and Sara's voices picked up again, like dinner guests recovering from the sound of broken glass.

"Give us food," Broken Nose said again to Willoughby. He was solemn but enjoying the tension he and his friends could create.

"We ... we have no food, good man," the reverend said. "I am sorry to have to refuse you."

"Hm," Broken Nose said and nodded. He couldn't help looking back at Sara again.

Small Face and Eats Fish walked around to look the horses over.

"Our wagon is broken," Reverend Willoughby said. "We are poor."

"Give us whiskey and guns," Broken Nose said.

"Good man, I assure you that I have no whiskey!"

"Vamos," Small Face said and Eats Fish lumbered behind him out of the light. Broken Nose stayed for a moment. He went over and touched Sara's hair to see what it felt like. Then he left. The Willoughbys could hear their laughter and joking fade away.

Reverend Willoughby bolted off, ripping at his pants buttons. After he had let go of everything in his intestines he came back. For a few minutes he leaned forward and grasped the back of the wagon. Then Sara heard him weeping.

She stood up and went to him. She rubbed his back and he wept harder, finally turning to her and weeping in his wife's arms.

"The devil is testing me," he sobbed. "I must not let him twist me."

He firmly broke away from Sara and straightened himself up. Sara looked at the ground.

"Sara," Willoughby said, "you must try not to always put yourself in the center of people's attention. I realize that you are demented and cannot control yourself, but in having to look after you I was not able to concentrate on the test God set before me. Thank the Lord they have left us now. We should pray and give thanks."

"I am not demented, Edmund," Sara said. She had seen what she had seen, and she had felt her husband tremble in her arms; the man who would put her away in a building with bars on the windows and faces dripping tears and drool had turned to her for strength. Perhaps there was a new way for her to think about things.

"These men are not through with us," Sara said calmly—so calmly that her husband lost track of his convictions for a moment.

"Don't be foolish. Let us go in and pray and then lie

down. God will send us help in the morning. We will know what to do."

"We should take the horses and get away from here," Sara said.

"You are talking like a child, Sara. We cannot simply go across the desert at night. We could not possibly survive in the desert, alone at night. What are you thinking of?"

"I want to go home," Sara said.

Reverend Willoughby ignored her. He went into the wagon and had just picked up his Bible when a whoop swooped out of the darkness. The three Apaches swarmed into the camp like twenty. When Eats Fish saw the look on the Willoughbys' faces he started laughing so that he couldn't do the war whoops right. He kept trying to be serious again, but every time he looked at the reverend standing up in the back of the wagon, hunched over like an old woman with his mouth hanging open, Eats Fish had to laugh. Small Face yanked his hair.

Broken Nose leapt up to where the reverend was, pushed him out of the wagon then jumped down behind him. He picked up a rock and struck him on the back of the head with it. Sara groaned and muttered over and over again, "Oh, dear God, oh, dear God, oh, dear God."

Small Face went into the wagon and started throwing things around. Reverend Willoughby moaned. Small Face came to the back of the wagon talking and laughing and holding up one of the torn dining room chairs. He tossed it out on the ground. Sara started to run toward it, as though it was a stricken person. Eats Fish caught her and held her wrists behind her back. The horses got agitated by all the ruckus and made the wagon jerk forward about an inch. Small Face fell down in the back of the wagon.

"There is nothing here," Small Face called in Apache. "These pieces of dog shit are poorer than us."

"Then let's just take the horses," Eats Fish said.

"And her," Broken Nose said. "Take her."

Small Face laughed and then shook his head, "Don't tell me, you dog in heat, that you are thinking of putting it in her. I never thought even you would fornicate with a white woman."

Eats Fish laughed. Broken Nose stepped toward Small Face and then stopped.

"They have taken our women. Let them see how it feels," he said. "Perhaps they will trade for her—bullets."

"I say that we cut her open and leave her for the soldiers to see," Small Face said.

Eats Fish looked sidelong at Sara.

All Sara knew was that the three men looked at her. Her hair had burst out of the clasp and was all around her head like black tumbleweed. Her nightdress was soiled and sweaty. She looked imploringly at Broken Nose, perhaps because he was the one who knew English. She looked at him to help her understand what was happening to her.

"We will take her with us. There are many good reasons to do this." Broken Nose strode away.

Her fate was determined. Eats Fish let go of her wrists and he followed Broken Nose around the wagon to unhitch the horses. Small Face felt the line of each horse's back with the palm of his hand. He commented that one had the spine of a slack rope, but that the other looked good. Broken Nose was unhitching Mister, who had the good back. They all three guessed the ages of the horses, Small Face insisting that the mare was older than Eats Fish and Broken Nose thought. He was lifting up Mrs.' upper lip to show her teeth when they heard a shot.

The three squatted down and froze. A moment of silence followed. Finally, one crouching behind the other, they crept around the wagon to see what was going on.

The wild woman with the wild hair was standing over her husband. She had a pistol in her hand, and he had a hole in his head.

"Eeeee," Small Face whispered.

Sara bent down and slipped the Bible out of Reverend Willoughby's arm. She held it tightly to her chest with her forearm. Then she turned to the three warriors stuck to the side of the wagon.

"Eeeee," Small Face moaned again.

Sara walked up to Broken Nose and handed him the pistol.

Eats Fish said, "Din Monganii' istsanii' Ntii'—This white woman is a witch."

Sara folded her free arm over the one holding the Bible and looked heavenward. Though her legs trembled like gelatin, she was ready to be martyred, to be taken and done with as God willed.

XII

Gliding just below the stars, way up in the sky where she could see the roundness of the earth, a hawk cocked her pointed head. She heard the thin stream of a song, like smoke. She heard it come up from the bottom part of the night.

> All hail the power of Jesus' name
> Let angels prostrate fall
> Bring forth the royal diadem
> And crown him Lord of all
> Bring forth the royal diadem
> And crown him Lord of all.

The song's center moved slowly along, moving too slowly for the hawk, to the scalloped black line that was the fringe of trees along the river the Spaniards called the Rio Grande. Small Face asked Broken Nose what the song meant.

"Is it a song of power?" he asked.

"No," Broken Nose answered. "It is about a god they call Jesus. It is a prayer to this Jesus."

Sara stopped singing when she heard the name of Jesus spoken by the savage who walked behind her. He said it the way the Spanish did—"Hay-zoos"—but Sara understood it.

111

"Praise God," she whispered, "they know the name of the Saviour."

After walking a few yards with a beatific grin on her face, Sara heard some voice in her head saying she was a fool. It took on the face of her Grandmother Franklin, the one whose skin was gray and who could make a problem out of anything, even a miracle. She always looked like she'd licked alum. Sara didn't want her there, so she burst into the Twenty-third Psalm.

"Yea!" she began and Eats Fish, who was feeling more and more jumpy by the minute, thought his heart was going to drop out of his asshole.

"Yea! though I walk through the valley of the shadow of death . . ."

Small Face laughed at Eats Fish, and Broken Nose put his salty hand over Sara's mouth. The horses balked. Mister jerked at the reins by which Small Face pulled him along. Mrs. copied him weakly but Eats Fish kept her going steadily.

The river was a dim trickle. Small Face said, "It sounds like an old man pissing." Small Face's humor was wearing on Broken Nose. There wasn't one raiding expedition that didn't end with Broken Nose believing he would kill Small Face if he made one more joke.

Eats Fish scratched around one of the twisty cottonwood trees and found the blankets and leather envelope they'd stashed there. Small Face whipped the pouch out of Eats Fish's hand and dumped the contents out on the dry dirt. There were several big pieces of meat wrapped in greasy strips of bark, six ears of corn, and about twenty United States Army spoons.

Small Face hunted through the loot, picking out a piece of meat. Broken Nose and Eats Fish gave sidelong glances to Sara who stood straight, still clutching the Bible. Then Eats Fish went down to the pitiful river leading both horses. He walked across the dry bed to suck up some of the water that was left in the middle. The horses fluttered their lips over the muddy moisture and then let themselves be tied up to a tree where a little bit of grass was available to them.

Broken Nose pushed Sara down and built a fire onto which Small Face threw one of the pieces of mutton. Then the four humans sat around the fire watching the meat spit. Small Face batted it out with a stick and each of the men ripped off a portion.

Sara was hungry. She was so hungry she whimpered a little to smell the mutton and watch the men eat it.

"Look at her," Small Face chuckled as he chewed. "She follows the meat with her eyes like a hungry dog." He held out a piece to Sara, waving it around, then put it into his own mouth and let out a "Ha ha!"

Broken Nose threw a piece at her. She picked it up and brushed off as much of the dirt as she could. It was almost raw, hard to chew and swallow. It tasted like coal on the outside and warm blood inside.

"Praise God from whom all blessings flow," she said.

Her face was wide and dirty. The bones of her cheeks looked like wings ready to take her up to heaven.

"This white woman is crazy," Small Face said, shaking his head and grinning.

When they were ready to lie down, Broken Nose offered to keep watch first. He sat close by Sara because a woman who shot her own husband might cause some trouble. The mint he wore around his neck smelled sweet to Sara. Small Face pissed against a tree and then lay down on his blanket where he fell asleep chuckling to himself. Eats Fish spent a long time getting comfortable, spreading out the blanket one way then another, until Small Face yelled at him.

In the quiet, Sara looked up through the twisting, tangling cottonwood branches and prayed. She muttered the Lord's Prayer. Her arms were stiff around the Bible. Broken Nose stared down at her once and looked away quickly when she met his eyes. He was wearing his shirt open and his chest where the mint lay looked like greased rock in the vague light. His eyes stayed away from her, looking straight ahead. When he felt himself falling asleep, Broken Nose woke up Small Face.

Small Face got up and sat before the old fire and as soon as he heard Broken Nose's deep breaths he also lay down and went to sleep.

Sara woke at the very first light. She squirmed backwards, crouched and relieved herself, praying that she would be done before anyone saw her. She was so nervous to be done that she wet her nightgown a little when letting it down too soon. She had to pull up her bloomers after she lay down again. She had no thoughts about anything except what she saw and smelled and touched.

In daylight the three warriors looked awful, all smudged and cross. They looked to Sara like Mexicans gone awry, since some of their clothes had been got from Mexicans. They had shirts on and buckskin leggings with leather breechcloths tied around their waists. Small Face also had an empty cartridge belt around his waist. High buckskin boots came up to their mid-calves. Eats Fish wore a lot of jewelry, a necklace of turquoise and shell, an amulet made of quartz; several pollen bags hung from his breechcloth next to his knife, and he wore wristbands made of small, shiny beads. All of their faces were dirty and scarred in some way. Small Face's face repulsed Sara. In the full light it looked clearly like an elfish gargoyle. There was a nick in his pushed-in nose. Eats Fish had a straight scar over his upper lip where he was plucking out a few whiskers that had popped out overnight. These demons preened and fussed with their hair, undoing the red strips of cloth that went around their foreheads and combing out their long hair with their fingers. Broken Nose's hair was very long; it fell over his shoulders in clean, black strips. He too had a scar over his upper lip. It was shaped like an upside-down V.

The three ate some corn pancakes that were cold and greasy. A burned edge fell in Sara's lap. When she finished eating it she started singing, "My faith looks up to thee." The three men groaned and stood up. It was decided that Sara and Broken Nose would ride the gelding, and Eats Fish and Small Face would take turns sitting in the valley of the mare's back.

A hawk careened ahead of them way up high. She appeared to them in a flight broken by the branches of cottonwoods. Broken Nose was sitting in front of Sara and she could feel his attention change from the horse to the hawk. He watched the bird coast. Sara kept singing but she also thought how strange the men were. They were quiet—much quieter than white men. They hardly talked to each other, and when they did their voices were soft. And their language didn't sound at all like English or like Spanish. It had many stops and starts in it as though they talked with a discreet case of hiccups, or as though they stuttered. When they looked at her they always said, "Monganii'."

Sara started feeling bad in her stomach around noon. She thought, "Oh, no. I've been poisoned by the filthy food they gave me."

After a while the pain cut into her gut sharply. Broken Nose heard her stop singing but she still sat straight. He could see her little black shoes dangling down and he laughed to himself. He turned around to look at her and got a fright because he saw some kind of spirit, a ghost.

Broken Nose thought that Sara's nightgown looked like fog and her hair looked like pubic hair, black and curly, loose and light. His hand, Broken Nose thought, might pass right through this woman. But her eyes frightened him. They had substance, as condensed and heavy as ore. And they watched the curving, winding trunks and branches of the cottonwood with some kind of horror.

And indeed, Sara felt herself becoming lighter and lighter. The pain lifted her up. It was God's hand, grabbing her by her organs and lifting her up. "Here I am, traveling through the desert with demons, in this twisted hell with its twisted bars, and God reaches in. He has not forsaken me."

She hugged the Bible more tightly. The pain was bad and her palms sweated. "Please, God," she said aloud.

Reverend Willoughby, he was with God. He smiled down on her with a hole in his head. God's hand tightened and light shot up through her body. "Please God," she said again.

The party stopped for some reason. It was the gargoyle face. He got off his horse and pointed with his chin to the ground at some prints. He crouched down and touched the prints with two fingers. Small Face was stalking something and the other two dismounted to wait for him. Sara swayed, waiting, waiting. She didn't understand why they had stopped and waited silently. Broken Nose and Eats Fish waited without saying much. Sara was very tired, but the pain stiffened her muscles and kept her straight. "Please God," she whispered, and then she turned to Eats Fish and grabbed his wrist.

"I don't think I can do this," she said, and Eats Fish's

face went paler than hers. He pulled his arm away from her. Broken Nose said something humorous using the word *monganii'* again, but Eats Fish didn't laugh. Small Face came back sullen and disinterested in any dramas concerning the white woman.

But the white woman wouldn't move. As a matter of fact, she screamed—loudly, shrilly—so that even the river stopped flowing in the silence that followed. And the warriors stepped back because she was not screaming at them, and they didn't want to be in the way of whatever it was she saw.

"Grandmother!" Eats Fish said, "this woman makes my flesh jump."

"Let's kill her," Small Face said.

In Sara's head, the light had just about swallowed up everything. It came from the pain in her lower abdomen and she was afraid that she was going to die.

"I want to go home," Sara whispered. She crossed her forearms over her belly and wailed softly.

"She's witched," Small Face said. "Let's kill her."

Sara went down on her knees.

"Let's tie her to a tree and cut out her intestines," Small Face said.

Broken Nose finally gave Small Face a piece of his mind.

"You listen to your own farts and call it the wind," he said. "Why do you think you can run everything and not consider the grandfathers? It's enough that we left without their permission. I say that we have to be careful not to insult them further. Let's take this white woman back to Many Visions and Most Important Man and let them have authority over the matter."

"We bring horses," Small Face said.

Broken Nose knelt behind Sara and put his hands on her belly. He moved them in slow circles, going from

just beneath her ribs to just above her pubic bone. At
first Sara held her breath, then she let her torso move in
circles with Broken Nose's hands. He continued to
speak to Small Face.

"A fool knows what to do with horses. We must
show the elders that we recognize their wisdom in more
important matters. You don't act like one of the Superior People. You complain and insult others by acting
and speaking like a drunken man."

"You are one to talk," Small Face said. "You who
lived with Hopis! You are one to talk about respecting
the old men's ways. You run after women and keep
quiet as though you have no interest in your people.
And now you behave like a midwife!" He jutted his
chin out toward Sara, who was taking deep breaths as
Broken Nose continued to massage her belly. She was
concentrating on passing gas as quietly as possible.

"We don't need to talk about these matters now,"
Broken Nose said. "I say we take her back as a sign of
our respect for the wisdom of the old men—or . . . I
will tell them who said no to this."

Broken Nose picked Sara up and put her over his
shoulder. Her hair tickled his back and he could feel the
warmth of her buttocks near his face. He put her up on
Mister's back and got up behind her so that she could
lean against his chest as they rode on. The pain had
subsided, but Sara felt weak. She rested without resistance against Broken Nose's body, but she still clutched
the Bible.

"Oh, God," Sara muttered. "Oh, God, I will try to do
your will. I will try to be strong. I will bring your word
to these people. I will do my husband's work. Please
help me, God. Please, don't let them hurt me and I will
teach them how to be Christians." She closed her eyes

and felt the man's forearms close to her, railings that
kept her from falling to either side as he held the reins.

"What is going to happen to me?" she suddenly
thought and her eyes popped open. A shiver ran through
her body and she wondered if these men had been summoned by her father to take her to the insane asylum.

"Poor Edmund," she said aloud, closing her eyes.

They came to a place in the trees by the river where
some low, round dwellings had been built out of
branches of cottonwood and oak. Several small fires
smoked, and steam came from pots of water that
smelled of musty herbs. Sara saw many black-haired
people standing beside blankets spread out on the
ground. They watched the four ride in. The people
showed no surprise. They moved slowly. Their faces
were sad, even the children's faces. Some were standing
around a small fire that sent up a stream of piñon
smoke. Children dressed in long shirts meant for adults
stood around with their fingers in their mouths. There
were also dogs, thin, bony dogs sniffing at the ground
where the people had been sitting. Sara looked at the
people, trying to find in one of their faces a clue as to
what was going to happen to her. For a few moments
she was sure they were the people of the First Presbyterian Church of Roanoke, just a little unkempt and
darkened. Adjusting her eyes she saw Mrs. Fullerton
and her daughter, Judith, and the Matthewses with old
Grandmother Matthews. But there was something else
here, something else in the way they stood straight and
quiet, weary, but with no impatience. They stood looking at Sara as though she had stumbled upon the heart
and core of some strange cult, as though she'd passed
into the secret center of some power in the world. In
their sun-browned skin these people carried the materi-
als of the mountains and the desert. And they looked

burdened with old secrets—perhaps doomed. Sara muttered prayers.

Small Face got off of the mare and told Eats Fish to take it to where the other horses were kept. He took the leather satchel off and walked to his dwelling. Broken Nose slid off of the horse and pulled Sara down next to him. The Indian women pulled their shawls around their shoulders and looked at the ground. The men stretched their backs. Broken Nose pushed Sara forward so that she fell on the dirt, and two children ran up and stopped to look down at her. At that moment it began to rain.

XIII

When Many Visions was a boy, before his name was Many Visions, he couldn't shoot the carcass of an adult deer from two paces. He was a small, wiry boy who should have been agile. But his mother had had trouble conceiving and therefore all her children missed the mark in one way or another.

Many Visions had a choice. He could be a buffoon or a holy man. Being a buffoon meant a continual performance of his shortcomings in front of his people. Many Visions didn't have the kind of wit to be a real clown, to relieve tensions with good jokes that didn't insult anyone. Even as a boy Many Visions didn't have much of a sense of humor, so he just couldn't see himself as a buffoon. But he could see himself as a holy man, feared and respected. And he believed that all he had to do to become one was to have a religious experience. But not even during fasting did he have this religious experience. So for a while he continued trying to be a first-rate Superior Man. He claimed that other boys' arrows, the ones that felled the deer, were his. But each boy knew the design of his own arrows and could easily disprove Many Visions' claims. But Many Visions did not give in without argument, so afraid was he of hearing the others laugh at him and tell stories that made the women laugh. Long after these hunting expeditions, even after Many Visions got his name, two elders, Shoots Straight and Three Fingers, held a grudge against the medicine man for having tried to make himself look good at their expense.

It was during these hunts that Many Visions began to have belief in himself as a healer. He got terrible stomach pains that came to him in dreams. He suspected witchery from the start, thinking that a witch might be helping another boy whose arrow he had tried to claim. And sure enough, these stomach pains came on just before he was supposed to go on a hunt or raid. His mother gave him a sweet herb tea which helped for a time. His father refused to look at his son and came and went as though the boy didn't exist.

One night the pains in the boy's stomach were so bad that he wept. He left his home and went out among the prickly pear and piñon where he could smell the coyotes and hear them panting. He lay down and asked Life Giver to cure him, to cast out the evil. He rolled around and around in the dirt. He let horned toads crawl on him. He picked a yucca leaf and cut himself on his arms and chest until he bled and gave himself wounds that would leave scars. He thought that if he cut himself with real blades, the spirit knives in his stomach would leave him alone. Then he fell asleep, stinging and bloody, but calm. When he reappeared in the settlement people stared at him. No one laughed. His father looked at him for the first time in years and in his eyes was a hope that his embarrassment might be near an end. Many Visions had no more stomachaches.

There was an old shaman in the settlement in those days, a woman who had good medicine. Her specialty was curing wounds from fighting. She got her power from a bear spirit and this was demonstrated by the fact that she could walk close enough to a bear to smell his warm breath. When she walked up to one, the big grandfather of animals cocked his head at her a few times and lumbered off, with her just standing there laughing. Her name was Laughs At Bears.

The boy who was to become Many Visions went to Laughs At Bears and told her that he had been called to be a healer.

Laughs At Bears asked him, "Who called you?"

Many Visions, who had a poor imagination, said, "Shush—A bear. I was walking by the river and a bear spoke to me."

Laughs At Bears laughed so that her upper gums showed.

"Boy, you'd better wise up," she said, "or one day you're going to cause big trouble."

Careful not to look directly at the woman, Many Visions asked with a tone of great respect, "How does one become a holy one?"

"Don't ask me," Laughs At Bears said. "If you have to ask you'd better wait some more."

"Can you teach me how to talk to bears?"

"Sure," she bellowed, sticking her big stomach out at him. "Sure! You just do like this, see. You just walk up to old grandfather and grab him by the balls! Now you go and try it. I think I saw a bear over by those rocks this morning. The sun's probably warmed him up good by now. Go ahead! I'll wait here."

Then she laughed and laughed as she watched the boy walk home with his skinny arms hanging down limply at his side.

About a year later, Many Visions had been on a few raids and the name Runs For The Hills was about to stick when the visions started. He had so many visions he could fill up a day telling them. A few people laughed at him, and so he went out into the desert for eight days taking no food or water. When he came back he looked so holy that he got the name Many Visions. He looked skinny enough to pass through a knothole and he told about the kinds of visions a holy man should have—animals talking to him, plants revealing their healing powers to him, dreams about the future. Many Visions told about a buck that had talked to him and was his spirit helper. The buck thanked Many Visions for never shooting a member of his family. Sometimes Many Visions forgot that he had talked to a deer and said that it was a hawk. Some contradictions were not mentioned by others who would rather say they were too stupid to understand the ways of a healer than say something to cause disharmony.

Many Visions came at a bad time for healers in Apache history. He didn't know that the white man would have flesh-destroying diseases and exploding weapons and twisted practices. Bullets and smallpox and tuberculosis and mutilation and extinction of their game—these needed new medicine. And then there was the food that whites gave to the Indians that made them weak, white powder that had bugs in it. Men went to the white man's forts and came back with a sickness that spread and made people cough up their own blood. And when blankets came from the fort a great epidemic swept through the settlement killing children and old people, including Most Important Man's mother. Many Visions announced with great bitterness that there was no power yet given to the Superior People that could outdo white witchery. He believed, like the young warriors, that in the case of the whites one had to learn the techniques of the enemy and turn those techniques back on their source. No spirit guide, be it hawk or deer, or whatever animal Many Visions chose to call his power, had stopped the whites. Three Fingers had the sweat ceremony to pass on for as long as the people could withstand the changes brought by whites. One day, he believed, the prayers said in the sweat lodge would be answered, one day when all the people's hearts were in their prayers. And to bring their hearts along there were stories, stories to teach the people about why they were named the Superior People, about their bravery and wisdom. And then Shoots Straight and some others told stories about the whites so that no one would forget what they were up against. These stories told about how the white eyes came out of nowhere one day and did things no Apache had ever dreamed of. They took off the tops of people's heads so that a man had to go through all eternity with his skull showing. And in one story, a soldier killed an Apache baby by dashing its head against a wagon wheel. Mothers kept their children quiet by warning them that if they didn't stop crying the white soldiers would hear them and come and kill them or take them away.

But many children feared the medicine man more than the whites. Their first memory was of Many Visions coming at them with his knife and cutting their hair for some grown-up spiritual purpose. And just before the girls' puberty rites, Na ih es, there was a rumor spread around that the healer had sex with each initiate. It was whispered that his penis was as long as a stallion's.

This is something Many Visions did not do. He was too afraid of mothers wielding sticks, and his penis was not nearly as big as a stallion's. Still, he walked like a fearless man; he was not what he seemed. Many Visions was often afraid and resorted to witchery. He groaned, sometimes, to think of what might happen to him for pretending to have a spirit guide when none had come to him. He had dreams in which a real spirit deer came to him and lowered his antlers to dig out the faker's intestines. He told himself that he was a strong man with whom the world had not dealt fairly. He told himself that by praying and singing he would help the people and they would let him be. He thought that all the people believed in him and needed him. But this wasn't true. Walks Like A Buffalo, for example, had seen him stuffing his bag with dried elk meat when he was supposedly getting ready for a fast in the mountains. And Shoots Straight's daughter, One Braid, had lost her first child after Many Visions had given her an herb for the health of the unborn.

But it was wrong to stir things up, to risk disharmony. "Don't talk against anyone," the elders told the children. So those who doubted Many Visions let it pass figuring that he did not own all the ceremonies and couldn't do too much harm. It was sad to think that times were so bad that there was a holy man with so little wisdom, but there were people in the settlement who believed in Many Visions. Best not to insult them; harmony among one's people was more important than any individual's righteous opinions. This would pass. Those who saw his real face said to themselves, "The earth will settle with Many Visions in its own way."

When it started to rain, Many Visions sat up in his dwelling and wondered how it was that he had caused such a miracle. He had, over the years, begun to believe in himself despite the facts. He had been so fervent a fake that he came to suspect that he really did have power and that an event such as rain coming after a drought must have something to do with him. But he had just been dozing. So he thought he must have left his body and gone into the spirit world to do a ceremony to bring the animals back with the rain. He rose stiffly, first having to get on his hands and knees before

standing up. Then he got himself into a certain deportment that showed the people he had something of spiritual importance to say. He came out wearing corn
pollen on his forehead and holding his head high. He
noticed that there was no one around his dwelling, that
everyone was by the central fire pit. Pots of half-
mashed yucca fruit collected rain and baskets of beans
sat unattended. An emaciated elk's carcass swung from
a pole. Then Many Visions' nephew ran up to him and
said, "The white woman brought the rain!" The dignity
dropped off of Many Visions' face. He angrily pushed
the boy away and walked to where everyone had gathered.

By this time Sara's nightdress was all wet. She was
still on the ground and rain pattered down on her and
the standing people. Sara saw many legs around her,
some bare, some covered by high-topped moccasins and
leather skirts. She heard a woman's laugh and looked
up. She saw children, but they were listless, leaning
against their mothers' legs or sucking on their fingers
from a safe perch in their mothers' arms. The children
let the rain stay on their faces. Two young women kept
poking Sara with their feet and laughing. A boy threw
mud onto her back, prompting others to pelt her. This
made Sara think of Saint Stephen, whom people had
stoned to death.

A woman with a baby strapped to her back on its cradle board bent down and tugged on Sara's hair. Others
laughed and did the same, some with a vengeful force
that stung her scalp. They spoke of her and the rain in
the same breath, considering the similarity between her
hair and a storm cloud. One man snatched a strand of
hair from her scalp and Sara feared that her story would
be that of a saint snatched bald.

But two of the women in the crowd had made a claim

on Sara and wanted her kept in one piece until they had settled between them. Walks Like A Buffalo, Most Important Man's first wife, wanted to take the white woman to her dwelling as a slave. But so did her daughter-in-law, Long Skirt.

"Dashi' shi'neka'——I have privileges," Walks Like A Buffalo said.

"You have Little Bird whom you treat like a slave," Long Skirt argued, "and I have two young boys."

Walks Like a Buffalo stiffened and wiped the rain off her face with her big palm.

"You have three sisters and you make my son carry wood for all of them, plus your mother! You have no need of a slave."

It was good to be entertained by a white captive and an argument between a woman and her daughter-in-law all on the same day.

Sara heard the strange, clipped talking and lay still, as though she were hiding, out of sight, instead of shivering in the cold rain in the middle of those people. Then a man with bony legs squatted down and lifted Sara's head up by her hair. The man's face was as bony as the rest of his body and had deep grooves in it. Two little eyes were buried in this structure that seemed as a whole to be a geological formation that culminated in a large, hooked nose. Many small scars, like white rain, marked his upper arms and chest.

The women stopped talking and Sara knew that this man had some authority. She held her breath and looked at him with a religious pleading in her eyes. "If you are the leader around here," she said, "then help me. I can bring your people out of darkness." Many Visions put her head back down on the ground. The rain fell harder and all but Most Important Man, Many Visions, and the two women who wanted Sara left for their dwellings.

Many Visions stayed hunkered down, studying Sara. He lifted her shoulder to get a look at what she held on to. Then he stood up and walked around her. He stopped where he had started and poked the Bible with his foot.

"Jesus, help me," Sara moaned and she hugged the Bible more tightly.

Many Visions poked at the Bible again, and again heard the woman call out for Jesus. He tried to wrestle the book out of her arms, but Sara clutched it hard.

The shaman then addressed Most Important Man.

"I dreamed about this. I'm telling you, I dreamed that this woman was coming here. She's a witch, and if you doubt me you'll be sorry."

"No!" Long Skirt said. Now that she was married to Most Important Man's son she wasn't so afraid of the shaman. "She brought the rain, didn't she? Perhaps she has power to bring other things, to bring deer and elk. What will happen if we kill her?"

Many Visions glared at her but could think of nothing to say.

Most Important Man heard the heavy breathing of his wife and felt her eyes willing his mouth to move.

"I have a thought on this," he began.

And then he waited to get one for he wanted to be sure not to insult anyone with one of his thoughts.

"If she is a witch—ntii'—we will know it soon . . ."

Many Visions interrupted, "I'm telling you she is a witch and this," he kicked the Bible, "has something to do with her power. I have seen the Mexicans with this thing."

"Then take the power thing away," Most Important Man said.

Long Skirt, who wanted to show her youth and bravery, jumped into action and pulled the Bible out. With her head lowered and biting her lip to keep from grinning, she gave it to Many Visions.

"And where will she stay?" Long Skirt asked.

"She will stay in our household, of course, since it is my husband who's making the decisions," Walks Like A Buffalo said. She crossed her arms over her chest and watched Long Skirt whip herself around and head for home.

Sara, meanwhile, closed her eyes and wept for the loss of her Bible. She let Walks Like A Buffalo pull her up. Sara's teeth chattered and goosebumps showed through the wet nightgown.

Pulled away, Sara twisted her head around to see Many Visions as though he were a lover, and Many Visions felt the cold bite him at the base of his spine. Sara recognized in Many Visions the look of a holy man, of holy men she had known in Virginia and at the teachers college. Then it was him she must reach, as one religious to another. It was God's doing that he now had the Bible. So she and this small man would bring all these people out of darkness, down on their knees to the Lord. For such a mission God would protect her from death and defilement. "Be brave, Sara, God is with you. The Lord is thy shepherd," she said.

XIV

Before an Apache man goes to war, he transforms himself. He starts speaking in a special language that only warriors use. He paints his face black and white: a black band across the eyes, and white on either side of that band. In the Nahuatl language the word *apache* means "raccoon." The Zunis use the word to mean "enemy." And to the French, *Apache* means "gangster." Most likely some crusty French fur trapper started this association after his beavers kept getting stolen out of his traps by Indians whose hair was wild. When the locals told him these people were Apaches, the man probably began saying about any son of a bitch who took his money or his whiskey or gave him a bad deal on his furs, "Cet Apache va mourir."

These raccoons and gangsters took great pride in their hair. They washed it every day if they could, using the natural detergent of the yucca plant. The men let it flow and tied a strip of cloth around their heads to keep their hair out of their eyes. When a warrior lets his long hair fly behind him, daring his enemies to grab it, he shows his fierceness. Coyote, it was said, liked to tie the braids of young children together when they were asleep.

But Coyote had done worse. As a matter of fact, it was Coyote who brought darkness into the world by let-

ting it out of the bag it was kept in. The world went
crazy for a while wondering what the hell had happened. Then all the animals got together and discussed
this darkness thing. They couldn't even see each other's
faces. The four-leggeds and the owls thought that the
darkness was the best thing since natural selection; it
meant that there could be no end to their hunting time.
But the birds said, "Whoa, wait a minute here. We like
daytime." So they struck a deal. Figuring that there was
no way to completely get rid of the darkness, the animals decided to play a game of moccasin ball in which
a leather ball is hidden by one team and the other has
to find it. They decided that if the four-leggeds and the
owls won the game there would be darkness all the
time; but if the birds won, there would be some daylight
time. Obviously the birds won, and as soon as they did
a light creased the horizon and they cheered. Now they
still cheer whenever dawn comes.

Bringing darkness to the world might have been a
good thing in the end, but Coyote really messed up
when his big mouth brought death. As it was, things
had just lived forever, but Coyote thought he knew
more than Life Giver and more than White Painted
Woman and more than Monster Slayer, the very forces
that had created everything. He said that rocks float,
and he was so positive about it that he said if the stone
sank all living things would ultimately have to die.

So people learned from Coyote's mistakes that it is
not only wise, but necessary and proper to show some
humility and gratitude toward the Earth and all its powers and gifts. And White Painted Woman, who saw that
humans needed some visual aids, gave them ceremonies
and plants with which to express their gratitude and humility.

Sage, for example, is a useful herb. It purifies and it

wards off lightning sickness which the Thunder People can inflict on a person. Though she didn't know that it was sage she was smelling, Sara would forever think of her first days of captivity when she smelled that scent. Since it had begun to rain, Most Important Man's second wife, Little Bird, hung sprigs of sage on the oak poles that framed the household. Occasionally she threw bits of it into the fire and the sweet smoke went up through the hole in the center of the roof.

Walks Like A Buffalo lifted the hide that covered the doorway and put a clay pot outside to catch the rain. "It is good to have rain," she said loud enough for the Thunder People to hear that she appreciated them. Besides this, no one spoke. The presence of the white woman was so much food for thought that they were too full to speak.

Besides Most Important Man and his two wives, there were two of his and Walks Like A Buffalo's children: a boy just reaching puberty named Asks Questions and a girl a few years younger named Strong Legs. These two sat against the sides of the round room sucking their lower lips. They stared at Sara who sat opposite them, safely crouching against the poles. She had a leather rope around her neck, the end of which was lying on the ground near Little Bird's hand. Little Bird kept one eye on the fire and one eye on that tether.

Sara shivered, unwilling to make any sense out of what was happening to her except as it applied to God. She prayed. She prayed to God for guidance, for miracles, for some way to make that strange holy man come to the true god and lead the others into salvation. Once they were Christians, Sara thought, these savages would treat her with charity and apologetic deference; they would be suddenly awakened to civilized attitudes, as though brought to their senses, and the spell of their savagery would be broken. They would cover their bodies with more clothes and, singing hymns, escort her to the nearest fort. Or perhaps a soldier, a gentle man with large hands and a southern accent, would come for her and find her standing before an obedient group of Indians, all sitting in rows repeating verses from the Bible as she read to them. She must wait and not panic, she told herself. It was hard to remain calm being so dirty and damp. She felt like a dog with a leash around its neck. And she had only her camisole and bloomers on. Her little black shoes stood underneath her nightgown that was hanging on the side of the dwelling to dry.

And every now and then Sara said, "Dear Jesus," out loud and the others gave her a suspicious, sidelong look. Sometimes she rocked and sang hymns under her breath. This irritated Walks Like A Buffalo who said that having a white slave was not going to be easy. There was so much to teach her.

Most Important Man closed his eyes and drew in a hot wind of smoke from a cigarette he'd made out of a corn husk and wild tobacco. The children's eyes were wide, taking in everything but mainly waiting to see what the white woman would do.

Walks Like A Buffalo busied herself with the cooking of the meat that Small Face had given her. She wrapped it in leaves and put it in the hot coals of the fire.

During the meal Sara got the bones. A yellow dog tried to get in the doorway to get its share, but Walks Like A Buffalo kicked it out. Sara was starving and exhausted. She watched the children break their mutton bones and suck out the marrow and she did the same. But when she saw what she'd been reduced to, tethered and sucking on a mouthful of broken bones, she began to cry; she spit the bones out and lay down.

For many days, from new moon to half moon, Little Bird pulled Sara around by that strap. She talked to Sara while she walked her around even though Sara couldn't understand her. Eventually she began to understand the words for water and wood because it was her fate to do all of Little Bird's work, which was mainly to fetch water and wood. And Sara learned that *ow'* meant "yes," *daa'ko'* meant "enough," and *dotah* meant "no."

Little Bird didn't like to do what Walks Like A Buffalo told her to do, so she got Sara to do it all. Sara learned that Little Bird liked to have her around as a companion, like a pet. Sometimes they washed in the newly thriving river and sometimes they collected piñon nuts. These activities made Little Bird's mood good and she did not mistreat Sara any more than she would have mistreated a dog. She even gave her a blanket to wear around her shoulders because winter was breathing cold winds.

Between chores, or when the chores seemed boring to Little Bird, she paraded around the camp to show off her slave. Such arrogant, attention-getting behavior did not sit well with Apaches. The women talked among themselves about Little Bird incurring the wrath of the Thunder People by idling and showing off while they squatted outside their doorways combining work and gossip.

Several of the men were out hunting elk and deer. The older ones, like Three Fingers and Most Important Man, got together in groups to discuss political matters. Children ran away from their chores to fish in the river. Some had begun to eat fish during the drought when there was so little food.

Many Visions was concerned that his people would be reduced to worse than fish eating and that the system from which he drew his authority would break apart like a brittle pot. He had never felt a stronger premonition in his life than the one that told him the white woman was trouble. He crept around in his dwelling saying prayers, so the people heard him at all hours of the day and felt a little uneasy about his secret ceremonies. But while he sang, Many Visions peeked out through the yucca leaves that covered the oak poles, as he crept around watching Little Bird and Sara.

Sometimes the two women passed through the shady place near the river where the horses were kept. The animals grazed among the angled cottonwoods. There were ten of them, and all but one dark, pregnant mare still showed their ribs from the time of the drought when there was nothing fresh and chewy coming out of the ground. Mister and Mrs. showed no particular alarm in becoming the kind of horses who grazed in a leafy place enclosed by fallen branches instead of being the kind of horses who pulled a disheveled wagon. But one day Mrs., the unlucky swayback, got some special attention. Wears Hats, who donned a blue United States Army hat and who tended the horses, discussed the mare with Broken Nose, Small Face, and Eats Fish, who had some say in the animal's fate since they had gotten her. Sara stopped to see what they were doing around Mrs. while Little Bird absent-mindedly walked on. Little Bird was thinking hard about not appearing to be thinking about Broken Nose whom she lusted after.

"Hey!" Sara said, because the rope around her neck had gotten taut and was choking her. Little Bird stopped and walked back to her servant.

Broken Nose led Mrs. out of the corral while Eats Fish and Small Face lifted the branch that blocked one side of the enclosure. Mrs. loped along calmly and the other horses lifted up their big heads to watch.

"What are they going to do?" Sara asked.

But Little Bird didn't understand her and hissed to make her be quiet. She didn't want the men to see them staring.

Then Sara gasped because the three men pushed the old horse down and made her lie on her side. Mrs. groaned but still seemed willing to go along with this game. She was a tired horse. She'd been born in a green place with ups and downs, and then she'd gotten hitched to a wagon that she pulled across a flat place. Then she was in a brown place with twisted trees. She'd ceased to let change rattle her. But when one man sat on her neck, Mrs. kicked out her back legs and tried to right herself. But Eats Fish pushed down on her flanks. The horse groaned again.

"They are treating her badly," Sara said, walking forward, but Little Bird pulled her back by the rope.

Sara started to cry, biting the knuckles of her fist. She could see Mrs. breathing hard. Small Face, who was sitting on her neck, took out a knife and slit the horse's throat, drawing a deep red line in her brown coat. The animal thrashed once, then lay quietly, panting and staring straight ahead at this, the most remarkable change of all. Sara shrieked in loud desperation. The sound made the crows fly up from the trees and suspend themselves in the air until the echo died away and they settled back on their branches.

Little Bird hit the back of Sara's head to try to dislodge whatever made the woman fuss so. The men looked up from the dead horse at the two women whom they hadn't noticed before. Small Face laughed and turned to catch Eats Fish's eye. The two men were sitting on Mrs. like boys straddling a log. Broken Nose was standing over the horse's head, away from the thick flow of blood. When he looked toward the women he caught Sara's eye; and though he'd butchered many horses in his day, he suddenly felt badly about this one.

This feeling badly about a woman's heart and about a sway-backed horse angered Broken Nose. He called upon the other two men to help him drag the loose carcass to a place near the river where it could be skinned and butchered. Then when Little Bird turned around to head back home, the sight of Sara made her afraid. The blood had fled out of Sara's face and her body shook as though in some kind of convulsion. Little Bird dropped the leash and backed off. Sara sank to the ground and moaned.

"Get up!" Little Bird hissed. "Get up!"

The men, still dragging the carcass, paid no attention to the two women.

Sara lay flat on her back and looked up at the sky. Little Bird was leaning over her with a terrible struggle going on between her terror and her dignity as a slave owner.

"Daa'ko, daa'ko," she said again regaining enough poise to pick up the leather line. "K'aatii'."

Sara looked at the wide, blue, empty sky and for a moment couldn't think of where she was or who she was. "Dear Jesus," she whispered, "what is going to happen to me?"

"Jesus, Jesus, Jesus," Little Bird snapped. She especially hated that the white woman made her look weak in front of Broken Nose. She bent down and struck Sara on the side of the head with the back of her hand. It stung and brought lights into Sara's eyes. Sara stood up and let herself be led back to Most Important Man's dwelling. Broken Nose watched them.

"What is she doing?" Most Important Man grumbled as he was trying to eat some roasted horse meat. "Why does she look at me like that? It's making me sick."

Sara leaned toward him and said slowly, as though to a lip reader, "You must open your heart to Jesus. The Lord God will protect you and guide you."

Most Important Man dropped his bowl down roughly and got his tobacco bag.

"Many Visions says that she is a witch," he said.

"That healer doesn't know everything," his first wife said.

"She has the same sickness as the Mexicans who wear the black robes," Little Bird explained. "It is this Jesus sickness. The ghost of a god that the pale eyes killed a long time ago. He haunts them and makes them crazy. This I've heard from Shoots Straight."

"She is a witch and she will bring a bad sickness to us," Most Important Man said.

Walks Like A Buffalo lifted the door flap and spit outside. A livid, orange sunset stained everything. It was as though the earth was in firelight.

"And in a household where such a witch stays the first wife often wakes up to find that she's grown a tail," Most Important Man said letting the smoke linger in his mouth.

Little Bird covered her mouth and giggled and the children doubled over where they sat and tried to smother their laughter. Sara wondered what the joke had been, but it was not hard to see by the expression on Walks Like A Buffalo's face that it had been on her.

"If it was me I'd just give her back to the white men," Walks Like A Buffalo grumbled. "She gives people a bad look."

The girl, Strong Legs, chimed in, "Or give her to the Comanches."

"I'm not going back to the fort," Most Important Man said and he did not look at anyone to see the embarrassment they felt for him for his last trip to the white man's fort. He and the other elders had accomplished nothing and had come back with nothing but warnings from the soldiers that they'd better not do any raiding or they'd get more than starvation. The aging heroes had been too weak to wait outside at night to slit some throats.

"It's a long way to the Comanches," Most Important Man said, thinking aloud. "But maybe it would be worth it."

"And then there would be bad feelings between us for bringing trouble to the Comanches," Walks Like A Buffalo said. "This woman makes plans. She talks to spirits asking them to do things."

"She is useful," Little Bird said. "She's a good slave. And she brought the rain."

Nothing more was said about the white woman for several days and Little Bird kept pulling her around the settlement. Many more days went by. Sara didn't know how many. She let herself be pulled along. She prayed the same one-sentence prayers over and over for whole days. Once she and Little Bird passed by Broken Nose who was sitting with two other men, and she reached out her hand and touched him on the shoulder. She meant to show that she forgave him, she meant to show him the ways of a Christian, a saint—a saint in dirty underwear.

One time they passed by Many Visions' dwelling and his bony arm shot out and grabbed Sara's arm.

"I want to be alone with the white woman," the healer said.

Little Bird hesitated. Walks Like A Buffalo and some other women were nearby with burden baskets on their backs. They were getting ready to go pick piñon and yucca fruit. It was going to be a long walk because they'd already picked over all the nearby plants. Little

Bird didn't want to have to go with them without her slave. But she finally wandered away toward the impatient group of women.

Sara didn't know what was going on. She just stood limply, waiting for the holy man to do something. She was always tired and always hungry. She had become aggressive about getting her share of the food and in any situation hoped to have access to something to eat. But then Sara wondered if she was being left for the holy man to torture or defile. This was the first time in weeks that she had been alone, without Little Bird. Panic washed over her like cold water waking her up, warning her about some danger she had almost been too numb to notice. She began to shake and then she sank down and mumbled, "Oh, God, please."

Many Visions squatted down and, as he had done that first day, he lifted her head up. It was more an excuse to grasp her wild and thick hair than to see her face. It felt rich in his hand, like a bunch of rare power.

Sara stared straight ahead, beginning to tremble as she had done when she saw her horse being slaughtered. Then she caught sight of the Bible. It was among power bags and amulets. A strong need for the powerful protection of the old ways, of the ways of God and Jesus and the gospel, swirled through her. Then Sara threw up on Many Visions' feet. Her retching left her shaking and she tried to slither along the ground to get to the Bible. Many Visions cursed her. Then he wiped the half-digested corn mush off of his feet with pieces of bark that he threw out the door.

"Oh, Lord!" Sara cried. "Oh, dear Jesus!" She reached the Bible with her fingertips but Many Visions scooped it up before she could grasp it.

There was a big silence between them. Many Visions stood over Sara, clutching the Bible with both his arms as she had done. Sara held her breath. Her mind was so empty, so frozen, that she could hear a small voice talking to her from within her head.

"Sara," this voice said. *"Don't be a coward, Sara."*

It was a small voice, a man's voice, very quiet and persistent like water flowing. It took her attention away from the Bible and the shaman.

Sara looked up into the shaman's eyes. They were cautious and attentive like the eyes of a rodent who is not sure of the danger he is in.

She got up to her knees and sat back on her heels, reeling a little from dizziness.

The shaman pointed with his face toward the gold ring on Sara's hand and said, "Doonzhoo." He was saying that the gold on her finger was morally bad. To get it one had to grovel inside the Earth which was like groveling inside one's mother. It was something that Mexicans and whites did that made the Apaches nervous. To wear gold was to flaunt one's disrespect for the Earth.

Sara didn't understand him. But she looked at the ring.

"I killed my husband," she said, examining the gold band as though considering buying it. "I shot him in the head."

The healer squatted down and asked in Apache, "Where do you get your power?"

Sara looked at his face, so close to hers, and saw how comical it was with its clownishly big nose and little eyes. She burst into laughter and Many Visions fell back as though the lid had toppled off a pot of boiling water.

Sara kept laughing. Though all that had happened to her might not be funny to some, it suddenly seemed ridiculous to her in light of the holy man's nose. Job, she thought, should have sat down in the middle of the road, after all that had befallen him, and had a good laugh. She could see him sitting there, wiping tears from his eyes as he laughed hard and shook his head, "My wife, my farm, my children! Hoo-wee!"

The medicine man, in a rage of humiliation, went for Sara. Even when she saw him grab for her she couldn't stop laughing. She was laughing so loudly that people in the settlement stopped and couldn't help but grin and chuckle though they shrugged at each other not knowing who was laughing or why. Many Visions pushed her to his door and shoved her out. She stood there with the leash dangling from her neck, and wiped the tears from her eyes.

XV

Sara walked freely through the settlement. No one took much notice of her. The women worked all the time. There was never an idle moment. From morning until night they worked on blankets spread out on the ground, surrounded by pots and stones and baskets. Mostly, they dried out meat, the meat of elk and occasionally horse or rabbit. But they also bent over foodstuffs that had before been, to Sara, desert weeds, part of the emptiness. Sara learned that almost anything was food when an Apache woman got ahold of it. No matter what it was, it could be boiled, mashed, chewed, pressed, or dried. In these processes that lasted days, mescal, yucca, prickly pear, and mesquite became a kind of jerky or cake. And what couldn't be made into pulp was boiled to make tea or smoked. Around the camp there was always smoke, the smoke of piñon or cedar. Steam rose up from pots of tea, a sweet-smelling tea made from a long-stemmed weed with a little yellow flower on it. This tea could calm a person and was often given to crying babies. Sometimes there was music, the flute or prayers sung in doorways in the morning. Throughout the day there was always work and there were always prayers. It had been that way before the white woman and it would be that way after the white woman. After a month, Sara had become a part of life, a slave who worked well, an oddity to be commented upon when a woman looked up from her work and saw her standing there, the blanket wrapped around her and her eyes staring as though she'd been sleepwalking and didn't know where she was.

Many Visions kept thinking about Sara. He said to Most Important Man, "The evil is in her eyes. They are black and gleam like polished rocks. I have dreams. They tell the truth to me about things to come. Do I have to remind you of the dream I had concerning your impotence?"

Most Important Man lit his cornhusk cigarette and blew the smoke in four directions.

"I am an old man," he said, "almost as old as Shoots Straight who pisses on himself."

"Think of how it will raise the spirits of the people to leave a mutilated white woman for the soldiers to find. And didn't those soldiers just recently treat you and other honored warriors like begging dogs?"

"When the young men come back we'll talk of these matters," Most Important Man said. He looked down at the shallow ripples of flesh on his old man's belly. There was a scar there he followed with his finger, remembering his young man's belly when a half-dead buck had gouged him with its antler.

Many Visions looked outside as the white woman passed by. Her appearance made him shiver. She still wore those tattered white undergarments, and the tether hung ridiculously from her neck when half the time she was let go to wander about as she pleased. She looked like the spirit of someone who'd been hanged.

"See," Many Visions said, "she gives me certain looks with her eyes."

"She is a slave," Most Important Man said.

Sara walked back into view the other way, the leash

dragging behind her as she gnawed off a piece of dried elk meat; it crackled when she chewed it; it tasted good. Two children followed her, jumping up to touch her hair. Sara didn't care. She knew Many Visions was in the dwelling talking to Most Important Man and she wanted to be near him. She prayed to God to give her some way of reaching the holy man and telling him about Jesus.

"She has power and she is trying to sicken me," Many Visions said to his friend.

"You are getting excited about nothing. What is wrong with you?" Most Important Man asked.

"The people say that she brought the rain, then you say she is just a slave," Many Visions said.

"It's of no concern to me," Most Important Man said.

"I tell you some disease will come and then you'll ask for a ceremony when it's too late."

Many Visions stood up and left the dwelling. He did not look at Sara. He walked directly forward. When he heard someone running after him he pretended not to take note of it. The hard breathing was right at his ear and he turned sharply to see Feeds Herself First, the old wife of Shoots Straight, panting. Her white and black hair was cut short, just below the ears, to show that she mourned her grandson who'd died when there was not enough food and good water.

"My husband, my husband. He has fallen down and stares straight ahead but doesn't move," she screamed. Other people stood up and stared at her.

Many Visions felt awed by his own powers, for hadn't he, just moments ago, predicted disease? With a boy's excitement and pride he went with the woman, showing a calm air of importance. Half the settlement quietly followed and heard Many Visions say, "I have said that this would happen. It was shown to me and I knew it."

The sick old man was lying half in and half out of his doorway.

"I am dying," Shoots Straight told Many Visions softly. "Half of me is already dead. See, I cannot move this side of my body."

His right eye was closed and his mouth drooped on the right side and did not move when he spoke.

People came into the dwelling and stood around him. Two of his daughters rushed in and helped him to his blankets.

Many Visions got a pinch of pollen and bent down to streak it on the man's forehead. He shut his eyes for a moment and then stood up.

"It is the white woman," he told the crowd. "I just saw her doing strange things."

The people said nothing. They thought about this. Shoots Straight just stared at the top of his dwelling with his one eye.

"I will do what I can, but if she is a witch, then my power is too weak. There is a particular way of killing such evildoers."

No one spoke. Then Shoots Straight said quietly, "I am tired." And his other eye closed and he fell asleep.

"This is a terrible thing," people said to one another. And they were scared to think of Shoots Straight dying because he had been with them longer than anyone except Three Fingers. He had been, in his youth, the finest warrior of any of the living men.

Sara noticed the people sadden. She saw it as the old women seemed not to have the strength to grind with a stone or to shake the baskets of piñon. She saw it as some left the work spread out on blankets and went quietly into Shoots Straight's home to sit. Little Bird found her slave and hurried her along to the river to keep out of the way, especially out of the medicine man's way. Long Skirt came with them, and for once the feud between them over slave ownership was put aside and they talked about Shoots Straight.

"I am afraid to have him die because of his stories. Who has remembered all of them? What will happen to his stories? And what of the stories he hasn't told yet?" This is what Long Skirt said.

"If half of his body is already dead will it decay while the rest of him lives?" Little Bird asked.

"He is our grandfather," Long Skirt said. "He was a good warrior. There are no warriors like him today."

"I'm afraid to have him die," Little Bird said. "I'm afraid of having his ghost around. His ghost will want to tell stories."

"They say that she is a witch and gave him this sickness."

Sara felt both the women look at her. She looked back.

"I'm afraid to be around her," Long Skirt said. "How do we know that she won't do something harmful to us? It is said that she killed her own husband."

"Let's not talk of it," Little Bird said.

"We should go to him and sit," Long Skirt said.

"I wonder if I should take the white woman there. People might want to kill her if they see her there," Little Bird said.

Long Skirt told her, "Bring her where everybody can keep an eye on her."

Many Visions began to try to heal Shoots Straight, the man whose arrows never missed, the man whose arrows Many Visions had tried to claim when his own had landed in the bushes. How fast boyhood had left them both. How had they become old men? It was painful to watch an old warrior, a man who had killed many Mexicans, drool helplessly from the side of his mouth.

"It hurts me to see him like that," Little Bird said. "He is our grandfather."

"We must make sure he sees that we are helping him in case he dies and his ghost comes back to haunt those who insulted him," Long Skirt whispered.

They pulled Sara in with them and sat with some other women who held their shawls over their mouths. Sara could hear weeping.

Many Visions rolled some herbs in a corn husk and smoked them. He blew the smoke in all directions. Then he looked up toward the sky and said, "Before you did this to him this man's body and spirit were in healthy condition. Now he is sick. I pray to you to breathe some of your spirit into this man, to make him over as he should be."

His voice lay low in the dwelling like a slow-moving stream. Sara closed her eyes and listened to his voice, listened to the soft weeping, smelled the smoky meat smells on the bodies around her and the sage from Many Visions' cigarette. She opened her eyes because she was aware of someone staring at her; and she saw a man wearing a mask, sitting across from her on the other side of the room, watching her. He wore a large mask, with long desert grasses coming out of the top and sides. There was a triangular spike on the top and a wide mouth painted on it. Though the light was very dim, Sara could see the man's eyes gleaming from inside the mask. No one else paid attention to him, though he seemed to be some important ceremonial figure. It was Many Visions who talked, Many Visions who stood and blew smoke. The masked man was quiet, inconspicuous, but he stared hard at Sara. And in his eyes Sara became aware of herself and was ashamed to be dirty, to be in her underwear. She felt in his expression, in the mask's expression, an impatience, a waiting for her to stop being low and weak and do something. He watched her as though saying, "When are you going to reveal your power?" Sara wondered if he was a spy, a soldier, a Christian infiltrator sending messages to her that he was here. He was ready to save her, but she must act first. Why did the others ignore him?

Many Visions took a piece of bark from one of the pouches around his waist.

"This is from a tree that was struck by lightning," he said.

He bent down and put it in the fire. Everyone was silent as the bark caught fire and flared up. The people who couldn't help but weep bowed their heads or hid their faces behind a shawl. What would happen without grandfather's stories? When the bark was done burning, Many Visions took a little wooden trowel and scooped up the ashes.

"Get water," he said, and a young woman close to the sick man jumped to her feet and went out.

"What is wrong with the man?" Sara asked, forgetting that no one understood her. She could not see Shoots Straight very well; she looked for the masked man and didn't see him. The emotions, kept behind the shawls, fought back inside the eyes of the men, were beginning to affect her. The day-to-day routine had been broken and she felt shocked to awareness of the life-and-death drama of things, of the life-and-death drama of a woman who had ended up as a captive.

Many Visions put the ashes in the water and added some white powder. He dipped his fingers into the mixture. With this stuff Many Visions painted lightning designs on Shoots Straight's face letting the liquid dribble into his mouth. The sick man was trembling so hard that Sara could see the blankets on him shake.

Many Visions raised the cup up four times, muttering prayers. He held it out toward Shoots Straight three times and on the fourth got him to drink. Sara heard the sound of retching.

"He is dying," she said and both Long Skirt and Little Bird shushed her.

Many Visions sang a song:

> He in the sky who is holy,
> He who is Dark Thunder
> Who put up the earth,
> He strikes down with life
> To give life to her body;
> He in the sky who is sacred,
> Dark Thunder, my father.

He sang this same song four times to the four directions.

Many Visions went silent. Everyone watched him. He didn't move but stood still, his wiry body rigid and his face turned upward. He closed his eyes. Suddenly he leapt at the sick man. He put both his hands on him and pushed hard. Shoots Straight moaned. Others moaned, weeping and choking. Many Visions pushed again and blew at the old man's skin. He leaned into Shoots Straight with all his might until the bones cracked.

Though it was cold outside, inside the air was steamy with so many peoples' sweat. Rage heated Sara, outrage at what the healer was doing to the sick man. She looked for the masked man. She felt hot and confined, horribly uncomfortable as the weeping rose and as Many Visions' attacks on the sick man seemed more and more perverse. She had the impression that the healer was taking advantage of weakness, was showing his power by abusing someone who could not fight back. She thought of the way her father laughed when one of the children got sick and he made them drink horrible medicine. She could tell that he liked to get the chance to bring it out of the cupboard and watch his little girl's lower lip tremble as she knew that there was no way to get out of drinking that nasty stuff that made her vomit.

"What is he doing? Why is he doing that?" Sara asked.

Little Bird put her hand over Sara's mouth and then pinched her upper lip for good measure.

Many Visions pushed another time and Shoots Straight screamed out.

"He is helpless!" Sara cried out. She stood up and stepped through the women and grabbed the medicine man by the hair. She pulled him up to his feet.

All weeping ceased. Many Visions thought he was going to spit out his heart.

The healer and the white woman looked into each other's eyes; Many Visions revealed his terror, and it surprised Sara to see it. She became dizzy, as though she had stood up too quickly. She had the sensation that a thick, hot liquid was sliding into the low part of her torso where feelings of fear usually sprung up. She let go of the healer's hair and crouched down and looked at Shoots Straight. His one eye was as wide as a leather button and looked straight at her.

Little Bird hid her face in her hands.

"Don't worry," Sara said softly to the old man. And she awoke to the boldness and craziness of what she had done. She was suddenly frightened again and didn't know what to do.

Shoots Straight looked around frantically, away from

the white woman's eyes. Sara put her hand over his open eye to make him close it and said, "Just sleep, rest. Try to rest."

Many Visions, having gathered up his fragmented wits, grabbed for the strap that was hanging from Sara's neck. He yanked it up hard and the rope dug into Sara's skin, choking her. She fell onto her back, but Many Visions kept pulling. He pulled with all his strength, dragging her outside by the neck.

Sara tried to get up, but the medicine man was quick. She gagged and felt her face about to burst. She grabbed the leather to try to pull it away from her neck, but Many Visions gave it a jerk. He dragged her over rocks and old fires. Her neck got wet with blood where the leather cut into the skin and rubbed into raw flesh.

Little Bird was running after them, afraid to call out.

Many Visions stopped in front of Most Important Man's home. He let go of the leash, throwing it down on the ground where Sara lay, panting. Then he gave her a hard kick in her stomach. He looked down on her, his face red and wild.

Sara lay still. She was afraid to move. She had an impulse to whimper and then an impulse to put all the strength she had left into raising herself up and strangling the man. But she was scared by the blood that got all over her hands when she touched her neck.

"Oh, Lord," she prayed to herself. Then she said aloud, "I want to go home. Why hasn't someone come for me?"

Then she whispered, "Someone will come. Someone will come for me. The Lord will save me. God, you had better save me."

Little Bird waited until Many Visions went back to attend to Shoots Straight. Then she helped Sara inside where they both fell to the ground. Little Bird gently took the leather strap from around Sara's neck. She had to pull part of it away where it had gotten stuck to the raw skin with drying blood. Sara grabbed Little Bird's hand to make her stop because it hurt so badly. It stung and ached. But the Indian woman knew what was best. When she'd gotten the leash off, Little Bird threw it into the fire.

"Why did you do such a stupid thing?" she asked. Then she sighed and shook her head as she remembered and said, "White people are stupid—monganii' dogoya'."

XVI

By the time the scabs hardened on Sara's neck, the healing ceremony for Shoots Straight was in its fourth and final day. Six young men who'd been hunting up and down the newly thriving river learned the news of the old man's disease as soon as they came into the settlement. Besides killing one doe and several jackrabbits, they'd come across a band of Navajo traders and stolen a huge sack of corn. And they told the women of a place where a lot of mesquite beans were ready for picking.

But the news of Shoots Straight made their pride seem foolish. Everyone knew of Shoots Straight's escapades, of his successes that included the felling of huge buffalo, of his revenge on a band of Spanish herders who'd killed his brother. They felt that no one could replace Shoots Straight, and if he died no one could tell his stories. Death was always a horror, always an incomprehensible cheat, so horrible that people weren't supposed to speak of death or the dead. And so, should Shoots Straight die, he would be gone forever with any of his stories that were forgotten or never told. And his name, which was his own property, would go with him; it could not be spoken again.

Shoots Straight felt that he had better try to tell all the stories he could. The people who came and went to

sit beside him during the healing prayed and let Shoots
Straight talk. They had to sit close and be very quiet,
because the old man's voice was getting weaker and
weaker.

After the healing ceremony, Shoots Straight was
much weaker than before and was almost certain he was
going to die. But he had something left in him that he
wanted to shed, that he didn't want to carry with him
out of life because he was afraid it would make him
come back again and wander around as a spirit. Shoots
Straight didn't like what had happened to him and his
people. What the whites had done angered him. He had
anger in him that threatened to bury him before he died.
Telling stories about the old days wasn't enough. He
used to think that it didn't matter if the stories died out
with old men because they'd come back again. They'd
happen all over again, maybe even better, with more
bravery, more loot, more beauty, bigger animals. Now
he suspected that the cycle of stories was coming to an
end, that something else was taking over, something terrible and stupid, something totally unaware of the dev-
astation it caused, of the stupefying sadness of its
carelessness. Shoots Straight was too old to do anything
about it. He'd gone to the fort with Most Important
Man. They'd stood outside in the purple night still tast-
ing the grins of the white captain and his sergeant when
they had shooed them away like old women. They'd
shooed away two of the greatest warriors in Apache history. Two warriors who had come to ask with dignity
for some food in exchange for letting the smelly white
soldiers keep their blood inside their skin.

But when he and Most Important Man had gotten
outside with Three Fingers they knew they couldn't slit
any throats. They were old and had seen how white
power turned things around quickly, with guns, with

disease, with broken deals. They'd lost their nerve, and that was part of the whites' trickery too.

The old men went home. They went home and waited for the young men to come back and prove that their people were going to live the stories again. But what did that dog Small Face come back with? A little meat and corn, a bunch of spoons, one good horse and a swaybacked mare. And the white woman who made it rain.

Shoots Straight lifted himself up on the left arm that he could still move and spit out of the side of his mouth that worked. He growled weakly to his wife.

"Get the white woman. Bring her here." Then he turned to Broken Nose, who was taking a turn sitting with the old man. "You stay here. You speak her language."

Feeds Herself First hobbled off to Many Visions' place before going to get the white woman. Many Visions got breathless when he heard what Shoots Straight wanted. Shoots Straight had never really liked Many Visions. It was possible that he meant to do him harm somehow with the white woman, to make a deal trading his life for the medicine man's. Then again, maybe the sick man would tell everyone that she was responsible for his illness, and Many Visions could finally see the woman die. Whatever the maneuver meant, Many Visions had to be present. He had to control it. So he told Feeds Herself First that he would go get the white woman and bring her to Shoots Straight himself.

Seeing Many Visions come after her, Sara stared from her corner of Most Important Man's dwelling like a rabid cat. Many Visions pulled her to her feet and asked the two other women there where Most Important Man was.

"He is in the sweat lodge with Three Fingers," Walks

Like A Buffalo said. "They are praying for our grandfather."

"I am taking the white woman. There is a need for
her in Shoots Straight's healing."

"Do what you like," Walks Like A Buffalo said.

Little Bird followed him at a safe distance and crept
into the sick man's dwelling when Many Visions
pushed Sara in. Shoots Straight lay with his head tilted
up by a pile of animal skins. A thin stream of drool
came out of his mouth and went into the streambeds
made by all the lines in his old chin. There was a look
of panic in his one open eye, but he spoke calmly.

"I am going to tell a story to the white woman," he
said, "and I want you to tell it to her in her language."

Broken Nose moved forward and said, "I do not
speak her language easily."

"Make her sit down near to me so she can see my
fine body," Shoots Straight said, and Many Visions
pushed her down near him. Sara could feel Broken
Nose's arm against hers, until he moved away. She
looked at him, looked at his eyes from the side, and
Broken Nose kept them forward, showing no interest in
the white woman.

"First ask her why she shot her husband. This is
something I'd like to know. It's good to shoot a white
man, but I never thought a white woman would do such
a thing."

Broken Nose looked at Sara's slender hands that lay
in her lap and said in his deep but faltering voice, "You
shoot the white man. For what?"

Sara thought for a few minutes and then answered.
"He belonged with God. He . . . he was not happy with
his situation . . . with me. He was suffering. I was afraid
that he would suffer more if . . . I suppose in God's

eyes I am a murderer." She put her hand out, poised above Broken Nose's forearm.

Broken Nose understood English better than he spoke it, so he told Shoots Straight pretty much what Sara had said.

Shoots Straight shrugged his one shoulder and said, "Okay. I do not understand these people's God. I want to tell her a story. Tell her that I am going to tell her a story."

"Grandfather tells you a story. You must take it like food," Broken Nose said. Sara nodded. She was afraid and looked around to see where Many Visions was. The medicine man glistened with sweat and suspicion in a far shadow of the dwelling.

"Here is the story," Shoots Straight said, and Broken Nose told it in halting words, sometimes using his hands.

"There was a man named Black Sleeves. He was my uncle and he was very funny. He was a kind of clown. Part of the reason he was a clown was because he looked funny. He had bowed legs and a big head. He was smart, but he got tired of fighting. He'd lived through the massacre of the red moon when the whites taught us about taking the top of a man's head off. He'd seen some bad things at that massacre and just wanted to clown around. Everyone respected him, and he could get along with anyone. He could always make people laugh.

"This uncle got to know some white men, some miners in the western mountains, and hung around with them. He liked to clown around with them and drink a little whiskey. He figured that since the whites were using Apaches as scouts, Apaches and whites were now on the same side. He was an old man, anyway. He was an old warrior.

"The white men didn't like him hanging around, though. They didn't trust him. They didn't like the way he looked or smelled. And even though he was an old man who couldn't hardly piss straight, they were afraid of how big he was. He was a big man. They didn't know that he was related to important men. He was related to several leaders and was greatly respected among his people. The whites didn't care about this because to them he was just a redskin. They don't concern themselves about a man's reputation or his father's.

"So one day these miners strapped him to the back of a wagon. Old Black Sleeves thought they were playing some joke on him and he laughed and tried to make jokes. They laughed too, but what they wanted was to make him go away and stay away. They wanted to teach him about white man's power and about how Indians aren't good enough to hang around whites. So about ten of them took turns whipping the old man's back until the flesh hung off in strings. I remember when he came back you could see the bare muscle in his back, and flies got stuck in the open wounds. I remember he had no peace from the pain unless he lay in cool water. And he had scars like vines grown into an oak tree. He was an old man. He had been a warrior."

Shoots Straight stopped and let Broken Nose finish off the story. Sara looked at the old man's face. He asked, "Ya na iika' ana inla'? Why did you come here and steal our children for slaves? Where you are from, do whites steal each other's children and make them slaves when they have only just begun to walk? I don't understand this practice."

Broken Nose asked the questions, looking straight into Sara's face. All the people in the room waited and Sara felt as though she had to speak.

"I have never heard these stories," she said. "I've heard different stories."

"Old men don't have to listen to other people's stories," Shoots Straight said when Broken Nose had translated Sara's words.

"The Spaniards were bad. They were bad. My grandfather's sisters were taken by a Spanish soldier when they were children. There are many stories about such things. I have seen good women go mad or die from grief when their children were missing. It's not like what happened to you, son," he said to Broken Nose. "The Hopis are all a bunch of old women, but they aren't cruel."

Shoots Straight looked up toward the sky with his one eye and told the story of Broken Nose while the younger man stared into the air ahead of him.

"When this man's mother was stealing corn from the Hopis her time came. She gave birth to a boy among the Hopis' corn stalks. The Hopi men ran between the rows chasing our women away. The baby's mother was dragged away by her sisters who didn't hear that her screams were for her child. The boy spent six years as a Hopi until we got wind of whose house he lived in and we took him back. You remember, son? You cried and reached out for the Hopi woman because you did not know yet that you are one of the Superior People."

Broken Nose stayed silent; he did not tell this story to Sara. Shoots Straight continued.

"Tell her I would kill every white man I saw. Tell her that I would take a gun and put a hole in the head of every white man, every Mexican I could get to." Shoots Straight got up on his elbow and shook. "Tell her," he said, "that I was a good warrior and that already I've killed maybe fifty men. Tell her, tell her!"

Sara did not need to listen to Broken Nose. She heard

the hatred in the sick man's voice. The drool came down Shoots Straight's chin more profusely and dripped onto the blankets.

Shoots Straight continued, his voice stronger, louder. "Tell her she is ugly like all whites. That she has a bad smell. Tell her that white men, like the ones at the fort who treated me like a dog, that such white men wear ugly clothes. Their skin looks like the underside of fish. They never wash. Their hair is always filthy with grease and pieces of dead skin. Many of them are fat and have no muscles." He spit on the floor. "And yet somehow they overpower us. We must have done something completely crazy to be punished like this, to be overpowered by such ugly men. I don't know what we did, but it must have been bad. Tell her. Tell her how ugly white men are."

Broken Nose told her.

Sara was scared when she saw how excited the old man was getting, how all his hatred was aimed at her. She was afraid he was going to die of his hatred and that all the people hanging around would jump on her and beat her to death in their crazy sorrow. She was afraid that the point of this meeting was to do the poor old man one last favor and let him watch the lifeblood flow from a white person's dying body.

Broken Nose finished, saying, "White men look bad, smell bad." He pinched the skin on his firm stomach and said, "White men have white flesh, like fish."

Sara followed his gestures and then looked into Broken Nose's eyes. Her mouth parted in preparation for a question. Then she looked at Shoots Straight's twitching face and tried to guess what he wanted from her. She knew ugly white men. A picture of Reverend Barkstone popped into her mind—Reverend Barkstone, all smooth and without muscle. She remembered seeing Reverend

Barkstone's limp, pink genitals as he pawed her. She wondered now why it had upset her so; why she had been so stunned by such a pathetic man.

What would she and Shoots Straight say if Reverend Barkstone were standing there right then with nothing on his flabby body? Sara imagined herself saying, "My, you certainly are a particularly ugly white man, Reverend Barkstone."

Sara looked at Shoots Straight and laughed. The old man registered some confusion and asked Broken Nose, "Why does she laugh? What was the last thing you told her?"

"I told her about white men's ugliness," Broken Nose answered and they both looked at Sara again.

She couldn't stop laughing.

"I'm sorry," she said shaking her head and sighing. But then she looked at Shoots Straight again and burst out laughing again. "Truly, I'm truly sorry . . . I . . ." She kept laughing. She tried to think of something sad or serious, like her grandmother dying. But she kept seeing Reverend Barkstone standing naked and chagrined in front of these stunned people, with her making jokes, pointing to his genitals and saying, "And what, exactly, is the purpose of this?" And all the people around her, including Shoots Straight, would be laughing.

The hair on the back of Many Visions' neck prickled. The white woman's laugh curdled his morning meal. He stepped closer. Broken Nose rubbed his chin and Little Bird giggled.

Sara laughed so hard that her eyes watered.

"Oh, I'm sorry," she said, "I am sorry." She had to bend over because her stomach was hurting from her laughing. Then she stopped suddenly and looked at

Broken Nose, very seriously. "Do I really have a bad smell?" she asked.

Broken Nose loomed close to her, sniffing like a dog at her neck. The women giggled and made little cooing noises. It was almost like a party instead of a vigil by the bed of a dying man. Sara pushed Broken Nose's face away from her. Then he imitated her in a falsetto: "Do I reeelee ha' a bad smell?"

No one could remember Broken Nose ever being such a good clown and many burst out laughing because his effort showed his embarrassment about being touched by Sara. And they laughed because he mimicked the white woman well.

Even Shoots Straight began laughing. He started with one side of his mouth. Sara pursed her lips together in indignation at being made fun of. She turned toward Broken Nose and slapped him on the face. This made people lie on their sides laughing. Broken Nose touched the place she'd slapped and grinned, grabbing her wrist and waving her hand around in the air. Many Visions tried to say something, but no one listened. Sara prepared to hit at Broken Nose with her other hand, but he grabbed that wrist, too. Someone in the crowd called out, "Is this the position you take with white women?" and the laughter burst out again. In the midst of all this Shoots Straight had been laughing as well. Suddenly the dead side of his mouth turned up and his right eye popped open.

Feeds Herself First jumped up and ran around from one side of her husband to the other.

"You're all alive again," she cried. "Both sides! Look! Look everyone. My husband isn't dying. Look!"

Sara looked over and said, "Praise God." She clasped his hand. "Oh, look. You are better. Look at you. You're all better."

Little Bird got up and came over to Sara. She squatted beside her and looked at Shoots Straight.

Feeds Herself First was stroking her husband's revived arm.

Many Visions moved out of the shadows.

"My ceremony has cured our grandfather," he said. No one paid any attention to him.

"The white woman comes and brings rain," someone said, "and brings a cure for our grandfather."

But someone else said, "Do-na shi'shi'—She is not one of the Superior People."

Many Visions slipped out and went home.

XVII

They made her a skirt out of soft doeskin and Little Bird gave Sara her ceremonial moccasins that went over the calves. Small Face's wife made the skirt, holding up the material to show Sara and saying, to teach her the word for deerhide, "Epun'." Then she stroked it with her rough hand and said "Di-ii' de', di-ii' de'—soft, soft." She had one narrowed eye all the time from some injury when she was a girl, but Small Face had done well for himself with her because her skin was very smooth and her hair so long that she had to tuck the end of her two braids into the waist of her skirt. While she sewed, a group of women and children sat around. A little girl was playing with the pile of spoons Small Face had brought back, and a naked boy toddled over and got a handful of them. He handed three to Sara. Two young girls, almost at puberty, sat close to Sara so they could touch her hair. It was almost as though Sara was becoming a woman, taking part in Na ih es. This was a ceremony given by White Painted Woman to show the great time when a girl becomes a woman. But Sara was a married woman, certainly not a virgin. And she spoke like the white eyes.

"My grandfather," Sara said, "Grandfather Williams, taught me this. Look." No one understood her, but they listened as if they did. She held two spoons in the fingers of one hand and clicked them across her other palm and against her leg. The toddler bent his knees in time with the clicking and the women laughed. Sara started singing, "Jimmy crack corn and I don't care. . . ." The older children picked up spoons and tried to figure out how to play them. For days the tribe clattered with the sound of spoons, putting a noise to the thoughts that rattled in Many Visions' head.

The settlement got louder, busier. The dogs barked more, the women scolded more, the children screamed more. One of the horses ran through the settlement with men and boys chasing it. When it was caught and brought back, the animal snorted and muttered horse curses. Walks Like A Buffalo stood like a boulder between the rampaging horse and a trench she had dug near her dwelling. She gave commands, pointing her chin here and there. She loomed, staring hard at the grinning boys who led the errant animal back to its corral. Something important was happening in that trench.

Walks Like A Buffalo was tending the making of cooʃhpi, a grey liquid made of fermented corn, a beer that Apaches had had long before whites brought whiskey. There was some ceremony, some patience, some respect in the making of cooʃhpi; whiskey came too easily out of a glass bottle and made a man lose his pride.

To take their minds off of waiting for the cooʃhpi, the men spoke of the next place they would go. The season was over. Any of the shriveled corn and squash in their small garden that had survived the drought was already picked. It was time to go on to a winter place where there was more protection from the cold and more hunting—to the west where the white eyes were scarce. And among the men there were now some who agreed with Many Visions that the white woman meant trouble. She was no good. She was making people turn away from their own healer. This was her witchcraft, to turn brothers against brothers until the strength they had left was wasted on fighting among themselves, until the people separated and clans were torn apart. To not have harmony was the greatest danger, the greatest sickness of all. When people cared more for their own ideas than for the harmony of their people, big trouble came. Ussen, the Life Giver, had no patience for squabbling; he had arisen from a contentious chaos when the universe was new. Then there was nothing but power. Power fought power until Ussen gave the chaos form by creating himself and then White Painted Woman who created the world where each plant, each animal, each grain of sand had to find its own power, its own role in the great universe. And instead of fighting, there would be harmony, as one power complemented the other. Some were meant to be warriors, others to sit in the sun and dispense wisdom, and others were meant to use the power in plants or the power in ceremonies to maintain or restore the delicate but beautiful order of things.

"We have had good healers in the past," Three Fingers said; everyone knew what he was saying about Many Visions, who was not in the past.

"There is no reason to discuss these matters anymore," Most Important Man said. "We are leaving this place and going to our winter place. She will not be with us."

Three Fingers took the corn husk cigarette with his maimed hand when Most Important Man passed it to him. These two squatted down with some of the younger men and Three Fingers didn't feel comfortable. His joints ached, but he stayed there and smoked without moving or complaint. Small Face and Most Important Man's eldest son, Dark Skin, exchanged a glance. They had discussed what they wanted to do to the white woman.

It was a good time for a party.

Sara, dressed in the new skirt and boots, let the women turn her around and touch her admiringly. They laughed about her hair which Little Bird had tried to oil and put in a braid, but which had too much curl in it. And Sara was drawn into the circle where everyone was passing around gourds of the grey beer. A drummer played and some of the children tried to play the spoons, but Many Visions gave them such evil looks that their mothers grabbed the spoons out of the children's hands and threw them on the ground. Eats Fish played the flute. People got up and shuffled their feet and grinned, reaching out to others to get up and dance with them. Sara drank the coofhpi. It was sweet and bitter and had a sharp, stinging fizz to it. The night was wild and loud. People acted foolish like men did when they drank moonshine in Virginia. These Apache men did silly dances, wagging their backsides at the blushing women. One or two girls slipped off with young boys. The women pulled at their husbands to go look for the ones who'd slipped away. Sara watched them and noticed that they did not touch each other to show affection in public. The men did not touch the women the way they did in Virginia, and even children were seldom embraced. After a few more drinks of coofhpi Sara became keenly observant about the people and the way they did things. They hardly ever looked at one another, and in this and in the lack of touching, Sara recognized an ironic obsession with privacy among these people who lived and ate and worked under each other's noses. Come to think of it, she observed after taking a long swig and getting a burst of laughter for it, she had never seen or heard these people fornicate and had rarely seen them engage in any other bodily function. They were extremely discreet for savages, she thought.

The sun going down turned the clouds purple and orange. The rest of the sky was pink and Sara held her knees and rocked back to look at it. This light made them all glow like precious rocks, large gemstones assembled in a circle in a place far away from Roanoke, Virginia, far away from Mr. and Mrs. Franklin. When everyone's eyelids came halfway down over their bloodshot eyes, Shoots Straight began to tell stories about the old days. He told good stories, about the fights with Comanches, about the far range of hunting land they'd had, way over the river and then both north and south for as far as the eye could see. He talked about the time Most Important Man was gored by a dying buck. He told stories about old medicine men and women whose powers were great, gotten directly from the Thunder People and Ussen, Life Giver. He talked about the days when they had many good horses, twenty or thirty or more. They were good horses, not for eating, but for going a long way on.

Many Visions was listening from a dark place on the outside of the circle. No one knew where he was. He listened to the stories about powerful healers from the past. He wanted to choke someone. He wanted to kick Shoots Straight in his stomach. He watched the white woman, all dressed in new clothes, honored like a chief's bride. He wanted to shout at them. Apaches are getting soft, he thought, not like when they tortured and killed those who would do the same to them.

The fire died out. There was one story left, trailing out of Shoots Straight's mouth quietly. All the children were asleep and some of the adults snored. Sara listened, drunk and tired, but feeling that she could actually understand the words Shoots Straight used. Broken

Nose stood up across the circle from her and stretched, arching his back and holding his hands up so that everyone could see the lightning bolt tattoo on the underside of his arm. Sara looked at him, swaying a little as she tried to move her eyes steadily up his body. She was too drunk to think anything clearly, but she felt oddly aware of her own body. It felt light and yet strong, like lightning, or wind.

She jumped to her feet and a few of the children woke up. Because of their dreams some still held their hands as though they had the spoons in them. No one spoke; the people gave her time to do whatever it was she was going to do.

"It is time," Sara said in a high-pitched voice. "God has spoken to me. It is time to tell you about Jesus. I know that you will be able to understand me. I feel that God is ready to make a miracle, and that I can tell you about the wonderful life you will have when you understand that Jesus is your saviour."

Hearing the word *Jesus*, the people groaned and stretched. They got to their feet while she continued to talk; they nodded their goodnights to one another and stumbled off to their homes.

"Jesus will change your lives!" Sara called out, reeling out of balance by the force of raising her voice. Then she said, "Dang," and kicked the dirt. No one was left by the dying fire, but eyes were on her. Many Visions was creeping around; Sara could see his face come in and out of focus at varying distances. Then other faces—Small Face's and Dark Skin's. But she couldn't keep up with their movements. These faces seemed to circle around her until she got sickeningly dizzy. She strained to see them in the darkness, thinking that a face was there when it wasn't and then seeing it clearly in another place.

"Dang," she murmured again, too dizzy to follow what was happening anymore. She sank down, ready to pass out on the spot. The faces came together and whispered. Then Sara heard someone say, in clear English, "Hey, get up, get on your feet!" She opened her eyes and then felt someone's hand circle around her arm and lift her up.

She turned around to see who it was. The masked man's head was right behind her, touching her hair with the long pieces of grass. He wore no shirt and had many beads hanging from a flap he wore over his groin. His tall moccasins rattled with beads.

"Go on now," the man said, and she could see his eyes inside the mask, worried and angry. "You're in danger." She could hear him breathing, and she froze watching him, wondering who it was. "Crazy woman," he said. And he pushed her forward.

It was all strange to Sara who could not remember how she had gotten to Most Important Man's dwelling. It seemed to her that she was suddenly lying down and about to fall asleep. She could hear laughter outside and people breathing heavily inside when she went into a dream of cows and laundry.

The next thing she knew there was no dream and no sound. The whole world had stopped, and the sun was weakly shining. A crow cawed and dawn shone through the branch walls around her. Nothing else.

Sara sat straight up. Blankets fell off her shoulders. Her head thumped with every throb of blood in her neck; her eyes felt red and her tongue tasted like vomit. She couldn't remember when she'd lain down to go to sleep the night before. And during the night it had gotten colder. A chill raised goose bumps on her bare arms. Perhaps like Rip Van Winkle she'd fallen asleep for a hundred years.

Perhaps the whole tribe was waiting, crouching outside the tent poles, ready to pounce on her when she came out. She stood, pausing a minute to hold her throbbing head between her hands. She slapped the door flap aside and stepped out.

That night the first light snow had dusted every surface. The frozen chill stung Sara's feet and came up her legs. But she stayed there, staring at the total emptiness. Nothing was left but the bushlike dwellings and a pile of brush that had served as people's beds. While Sara was sleeping, the whole tribe had packed up and left. They'd filled in the central fire pit, pushed dirt over it and neatly brushed the surface clean. Then they'd gone.

Sara pranced in place to relieve her freezing feet. She clutched herself and looked around. To the east the mountains stood firmly, to the west the silver mesas looked away from her, taking no responsibility. Between the riverside cottonwoods and those mesas, the desert still slept in the cold dawn.

Sara stood alone, a tiny person who was growing tinier as she realized she'd been abandoned. Way above her, in the lower mists of the clouds, a hawk saw her head as a little black spot amidst a bleak, whitened world. And in that black spot of hair and skull thoughts began scurrying around like hunted mice.

"What will happen to me?" she whispered aloud. "How could they have left me to fend for myself? I'm going to die."

She stepped back into the dwelling to pull on her boots. All that was left of Most Important Man, Walks Like A Buffalo and Little Bird were the indentations that their sleeping bodies had made in the earth.

"I have been a captive of Indians," Sara told herself, because the situation seemed confusing. "Oh, God, what has become of me?"

She stroked and observed her sunburnt arms and imagined her face as dark and dirty. She'd lost the silver hair clasp and was wearing underwear and a leather skirt. She looked at her hands, dark and scratched, the nails broken and caked with dirt. Then she made the final assessment by rubbing the scars on her neck where the leash Many Visions pulled had cut into her skin.

"Oh, God," she moaned. "Oh, God. What am I to do?"

But God did not appreciate, as Shoots Straight had, a woman who shoots her own husband, or a woman who drinks beer and shows her legs. A woman who had had the opportunity to be a witness to the savages and bring them into the fold of Christianity, and had failed.

"Oh, God," Sara said. "Jesus, help me."

And while she spoke she thought desperately about what she should do to encourage a miracle.

"I am a woman alone in the wilderness," she told herself. "I must wait for rescue. A soldier will find me and take me back—or the masked man. I can go back. I can go back now and bathe in warm water and eat biscuits." She rubbed the skin on her face and softly repeated, "Biscuits." She looked at the brown, grey, and white vistas around her: bare trees, rocks, dry bushes, mesas, distant mountains—all as silent as the huge, pale sky.

And where would she go back to? To Barkstone? To Roanoke? To her father's house? And what would he say to her as she stood on the porch, her mother behind him? But surely, under the circumstances—her husband dead, murdered—there would be pity. She would be wrapped in pity; and if she wept and acted distraught no one would dare bother her with suspicions. She would be taken care of by . . . whom? She could hear her father say to her mother, "You can't be takin' care of a growed woman. You got your chores. She's got to go to the asylum bein' as she's all crazy in the head now."

"And if he ever found out ..." Sara whispered to herself. Then she went down on her knees.

"Oh, God," she wailed, "what am I to do?"

Perhaps no one would ever know that she had shot poor Edmund. Surely they would believe that one of the Indians had done it—that some beast like Small Face had done it. No one in Roanoke could ever imagine Sara killing anyone ... well, except maybe that boy whose hand she'd smashed, and maybe his wife, if he'd told her. The people here had known the truth about her, what she'd done about Edmund; they knew her dirty and ragged. They knew and didn't care. They liked that she had shot poor Edmund, who had become a horrible burden. They didn't care that her legs showed and she didn't have a real blouse. They even liked her and thought she could do important things.

Then why had they left her?

"It's that snake," Sara said rubbing her scarred neck. "He hates me. He made them do it." She pounded the ground with her open palm until it was red. With each strike she said, "They liked me, you demon." Crows flew up in the air.

"Oh, God," Sara moaned, "what am I to do? Help me, Lord."

She lay down, curled up, squeezing the blankets to her. Then she imagined the masked man standing over her, and he said, "God helps those who help themselves."

"How could they have left me alone to die? I was good. I helped them. I could have brought them to Jesus. Now I have no food. I will starve," Sara sobbed.

"Don't be an idiot. God helps those who help themselves. That's all."

She sat up.

"What should I do?" she asked aloud. She blew her nose on one corner of the blanket. She wondered what Little Bird had thought of leaving her slave behind. She thought of Many Visions, traveling through the desert with her Bible.

"Mother," Sara said and a new weakness swept through her. She thought of her mother hanging up laundry. She saw her mother's skirts blow around in the wind and hide her when she clung to her mother's legs. "Mother, hide me," she thought. "Hide me."

The masked man stamped the ground like a horse and folded his arms over his chest.

"They didn't kill me," Sara thought. "They didn't molest me. They know I'm not evil. I'm not evil."

She thought of Little Bird and Walks Like A Buffalo. She thought of Broken Nose speaking to her in English, of his eyes that looked at her as though she was important.

"I will have to wait here or try to find a fort or town." She looked around at the big landscape again. All space and no sign of life but the crows and the footprints of the people all around her.

"Maybe someone will come for me," she said weakly. But this was what she'd always suspected her end would be like: she would be left alone.

"You could go across the river and toward the mountains," she told herself. The mountains were in the east, where white men were.

Sara saw a white man's hands lifting her up, carrying her along, and white women in bonnets and dark, layered dresses staring at her in horrified pity. She was a Presbyterian, she would explain, and she'd been in the wilderness with savages. Her husband, she would say, had been killed. Shot in the head.

Crows cawed and a wind rustled the few dried leaves that were still stuck to the branches. Sara held the blankets around her shoulders.

"They left these for me," she said. "They could have taken them and killed me." She imagined Little Bird laying an extra blanket on her before leaving. Bracing her throbbing forehead with one hand, Sara stood up and walked to the edge of the river. There she stared down at all the footprints where the snow was already melting and making mud. She thought of those to whom the feet belonged that made the prints and imagined them milling about the river before leaving, quiet so as not to arouse the sleeping white woman. Perhaps they had even made sure to get her drunk so that she would sleep hard. She thought of Little Bird and Walks Like A Buffalo, Small Face, Long Skirt, and Broken Nose tramping around making those footprints, and now they were gone. Maybe they had never existed.

For several minutes Sara crawled around in what was left of the settlement looking for bits of dried meat or trailings of ground corn. There was nothing, and having her head bent forward escalated the throbbing.

Then she sat still in the middle of their old homes. She waited. The masked man walked away, toward the mesas. The rattling of his beads aroused the wind. She sat still for a while, humming, coughing occasionally, squinting at the horizon for any sign of rescuers, thinking of building a fire, of yelling "help." She spoke aloud to her father, to her mother, to Many Visions, to Broken Nose, to Hattie from the wagon train.

"I could die here," she said. She stood up and walked to the water again. The only thing that replaced the hunger in her stomach now was a great bubble of fear that she felt would kill her sooner than starvation if she didn't do something.

"Dear God," she said staring down at the ground, "I am so afraid."

She followed the footprints away from the river, past the abandoned dwellings to the open desert where the cottonwoods ended and many footprints led southwest to a crease between two grandfather mesas.

"Yes," Sara said. "Yes, thank God."

She stood, facing the west and clasped her hands together. She shut her eyes and said, "Be with me, oh Lord."

The crows said, "Amen."

XVIII

Sara and the Twenty-third Psalm moved in a bundle under the cold sky. She walked with her dark eyes on the space between the two slate grey mesas, sometimes pausing to squint and look for the people moving ahead of her. Such a horde moving in that big emptiness should be visible, stand out in both form and movement. But the shadows on the desert hid things and distances were as tricky as fog in the mountains near Roanoke. A herd of rocks a hundred yards away could look like a group of travelers three miles away, and vice versa. But Sara could not conceive of doing anything but walking forward. Any other ideas fell under the wheel of the Twenty-third Psalm.

She walked between the prickly pear cactus and the cholla with its skinny, needled arms, now shriveled and sagging. Some of the cholla was dead, lying in heaps of porous grey sticks like the grey arm bones of some wasted human. And there was sage and other light green bushes that thrived in the gravel and sand. Sometimes Sara came to outcrops of boulders that she climbed on top of to see the whole of the direction in which she walked. The wind was strong and tossed sand in her face and hair. It was a frigid wind that encountered few trees to sift apart its sting.

"This is a godforsaken place," she mumbled, adjusting the blankets around her shoulders.

Sara wanted to see green forests, the forests of oak at her father's farm where a child could hide in the shade or burrow like a rabbit in patches of bushes. The desert was too bare. In the desert, God's eye fell hard and direct. His presence was raw and big. The desert was as powerful as an ocean. The purple mountains and black mesas always in the distance were frozen, never-breaking waves. Heaven and earth were not so vast in Roanoke.

"I am Sara Williams Franklin of Roanoke, Virginia," she called out. And then she shook her head. "Sara Williams Franklin Willoughby."

Sara bit into the blanket and dragged it up as she raised her head to look at the sky. To the east were the clouds, grey and fluffy. But to the north and west there were strips of blue, and she could even see sunlight on the top of one of the mesas. To the south the clouds were blacker and spewing trails of freezing rain on the earth. It was as though one could see the weather of three different days in one sky.

"I am hungry," Sara said, "and thirsty. I should have brought water." Then she warned herself. "Don't think of such things or you will despair and be lost."

She trudged alone, a little thing in a big space. So she performed an entire church service for herself.

"We will now sing hymn number 351."

She recited scripture, and gave a sermon. Mary Magdalene popped into her head as a subject for the sermon. She'd always wanted to hear more about Mary Magdalene. And here was her chance. She talked to the congregation about Mary Magdalene's life as a whore, about her beauty, about the change that had come over her when she looked into Jesus' eyes. She described Jesus and Mary Magdalene looking deeply into each other's eyes. She described the overpowering influence of Jesus that made the woman want to touch him and no one else—to wash his feet.

"Could I have washed Edmund's feet?" she wondered. "Yes, perhaps I should have washed Edmund's feet.

"And should we not all have such desire," she asked a clump of scrub oak, "to touch the feet of our Lord, to feel the skin of God's own flesh, to taste the sweat of the Son of God who labored for our salvation, to inhale the breath of the Saviour?" She saw the strong and patient Christ embracing the woman of the streets. She saw him lay his fine hands on her exhausted brow. "And Jesus took pity on this woman. Yes he did! Many said she was a sinner, but Jesus loved her."

Sara started weeping.

"We must forgive sinners," she told the congregation impassionately, "for they are Jesus' chosen companions. He will lift them up, to hold them to his breast, to fill them with God's power and love."

Sara reached upward with both arms and the blankets fell off. She stopped to gather them up and to send the collection plate into the congregation. She asked for food and water but got back sand and a breeze that smelled like sleet.

"How far could they have gone?" she asked. The mesas seemed to slide away from her as she walked, keeping their original distance. The sky turned orange and pink, then purple, and she could no longer see the footprints, or the tracks of packs being dragged.

Sara squeezed against an overhanging rock and curled up. It was very cold. She could only stay warm by staying very still and sealing herself against the air with the blankets. Hunger and thirst made her whole body ache. She wondered if she would die in the desert that night and be eaten by the coyotes she could hear occasionally. Her only hope was to find the people again, and to keep God interested in her. She was all alone save for God and the people. She wondered what God was thinking. Maybe He wasn't thinking about her at all. She spent the night quivering and crouching and praying.

By morning she was so weak that it took two hours of the sun's warmth to get her going again. She walked a few hours, dragging her feet and the blankets, until she realized that she'd forgotten about the footprints and had lost track of them. She lay down on the ground again. Her thirst was so powerfully irritating to her body that she imagined she would vomit up the emptiness inside her until she was turned inside-out. She took sand and put it in her mouth to suck on, as though it might quench her thirst. She tried to get to her feet, muttering, "I should go back, back to the river. I should go back to the river and get water." But then she whimpered thinking that it would take two days to go back, and she had far less strength than when she had started out.

She sank back down and murmured, "I will just die. I can't go on."

She looked up at the sky. There was a dark speck coasting slowly on some air current. She lay there, wondering how long it was going to take to die. She closed her eyes and tried to recite every piece of religious liturgy she could remember, other people's words. "Almighty God, father of all mercies, we thine unworthy servants do give thee most humble and hardy thanks for thy goodness and loving kindness to us and to all men . . . all men."

She thought about her life, about how she had kept

her life inside of her for many years. It had an internal landscape, sometimes touched by things from the outside, as though seeds had blown from the flowers in the meadows or from her mother's words into her mind and grown there. It seemed that when she tried to touch the outside world she caused misery and confusion. Until these people and their world that had no separation between the outside and the inside. Their minds, Sara imagined, were formed of the dirt and plants around them, just as God had made Adam from the clay of the Earth. And with clarity, Sara knew that she wanted to live some more in the world outside her own childhood's mind. She could only hope that heaven, if she still deserved to go there, would be a place like this, not like Roanoke.

XIX

Sara lay on her back and concentrated on the crystals in the purple sky. She laughed to hear coyotes howling in their appeals to the universe. The wind howled, too, so hard that it blew the stars around in the universe. A white half-moon sailed through the night. Sara imagined what it must taste like—like a biscuit with butter all over it, one of her mother's biscuits with good, fresh butter.

"I'm hungry. Why doesn't God give me any food?" Sara said aloud.

She could hear little creatures skittling around near her ears and thought of catching them and eating them. Toward dawn she dozed and felt a small horned toad squatting on her cheek. Its cool belly felt like a caress, and Sara awoke thinking that Broken Nose was bending over her. Dozing again, all she saw were the beady, chickenlike eyes of the miniature monster as it backed up and rested on her chest. Every time it breathed, Sara felt its squat, spiked body expand.

She fell asleep again and dreamed about the things the horned toad was telling her, about what was really going on in the world, things that sounded nothing like what was talked about in the First Presbyterian Church of Roanoke. It said, "You could be anywhere, but you are here, and so here you need to know certain things.

Somewhere else you would need to know other things. But it all amounts to the same thing." And she dreamed in Apache and understood everything that was said.

On her fourth morning in the desert, Sara awoke and saw smoke to the south. It was white smoke reaching up into the blue, blue sky like a misty roadway to heaven. Indeed, the horned toad had mentioned that some help lay to the south. Sara got to her hands and knees, empty in the stomach and empty in the head. She stumbled and walked southward, now parallel to the great long mesa she had been walking toward. She spoke to herself in both English and Apache, giggling, giddy at the wonder of it all. She imagined that when she got to their fire, when they saw her, she'd smile and say something in Apache—something like, "It is a good day for the dogs to lie in the sun." Little Bird would fall at her feet and give her food and water. Maybe some of that crackly dried elk. That would taste good.

The smoke was white and swirling. As she got closer Sara saw something humped on the landscape. Perhaps it was a home. But where in all this flatness and scrub oak was any water to support a settlement? Why stop here, in the open? These Indians were crazy.

Sara carried the blanket in a bundle in front of her. The sun shone warm, even though it was low in the southern sky.

"Dear Lord," she whispered, and she stopped. "That's a white man's wagon."

In the middle of nowhere was a wagon, not a teepee or hogan. Sarah thought of Reverend Willoughby and could feature a white man being stupid enough to camp in this unimpeded wind tunnel, offering a place of shelter to rattlesnakes. Smoke was rising up from near it. Would he be an outlaw? A prospector? A preacher?

She wanted food and water, never mind that here was

the beginning of a long story, a story she would have to tell again and again and again for the rest of her life until she was in a rocking chair and other people's grandchildren came to see her.

Food and water.

She dug her broken nails into the blanket as though it could hold her up. If she thought coolly, below the sickening thirst that almost overwhelmed any hunger, if she moved her mind underneath that thirst and saw this whole drama from the eyes of a person who had recently eaten and drunk, she could see that she was a story. Her face and arms were dark, her hair wild, her lips split and dry, her hands cold and rough. She had no bonnet and she wore a squaw's skirt that showed her legs. And in the white man's world, the thing she wore as a blouse was underwear. She was a woman wandering around in her underwear. It was a good thing she was desperate and insane or she'd be immoral. She walked closer, hiding her bareness with the blanket, creeping coyly up to the wagon. A hope that the man was not drinking whiskey came into her head and made her consider going on, skittling across the desert like a lizard. But water, water, liquid. She could not yet see any human, but she could see the wagon in detail. Then a cry leapt out of her throat all on its own.

"Dear Lord," she said. "Dear Jesus, Son of God. That is my wagon. That is my and Edmund's wagon. That is the Willoughby wagon."

The last time she'd seen that wagon was at night, when Small Face, Eats Fish, and Broken Nose had been formed out of darkness and leapt into the light of the Willoughbys' sputtering fire. The last time she'd seen that wagon was when she shot Reverend Edmund Willoughby in the head after seeing one of her mother's dining room chairs being thrown out of the back by that grinning gargoyle, Small Face. She remembered seeing the ripped seat, the straw popping out of it, remembered that Reverend Willoughby had ripped every one of those chairs. He had ripped the innocent silk skin of those chairs apart looking for hidden money. Reverend Willoughby and Small Face had massacred those chairs and she shot him. He was going to drive her crazy and then tie her up and put her in a wagon to take her to a crazy house. That was what she remembered when she saw the wagon, broken, crumbling, leaning, weedy— drifts of sand blown against the wheels.

She walked slowly, no longer coy but with her mouth hanging open, taking in the broken wheel, the torn canvas cover, the weeds grown around the horses' harnesses. It was like looking at the old, abandoned set of a play she had been in. Sara tiptoed around the wagon, close to the dirty canvas. A sleek lizard whirled around and then shot off. Sara leaned out and looked at the source of the smoke.

And there was Edmund, or what was left of him. Sara was looking at the white, bleached skeleton of Reverend Willoughby—a smiling, relaxing skeleton—bones as white as old dog feces. And he was steaming like dry ice in smoky, silent swirls.

Sara stepped from the side of the wagon.

"What are you doing, Edmund?" she asked.

He didn't say anything.

"You are a strange sight, way out here in the desert, Edmund," Sara said, and still the skeleton was as silent as Brer Rabbit's Tar Baby.

She shook her head.

"I'm sorry about shooting you, Edmund. But I couldn't think straight with trying to do what you wanted me to and trying to watch out for those crazy men."

She kicked at the dust a little, but the bones lay still, smoking cold steam.

Then she recalled something useful. She scrambled into the back of the wagon. Everything was thrown around the way Small Face had left it. Sara grabbed the canteen and drank from it. The water was thickish and tasted like metal. She could feel it wet her insides all the way to her stomach. She drank, laughing and then screwed the top back on. She shook the canteen and hearing the water left in it she opened it again and drank more.

"Save the rest," she told herself.

Then she felt around on the floor for anything edible and gathered up about twenty beans. She thought about how she could eat them. She wouldn't dare use the water for cooking. She finally decided to drop them into the canteen where they'd soften up and she could chew on them when she took a drink. Her hands shook as she dropped them carefully from her fist.

Finished with that task, Sara looked around. Then she opened a trunk and picked at some of the clothes. They were wrinkled and smelled like bleach. She held a woolen skirt up to her, then carefully laid it down. The dining room chairs were still there, except for the one Small Face had thrown outside. Sara touched the tufts of straw that stuck out of them.

"Oh, Mother," she said. She wiped tears out of her eyes. "What you must think of me. And Timothy, little Timothy. You must think me dead, or that I don't care to write to you. Oh, Mother, I miss you so. I wish. . . ."

She located paper and an old school pencil. Something had chewed on it and left little teeth marks. She sat down on the edge of the cot where little balls of some animal's droppings had hardened. She paused, looking into the air and thinking. There was so much to say.

"Dear Mother," she wrote with a shaking, rough hand.

I want you to have news of me when the wagon is found. I am not dead. Edmund is dead, but I am alive and doing God's work. Tell Timothy that I miss him. And tell Adele that she should not be so cruel. I hope that father treats you well. I miss you terribly and wish that we could be together.

A gust of wind made the canvas snap and pop. Sara looked up at the deep blue crack that let in the limitless outside.

I think you might even find in this wilderness the beauty of God's world.

Your loving daughter,
Sara

She held the note to her, as though it was her mother, and looked around.

"Should I take the sewing box?" she asked the paper, "or some clothes?"

She sighed and lay down on the cot, her legs still on the floor. She took the blanket up again and hugged it to her. She thought of hugging her mother's legs. She wanted a human being to hold her, though it should have been enough to believe that she was in the hands of God. She fell asleep and had a dream that she would not understand because it was, of all things, a dream about Broken Nose, a dream of the lightning scar on the underside of his arm. The dream smelled like the mint hanging on his chest.

A movement outside woke her, a hard snapping. Her heart pumped fast and she sat up, staring out the opening at the blue emptiness that whooshed out into the universe. A little of the white steam swirled into view, then the whole skeleton stood there smoking and waiting.

"Edmund," Sara said, "what do you want?"

The skeleton remained silent.

"Edmund, I know that I shot you in the head and all, but that's done. I can't undo it. And now I'm alone, all small and alone in the middle of nothing."

She stood up, making the old wagon rock and creak.

"I have seen many unusual things, Edmund, so don't think that you are impressing upon me that the world has become odd."

She grabbed the canteen with the beans rattling in it and jumped off the wagon, careful to avoid the skeleton. He exuded coldness and moved stiffly, like a marionette.

"I have a new home, Edmund, and must go on—over there, where the people have gone. I don't understand how all of this happened, Edmund, but I'm no longer a member of the Presbyterian Church."

She stuffed the letter to her mother in between two of the skeleton's ribs.

"You can take this for me. I don't see as how you'll have much trouble meeting your needs in the desert. Take this letter. I don't want my mother to suffer on my account."

The skeleton looked blinklessly at Sara. His big grin seemed servile and perhaps a bit idiotic.

"We can't question God's ways, Edmund," Sara said. "Now, go on."

The skeleton clicked and clattered into motion, still

grinning. And it soothed Sara's guilt somewhat to see that he never stopped smiling.

The skeleton danced off to the east, steam flowing around him, his knee and elbow joints jerking up and down. Sara headed in the opposite direction, to the west toward the two mesas. The woman and the happy-go-lucky skeleton moved steadily apart, putting a distance between them in which the wagon was always the center.

XX

When Sara was only half a mile away from the wagon, she saw a man standing in the middle of her view. His legs were apart and his hands were folded over his groin. When she got closer to him, he motioned to her to hurry on. She trotted, listening to the beans rattle in the canteen. She saw that he was the masked man. His mask was the same—a big hollowed-out piece of wood, painted like a horned toad, and the long grasses still came out of the side and top of it. He stood with his back against the sun so that Sara could hardly see anything of him but the shape of his mask and his bare muscles. She put her hands above her eyes to block the light and saw his eyes looking steadily at her.

"Are you going to take me home?" she asked.

The light all around them suddenly dimmed and Sara shivered and hugged the blanket. Looking up she saw streaks of clouds covering the sun.

"Go with me. Show me the way," Sara said. "I can tell them about Jesus."

The light changed again, brightening.

"The world is much bigger than I thought before. There is always more, isn't there, up there, past the blue, past even the stars. There is always more. There is a lot of room for sinning. It is hard for one woman in so much space not to commit sins."

The masked man didn't say anything. He walked just a bit ahead of Sara. He was guiding her.

"Who are you? Where do you come from? Are we going home?" She said all this running after him. "Do you have any food?"

He kept walking, rattling—ching, ching, ching.

He walked quickly, as though he had a job to do and didn't want to linger over it. Sara had to run again to catch up to him.

The masked man stopped. His breath was heavy inside his mask. He let her look at him.

"For all I know I am either in a dream or I truly am crazy," Sara said.

"It doesn't matter either way," the masked man said. "There are other things that matter." He kept his face toward hers and Sara was frozen by the look he let her dwell on. His eyes seemed so dignified and sad that Sara felt ashamed of her own small hardships. Those eyes had seen more than anyone, every kind of suffering. Sara stood stupidly looking at them.

"Keep walking," he said, pointing, "on that way past those boulders. See where there are trees? Keep walking there. You'll know what to do, you'll know what matters."

"Don't you have anything to eat?" she asked. He backed away—ching, ching, ching.

Sara took up the canteen and undid the cap. The swig of water washed two beans into her mouth. They were softened up but had to be chewed a lot. When Sara screwed the cap back on and looked around, still chewing on the beans, the man was gone. But she could hear his rattling—ching, ching, ching—as though he was walking in the ground underneath her.

XXI

〰〰〰

The new settlement fanned out from the bottom of the mesa. The site had many memories; it was a good place to be in winter, had been for many hundreds of years. There were cliff dwellings, old and long unused, to the north, nearer the river. Now they were just empty caves where birds nested. And there were ghosts there, spirits of the Pueblos' ancestors. The Apaches erected their branch-and-hide homes against the end of the northern mesa, so that the whole table of striped earth was between them and the north wind. To the north the mesa slid down to the river where some evergreens and big bushes bunched. The far bank of this river was a canyon wall where eagles nested. The boys took the horses down there every day when their sisters filled water baskets. It was a time for a lot of hunting, to set up stores of meat for the hard weather. It was a time when the pueblos were good for raiding, their storage places full of corn. Many goods had to be gotten for the winter and for the Na ih es of the girls, like Strong Legs, Most Important Man's daughter. Gifts had to be given by the fathers of these girls, and the gifts came from raiding.

These were old patterns, the hunting and raiding, based on spiritual vision. The patterns and ceremonies defined who the people were and showed respect for the past and for the powers that had no past, present, or future but existed before time and would exist after time. These powers created time, seasons for this and that, places to do summer things, places to do winter things. It showed respect to remember, to repeat. But another part of life were the new stories that came, that were added to what was told. There were always new things, and to make them part of life they became stories that had the old wisdom.

So now there were four new stories, one for each of the four directions. There was the story of the crazy white woman who had leaped on Many Visions and who was dragged by her neck through the camp, the crazy white woman who had shot her husband and was Little Bird's slave. That was a good story. Then there was the story of Long Skirt's home being blown away by a sudden wind that came right between the two mesas as it tried to run from winter. This wind blew the beginnings of Long Skirt's home, the poles she'd dragged from the river and set up; it blew them right over and out across the desert toward the scalloped purple mountains way in the distance to the west. That was a good story. Then there was the story of the new foal that came at sunrise one morning after the people first got to the winter camp. It came out with its nose first, and the mare ran around and around with that nose sticking out of her until Wears Hats caught her and pulled the rest of the foal out. That was a good story. But the bad story was that Shoots Straight died on the desert. He was riding one of the horses. Feeds Herself First was walking beside the horse that carried her husband. She heard him gag, as he had the other time when one side of him died. It was as though he'd been struck by lightning. He had a wild look in his eye and then slumped over. This time both sides were dead. The grandfather who told stories had passed on, and his name couldn't be said anymore.

So when things started disappearing, like Three Fingers' bearskin and some food out of Walks Like A Buffalo's pot, the people thought it might be Shoots Straight's ghost. There was some suspicion about Feeds Herself First and her daughters. They were suspected of showing their grief, of weeping for him and saying his name. Walks Like A Buffalo had a talk with the widow, but she swore that she wanted her husband's spirit to be at rest on the other side. Many Visions went through her home with sage smoke and prayers.

Up above the river, among the cedar and grey stalks of dead cholla, Sara paced. She held Three Fingers' bearskin around her and talked aloud about her hunger. The bear's head lolled on top of hers.

With grandfather bear looking over her head, Sara stopped and squinted as though she might be able to see the settlement and the people from there, or to see Little Bird sneaking up to her with food. Little Bird had found Sara sleeping up on the ridgetop one day. She kicked her hard in the side, and when Sara shot up and saw her, Little Bird pressed her lips together and shook her head. Sara wept with gratitude at the sight of this familiar face and the long braids that smelled like sage smoke and venison grease.

"Do-ye' ingashii sezii'," Sara said.

Now it was Little Bird who had been kicked. She backed away, dropping a bundle of sticks that she'd been carrying.

"You speak as though you were one of the Superior People."

"I am hungry. I am very hungry," Sara said.

"Are you alive?" Little Bird asked, backing up a few steps.

"Yes, yes," Sara said. "I am not a ghost."

"You are a woman of power," Little Bird said in a whisper.

"I need food," Sara said.

"That bearskin belongs to one of our grandfathers."

"Don't tell the others. Please. I need to eat."

Sara walked up to Little Bird.

"You'd better get out of here," Little Bird had said. "You will be killed. You'd better use your power to get out of here.

"I know Many Visions will kill you, and no one will stop him," Little Bird had told Sara that first day of reunion. "People say that you are a witch, and now I believe it."

But she brought Sara food every now and then, always saying, "You have to leave." As she got more used to Sara, Little Bird threw the food at her, and while Sara snatched up the threads of dried meat and hunks of corn cake, the Apache woman hissed, "You do not belong here. Go on," and shooed her like a dog.

"I am one of the Superior People now," Sara had said.

Little Bird looked sharply away, her braids flying. "Then you will starve. You will disappear forever, for that is what is happening to our people. Go home, white woman."

This was not how Sara had envisioned the reunion.

There were times now when Sara thought that if she had a belly full of food, she would go. She sometimes felt a strong urge to pass from this world to another, that it was time to end this spirit journey and go home. The urge came in dreams of her mother. She wanted the people to tell her how to make such a journey and to give her directions and food.

She paced again, waiting for Little Bird. It was late

afternoon and there was still light in the sky, though the sun seemed small and cold. What was there to eat in such a world? She looked around for something to chew up and make into the mush that the women turned into food. But she had to boil water to do the job properly. If she built a fire, Many Visions would find her and kill her. He would choke her with his bare hands and mutilate her so that she would enter eternity without hands or with a long gash in her stomach. No, she must slowly find her way back with the people, quietly, humbly, so they wouldn't want to hurt her. She could then be protected again by Most Important Man and his family. He was a good father. He showed his children the right way to live and didn't harm them. And Sara knew that if anything bad came to his door, Most Important Man would stand up to it and protect his family. And if that's the way it was supposed to be, she would disappear with them, sink into the earth, a pale layer of the brown rock they would become.

Still, she couldn't forget everything. She was still used to certain comforts; she missed them. Here there was no fried chicken or biscuits and butter, no outhouses, or porcelain washstands. No quilts or tea and milk. No nice chairs and good books. Little Bird had told her, "You are not one of us. You say that one of our medicine men is evil—donzhooda. But he is one of us. You are not. You are a white woman. Go home. Go back. Go back to your own people and tell them to leave us alone."

That old home, Sara tried to explain, was many, many miles away, over the mountains and over all that flatness and grass and through all those rivers, like the one the boy had drowned in when his dog barked and barked and barked. And now that it was cold and the mountains were caked with snow and ice, how would she get back home? It was lonely to think of it. Wasn't there a man among the Superior People who could take her as a wife, who could give her children, who would sleep close to her? She didn't dare bring these thoughts up with Little Bird, Most Important Man's youngest wife who had borne no children.

She heard a snap behind her and turned around to face eastward, expecting to see Little Bird, but instead it was Broken Nose who was only a step away from her. She could feel his breath, he was so close.

Broken Nose was equipped for hunting, with arrows and a bow over his shoulder. He wore a red flannel shirt, a Mexican's shirt, and his long hair fluttered against the material. He looked padded, solid, and stared at her before stepping forward.

"Totah," Sara said.

"Inda'a'," Broken Nose said and then he laughed and shook his head. He fingered the bearskin.

"You steal," he said in English. He showed amusement, but his eyes twitched.

Sara stood still, waiting.

"There was a story that this was so—a story of the white woman flying like a witch," Broken Nose said. "You take our grandfather's skin."

Sara took it off and dropped it on the toes of his moccasins. Then she stood shivering.

"Why you here?" he asked. "You walk alone?" He suddenly laughed so loud that Sara was afraid that others would hear and come. He picked up the bearskin and smelled it, then threw it over his shoulder. Sara grabbed it off of him and ran.

"Hey!" he called out. He ran after her and caught her around the waist. Holding her there with one arm he let her struggle, patient because he knew she couldn't get away. He had the sensation of holding a wild horse whose fate was to be tamed. One must have patience and show strength and respect. He waited until she became breathless, then he turned her around and, still holding her by the waist with one arm, brushed her hair away from her mouth.

"Quiet, white woman," he said softly.

"I am not a white woman," she screamed and he put his hand over her mouth. Her nostrils flared and her eyes widened as though she was trying to breathe through them, too.

He just held her. He held her and waited. She felt his ability to easily hurt her, but she also felt him wait with her.

Her breathing gentled and he took his hand away.

"Quiet," he said again. He stroked her hair as though stroking the mare's mane while holding tight on its bridle. She could taste the salt from his hand on her lips. She leaned against him and rested from the exertion and the cold. She smelled the mint and smoke on his hair and clothes. Each of his inhalations made her warmer. She stared to cry.

"Strange woman," he said.

"Tell them that I am a friend, not an enemy," she pleaded in Apache.

Broken Nose stopped stroking her hair. She kept talking, babbling away in Apache.

"I am tired," she said, "hiyaa." And, "I am going home—nadistaa." She began to walk down the edge of the ridge to the path that led down to the river and to the settlement.

Broken Nose grabbed her shoulders and squeezed hard as though to keep her from floating up.

"You speak. Who taught you our words?" he asked in Apache.

"I don't know," Sara said.

He let go of her, tossing her away from him like bad food.

"You must say that I am a friend. I'm afraid I will be killed. I don't know how it will be for a white woman who follows after she's been left. But I had no food. I had nothing."

Broken Nose walked away, very quickly disappearing—just like that, as fast as he had appeared.

And Sara was left, cold. She looked down and saw that he had dropped the bearskin. She picked it up and wrapped it close to her, staring toward where he had vanished.

She slept badly all night long, wondering if Broken Nose had told the others about her.

In the morning her hunger was great. Little Bird had not come with food, so Sara climbed down to the river's edge to look for her. She crouched down and stared at the water. She saw several fish come and go, pausing underneath the bank where it hung over the water. After watching them for some time, she was obsessed with the notion of catching one. With furtive concentration she squatted, her feet planted firmly and wide apart. She positioned her hands, poised inches above the water. Then she lunged for a resting fish. But all she came up with was water that glazed her hand in the yellow sunlight. She waited and watched. Nothing could divert her now or make her care how foolish she looked. Hunger for this food made everything else seem foolish. Finally, she caught a fish in her hand. She hardly understood how it got there. It was a speckled trout flapping around. She held on to it fiercely until the thing stopped moving and its big, round eyes were mesmerized by the sight of eternity. Sara jumped up and whooped. Then she sheepishly covered her own mouth and walked a few yards along the river holding the dead fish, talking to herself about it.

The dilemma of eating it sobered her. With no fire how could she cook the fish? She looked around, as though she might spot a woodstove sitting amidst the sage bushes. Then she reasoned that she could lay the fish on a rock the way the women dried out their meat. She put the trout down and squatted by it, staring. The fish still looked stupid and uncooked. She stood up and circled the rock, then squatted on the other side of it, watching. Finally, she took the cool fish and bit into it. It was watery and stuck her mouth with bones. It was slimy, too. She picked at it with her hands, getting hunks of clear, white flesh into her mouth. At the end, she left a pile of slimy organs, torn skin, and the still bewildered head on the pebbles.

Then Sara washed her face and hands, sticky with blood and fish juices. She hummed jauntily. She talked to herself; she lay down in the sun and fell asleep. The rushing water overrode all other sounds, such as the sound of someone sneaking up.

Sara went over and over in her mind how she had caught and eaten the fish, until she was asleep. She fell deeply asleep, tired and satisfied by the raw fish. Her mouth was slightly open and her hands were under her cheek as a pillow when someone grabbed the front of her hair and jerked her up. She gasped a long, swooping gasp and opened her eyes wide to see Small Face's squinched-up grin an inch away from her face. He was laughing hard. He couldn't believe what he'd gotten ahold of.

"You crazy mother dog," he said with wicked glee. He pulled her up to her feet by the hair. She winced and grabbed his wrist to stop him from pulling harder.

"N-la shii tsi' domanantii'," she said.

Small Face stopped grinning and narrowed his close-set eyes.

"You know how to speak," he growled. He looked her over and announced, "I am going to kill you."

He grabbed the back of Sara's neck and pushed her across the shallow river, through the cold water and up a steep path. There was an indentation in the side of the steep bank where three other men were sitting: Eats Fish, Broken Nose, and a younger, wide-faced man named Kills Bucks. They all stared at the white woman, and Small Face laughed.

"Where did you find her?" Broken Nose asked.

"Sleeping like a dog in the sun," Small Face said. "I say that she has been stealing things. I say she leads soldiers to us. She has made fools of us."

"It is unusual for a white to be alone here. Usually many white men come together," Eats Fish said. "And the women never come here."

"She speaks our language. She can understand everything we say," Small Face said. Then he said to her, "I'm going to cut you many times with this knife." He took a dagger out of his belt and put it into her nostril. She straightened up a little but did not scream.

"She doesn't look afraid to me," Kills Bucks said. "I am thinking that she's a witch."

Eats Fish laughed as though Kills Bucks was a fool, just a kid who didn't know anything. But he'd always thought the same thing about the white woman, since the beginning. Somehow, he wasn't all that surprised that she had showed up again.

Sara flung her head back, tossing her tangled hair like a proud horse. She said nothing. She didn't feel the old way of being scared, the wanting to sink down on the ground and weep and whine and go crazy. She looked at each man's face.

"Let's do it now," Kills Bucks said.

"Such a killing has important meaning. This is a matter for a healer," Eats Fish said.

Small Face looked as though he were going to spit. "I am tired of asking those who don't know."

Sara caught Broken Nose's eye. He didn't look away. He was studying her the way she had been studying them. He was squatting in the dirt, but looked bigger than the others. The mint he wore around his neck swayed like a pendulum away from his opened shirt.

"I will take her," Broken Nose said.

Small Face laughed. "What are you going to do with her, Hopi man?"

Broken Nose stood up.

"You who were raised by a soft woman, a Hopi woman, I don't see how such a man can have the courage to kill a witch."

"If anyone kills the white woman it will be me," Broken Nose said.

They climbed up the steep wall in silence, Sara in front of Broken Nose. They made their way between cactus and big rocks. By now Sara knew the best footholds and was quick to get up to the top. The river whispered below them and Small Face's voice came up. Broken Nose said nothing until they reached the top and were in the company of cedar trees and piñon. He took her to a big, flaky-barked cedar tree and pushed her against it. He leaned against a boulder that faced the tree.

He began speaking to her as though his mission was to tell her certain things.

"It is true what is said about me."

Sara could see that he was tense almost to great anger.

"I was raised by a Hopi woman, until I lived six

years. Then my people came and took me. My mother was killed, the one who picked me up out of the corn and told me that the world is always beautiful." He looked away, toward the west where his mother had pointed when she whispered in his ear.

"I am one of the Superior People, and yet my first mother haunts me."

Sara just watched him and pressed her back against the tree.

"You are a strong woman," he said. "Why are you a strong woman? Why have you followed us? Are there soldiers with you?"

"There are no soldiers," Sara said.

"Why do you look into a man's eyes? Is it right in your family to do this? It is a rude thing to look into a person's face."

"You are looking into my face," Sara said. Her heart was beating so she could hear it.

Broken Nose laughed and seemed nervous. Then he stood up and pulled her head back by the hair and looked close into her face.

"I will look into your face if I want."

Sara closed her eyes and he let go. She couldn't hear him for several seconds and opened her eyes to see what he was doing. He was thinking, looking at her and thinking.

"Are you going to kill me?" she asked.

He looked away again.

"There is a story," she said, "that my mother told me. It is the story of a woman who was going to be killed. A powerful woman wanted this other woman killed and told a warrior to take her into the woods and kill her. She told him to bring her heart back as proof that he had killed her. But when the warrior took her to the woods and drew his knife, he could not kill her, because he knew she didn't deserve to die. So he told her to run and he killed a wild animal and took its heart back to the powerful woman."

Broken Nose crossed his arms over his chest and chuckled softly, nodding his head.

"I remember how warm your ass was when I carried you. A long time ago," he said.

Sara blushed, and he leaned in close to her and took the blanket off of her shoulders.

"You shouldn't touch me," she said. "I don't want your hands on me." Her heart's beating nauseated her. She wanted to lean in, to collapse on him, but it was him she had to fear. He looked at her chest and touched the nipples through the material. They stood out brown beneath the yellowed linen.

Broken Nose said, "You are a crazy woman. With your people you must be an important person."

"I don't have any importance," she whispered.

He rubbed her breast with the palm of his hand. Sara's legs shook. He pressed up against them and could feel them shake.

"You are afraid," he said. "What are you afraid of, white woman?"

"I don't know," she said.

Her hands fluttered over his back and he stroked her neck with his knuckles. Then she pushed away from him, against the tree and placed her hands against the flaky bark. She looked down, posed like a girl in a melodrama. He lifted her camisole above her breasts. She pulled it down, holding it down with one white-knuckled hand.

He laughed and walked away. Sara watched him. He turned from some distance to face her.

"I will tell you something, white woman. You are like me. You don't have a true name for yourself. You are white, but you talk with our words. You are a woman, but in some ways you act like a man."

"I am a Christian," Sara said quietly in English.

"You are a woman of power, and I am not afraid of you. A woman of power cannot call herself one thing or another. It is the same with me. I have thought about this."

He came back and leaned into her against the tree, between her legs. He lifted her up and put her feet on the rock he had been sitting on. They both breathed noisily. Her buttocks were supported by his hand and she laid her head on his shoulder.

"In your story, do the woman and the warrior lie down together?" he asked, teasing her.

Sara answered, "No."

And he said, "Well, that is what is going to happen in this story." And he pushed her skirt up. The bloomers she wore were thin and full of holes. He didn't want to let go of her so he ripped them off, peeled them and let their rags fall to the dirt. He untied the rope that held his pants up and let them fall around his ankles. Sara pretended not to notice. But Broken Nose stood before her with his shirt open and his amulets rising and falling with his breathing.

Then Sara held on to him, linking her arms behind his neck.

"I don't care who I am," she whispered.

"You are new," Broken Nose groaned into her neck. "You had a husband, yet you are new." He leaned back from her, tossing his hair away from his face. He was amused.

He massaged her and moved her with his large hands, feeling her continue the movement herself by pushing her feet against the rock.

In her mind were pictures of herself doing what she

was doing, and these pictures made her moan. She stung as though she'd been cut, but the stinging was overcome by the warmth.

"It is good," he said. He took the mint he wore and rubbed it on her cheek while he still held her up with one hand. "Very soft, soft—di-ii' de', di-ii' de'."

Sara sucked the warm, hard skin on his shoulder, wanting forgiveness for what she was doing and for how good it felt. The warmth ran up and down her legs and they shook more. Broken Nose couldn't hold her up any longer so he stopped and led her away from the tree. He pulled her down beside him on the ground. For a moment she stayed close to him with her head on his chest. He laughed and rolled on top of her. There he finished, holding himself up by his arms, watching her breasts jiggle as he moved her. She felt an unstoppable greed for the man's warmth, his close, living body. She held on to him, held him like a blanket as he rested.

At this same moment, Many Visions, who was watching them, came all over himself. The medicine man was squatting a few yards away, watching. He didn't pay much attention when he got an erection seeing Broken Nose thrust into the white woman, when he saw her giving in to him, moving herself around him, rubbing against him. Then when he got her on the ground, when her breasts spread out and Broken Nose's thrusts were strong and deep, Many Visions came unexpectedly.

"That crazy white woman," he cursed and he brushed his juices off as though they'd been spilled on him by someone else.

XXII

Light cracked the bottom of the west door of the sweat lodge. This door faced the sunset, because that was where a man must eventually go. He had to be pulled out of this world, pulled down into the darkness. But, for now, a man came and went through the east door. Three Fingers pushed the hide more securely against the opening and the cracks disappeared. Then it was totally dark in there, like it is inside a woman. The fourth load of rocks glowed in the hole, then Three Fingers threw water on them and the glow turned into steam. Now there was nothing but total darkness and steam and heat and the moans of some of the men who tried to stay strong in the heat. Three Fingers chanted low, then stopped to let each man look ahead of him at the darkness where the only thing he could see was his own power or lack of it, and the only thing he could hear were his prayers. Each man sat as though in a waterfall of his own sweat. It came out of every pore like many springs, and it was hard to breathe. In the black, black absence of light they were in the earth again, unborn, before their own beginnings.

"Shi' Ma, Shi' Ma, we are just little things," Three Fingers said aloud, and men's voices came out of nothing to say "Ho."

"Mother, Mother, you are a big thing."

"Ho."

"Mother, Mother, hear our prayers."

"Ho."

"Mother, Mother, even though we are small, hear our prayers, great Mother."

"Ho."

Another explosion of water on the hot rocks, more moans as more invisible heat mushroomed up into all their faces.

"Hear us, Mother," Three Fingers said. And then they all sang a song without words that could hold any prayer.

Most Important Man prayed hard for his confusion to end. Something had to be done. Small Face and the other young men scorned him openly now for being a man who sits and lets his oldest wife tell him what to do. It didn't work anymore to be the only man with two wives. His youngest wife had not given him any children. He had, in the eyes of his people, begged to the white soldiers. Many Visions was telling him he should have killed the white woman, that she was back lurking around and meant trouble. He was saying he had gone into the woods above the river and had had one of his visions. He had seen the white woman bringing soldiers from the east down on the settlement. He had seen many people die in this vision and the bluecoats weren't the ones dying; they were laughing. Apaches liked a good joke. They liked to laugh, and there was nothing funnier than watching enemies running. But they were not at all amused at the idea of being hacked up themselves, of people laughing at their body parts.

Small Face was talking about waging war. He didn't mean stealing a few sacks of grain from the fort, or getting some Navajo sheep. He was talking about going north and getting the Utes to join in on something big. He was talking about war.

Most Important Man didn't trust the Utes. They traded badly. He'd gotten two bad horses from the Utes in return for two guns that he didn't have bullets for. The Utes had guns and lots of bullets. Small Face had a loaded pistol he'd gotten at the white woman's wagon, but that was all. The Utes were likely to laugh at Small Face when he suggested they join together to kill whites. Then Small Face would do something stupid and there'd be bad feelings between them.

This kind of thinking had given Most Important Man his reputation as a wise man, but he was also called a man of no action, a man who thought too much and let fate and his first wife lead. And now that Shoots Straight was gone there weren't the old stories, the good ones about the old days when the Apaches had the world tied by the wrists. Nobody could tell the stories like Shoots Straight, and nothing was happening to make new ones. A sick feeling was inside the men that there wouldn't be any new stories, at least not about the same things. It seemed that the things people told about were pathetic, that the world was changing for the worse for the Apaches.

Most Important Man prayed in the darkness, in the hot, hot emptiness, that he would have the courage to do something. In this dark heat, a man sees himself. Some of what he sees makes him sick. But then it comes out in sweat and rolls off his body. He may weep, and this is the sweat from his brain. He weeps because he's not sure that he will do what is right. But in the dark no one can see him weep; no one knows the journey that a man has made in the dark but himself. And this loneliness binds them. They all understand when they leave the sweat lodge that they had all been asked to take a journey. Some of them had the courage and went; some weren't ready. But it is each man's private business.

When Most Important Man crawled out of the sweat lodge, all slick and flushed like a newborn, he had decided what to do. He would lead the young men on a war against the soldiers. If the white woman had left a trail for them to follow, they would meet them and slaughter every single one of those soldiers, those sneering, smelly soldiers sweating across the desert in their woolen uniforms—the ones who had treated him like an old beggar. The Superior People would not sit and wait for the bluecoats to come sauntering in to humiliate them, murder them while they crouched around their food pots with their wives shaking their heads. Most Important Man would take the strong men; he would lead them like the important man he was. He would ride in front of Small Face and in front of Broken Nose. It would be like the old days, only this time they would all die. Maybe the people would understand this and forgive him. This dying was all right compared to sitting outside the white man's fort and in his plazas wearing blankets and trading baskets and jewelry for gold. Most Important Man was not a man of visions, at least not in the sense that Many Visions was, but he had a feeling in his chest that there would come a time when the white man won it all, won all the land and all the wild animals. In such a world, Most Important Man didn't want to live.

Most Important Man wanted to get this war on the move before something ugly happened. He wondered, for example, if Small Face and Broken Nose were going to kill each other. Ever since he had been a small boy Small Face had taunted Broken Nose, picked at the boy's unfortunate history with the Hopis. And now he didn't believe that Broken Nose had killed the white woman even though Broken Nose had shown the blood.

"This is blood from the white woman," he had said. He showed his long fingers, streaked with red. "I say this as a man of honor."

"Where is the body?" Small Face asked.

"I don't have to show you anything," Broken Nose said to him. "You believe my word as an Apache brother. You insult me by asking to see her body. I left it for the buzzards and coyotes. You don't need to know more, for I have said it."

"I would believe your word as an Apache brother if you hadn't been raised like a three-legged dog at the feet of the corn-growing women," Small Face had said.

Many Visions knew where to find the white woman and so he went up above the river and hid. He waited until dusk. He heard her talking, and it made him shiver because there was no one else around. She spoke, not as in a prayer, but as though in conversation. He wondered what invisible thing was there with them and he wondered how it would protect her. His hatred and fear of her made him stay, but he told himself that it was great courage that motivated him.

When Sara heard his footsteps, she jumped to her feet and smiled widely, thinking that it was Broken Nose. He had been away for three days and she had had a hard time of it waiting for him.

So she stood up looking around, like a girl at a dance looking over the crowd toward the door to see if her beau had come. Only this Sara was dirty and cold and hungry. There were little sticks in her hair, and she smelled like the earth. Then she saw Many Visions. He had come with a big knife, so big that it made him look smaller than usual. He held it in front of his face and crouched as he stalked her.

"You have a big knife," Sara said in Apache. She shivered, despondent that it was not Broken Nose.

Many Visions sensed that he was inconsequential to her. This gave him the courage of an enraged child, and he stabbed Sara in the side. He had aimed for the middle of her abdomen, but in the last instant he could have sworn that he had felt a man's hand push his over to the side, so that his knife went all the way through the edge of her waist. Sara felt a long entering and a long withdrawal. It was the most obscene and shocking feeling she could imagine. Her mouth fell open, and she looked at the medicine man and at her side with great puzzlement.

"I am the one who has power," Many Visions said. "You are nothing but a slave. I am tired of being concerned with such a small thing."

Sara doubled over, holding the place where the blood came out. She groaned. She reached out, as though feeling for her bed in the dark of the attic where she'd been a child. She slowly got down on the ground and lay there.

Many Visions stepped backward and then went behind a tree to lean on it, to shut his eyes and rest his racing heart. He looked around and saw that the white woman was not moving. He put the knife back in his belt.

Sara was afraid to breathe, because every time she did she imagined the cut growing like a tear in the seam of a dress and that she'd be opened from head to toe. She lay very still and finally got the courage to touch the place. There was not much blood, and she even made a joke to herself that she could put a tuck in her waist and make it more petite. She moved carefully, slowly, and looked around. She saw a piece of the medicine man's shoulder behind a tree and very, very quietly got to her feet. The wound oozed a little more blood and she covered it with her hand as she walked and winced against the stinging.

The medicine man was singing a prayer and smoking. Sara could see the smoke coming out from behind the tree. She thought of what she could strangle him with and the only thing thin enough was her camisole. She took it off from beneath the blanket she kept around her shoulders. Creeping up, telling herself not to mind the pain in her side, she twisted the cotton around and around until it was like a rope. It was good that he was smoking because he might have seen the smoke her breath made as she got right behind him. She held the cloth in one hand, shifted a little in a kind of shimmy like a cat about to strike, then flung the cloth around Many Visions and the tree and caught the other end of it with her other hand. Pulling tightly, she had him pressed by the neck against the tree.

"You little weasel," she hissed and he gagged and tried to pull the cloth away from his neck. He coughed and sputtered, the bottom of his body jumping around because he'd dropped burning tobacco on himself.

"I've killed better men than you," Sara said, exaggerating. "I'll choke the life out of you, you little weasel."

Many Visions couldn't speak. Sara pulled the cloth back and forth a little to rub the back of his head against the tree bark.

As luck would have it, thunder began to rumble in the sky. At this point, Many Visions would have eaten his own arm if she'd asked him to. He had no doubt that she was a woman of power, that he hadn't known the meaning of power until then. The thunder rumbled and he listened and said in his head that he was sorry—very, very sorry; he would do many humbling things to prove how sorry he was. He would sit with the old women and he would feed the dogs and he would let the children climb all over him.

Sara wished she had the pistol, the one she'd shot Edmund with, because she didn't have the stomach to choke a man to death. She let go of the cloth and Many Visions lay on the ground and moved himself around with his feet to face her. He held one hand on his throat and the other hand up toward her, to fend her off.

Rain started falling; it was cold, cold rain. Sara took the knife out of Many Visions' belt. Then she kicked at him.

"Get up, you miserable little snake," she said, tempted to keep him there all night to terrorize. "Get up and go home to your mother. And if you try to harm me again, I'll cut your big nose off." She put the knife blade in his nostril, as Small Face had done with her. Many Visions backed up, shaking his head. That's when Sara lost the fun of it and felt a little sorry for the man because such a man always has to carry a big knife and look a little ridiculous.

XXIII

Sitting between two bunches of cactus, Sara felt that it was good to be alive. Her fingers dabbled with the blade of the knife. Then she got up to hobble out to the desert for a while. She felt her side and laughed. Little skeletons wafted out of the wound that she'd bound with the remains of her camisole. Their stretched-out faces were mournful.

Sara talked to herself. She walked down to the river and crossed it at the fallen log. She walked out to the desert just to see the sunrise, because those colors were almost as good as food. She talked to herself and to God, or to both at the same time. It was hard to think like a white woman, like a Presbyterian woman, when she was so hungry and when she was dirty and bloody under the blanket.

"I will have to do something soon," she said in English. "I am cold." She stopped to pinch off a leaf and chew on it.

"Of all the times in my life, I need Jesus now," she said. But whenever she thought of Jesus all she could see was the Last Supper—a table full of food. And all the disciples, sitting there with their arms on each other's shoulders, were skeletons.

Sara paused to indulge in a fantasy about what the disciples had been eating at the Last Supper. She was glad to think that they'd gotten to enjoy a good meal before the crucifixion. Who could eat after the crucifixion of a loved one?

Then Sara saw Little Bird standing all alone away from the settlement. She was looking eastward, at the same sunrise Sara had come to see. Her back was to Sara. Little Bird wasn't sure that the white woman was still alive and Sara knew this, so she slowly walked up and made a small noise, like a dove, a singing sigh. It was still dim enough so that both women looked greyish pink to one another. The features were not clear. But even from behind, Sara marveled at how exotic Little Bird was. Those two braids were long enough to swing beside her waist, and her skin smelled like her whole life of meat and piñon fires. In the white world, this Apache woman was probably only eighteen or so, ready to marry but still girlish. And yet Sara felt that Little Bird was indeed a woman, wiser than she, older by many, many hundreds of years. Little Bird turned and at first did not see Sara, but a woman, a spirit with very wild, big eyes and a bony face surrounded by an explosion of hair and twigs. She saw a spirit wearing a blanket and high moccasins. Sara stepped closer and let Little Bird see her better.

Little Bird touched her hair and looked back toward the settlement. There was no light, no smoke. But they could hear the morning prayers of the men.

"I was told that Broken Nose killed you," Little Bird said, studying the eastern sky. "You keep coming back to life like this dead man to whom you pray."

"Where is Broken Nose? What is he doing?" Sara asked.

"He is in silence. He and the other men who are preparing to go to war. They are all in silence. This includes my husband."

"Nownifh dzo?—What war?"

"A war against the soldiers."

Sara repeated to herself, "A war against the soldiers."

"What are you doing out here alone?" she asked Little Bird, for it was unusual for a woman to be alone. It brought suspicion on her.

"I could not help it. I could not listen to my husband's first wife any longer. We are all hungry again. And there are many words and looks being shared about this war. I do not want my husband to die."

Sara nodded and placed her hand on Little Bird's shoulder, and the woman did not move. She let Sara touch her, but they said nothing. They both looked out at the desert and there was the sun coming up in yellow and pink. It was very beautiful. This reminded Sara of something; she remembered, a long, long time ago, standing with another woman, that woman named Hattie. She had hardly known her, but suddenly her eyes filled with tears with a longing for that woman Hattie who had stood with her in the night on the wagon train and looked at the stars.

But here was Little Bird. They stood, facing the same vision, Sara's hand on her shoulder, Sara thinking of the little bunch of yellow flowers in Hattie's waist. The tears slid down her face.

"I am hungry," Sara said. "I am so hungry. I have been hungry for years, I think. All I know is being hungry and cold."

Little Bird moved out from under the white woman's hand and was embarrassed to hear her speak of her feelings.

"You are a woman of power," Little Bird said. "Many believe this and wonder what you have come to us for."

"I don't care about my power now," Sara said,

openly weeping. "I am cold and hungry and I've been wounded." She lifted up the blankets and showed the bandage that was stained with a reddish, yellowish wetness.

"Broken Nose did this to you," Little Bird said.

"I can't stand to live out in the open anymore. It is getting colder and colder, and I will die if I don't have food and warmth. I don't care what happens to me, I won't stay away from the warm fires and shelter any longer. Take me back with you to your husband's dwelling."

"But Broken Nose—he will kill you when he finds that you are still alive. And Many Visions . . . he believes that your power is evil."

Sara stood up straight pressing the wound with her hand and said, "I don't worry about those two."

They walked back into the settlement. No one stared. The people went about their work as though nothing out of the ordinary was happening. Little Bird kept her eyes on the ground and felt that it took forever to get to her dwelling. As soon as they passed, the women leaned over their pots and whispered about how wild the white woman looked.

Most Important Man was counciling with Three Fingers and Many Visions, but Walks Like A Buffalo was inside the dwelling repairing a water basket that was beginning to unravel at the top. She looked up as the two women came in and then looked back at her work. But she said, "No one owns a woman who has been in the desert without food. She has earned her freedom."

"She is wounded and hungry."

Walks Like A Buffalo shrugged and Little Bird went about the business of tending to her friend. She fed Sara some dried cakes of something that tasted like squash once it got wetted in the mouth. Then she cleaned the wound and put a clear, greenish, jellylike salve on it. Sara lay down and went to sleep. She slept hard, past when Most Important Man came back and scolded Little Bird. Past when he found the knife on her and knew that it was Many Visions' knife. Most Important Man took the knife and hid it under his bedding. Then he laughed to himself louder and louder and refused to tell his wives what was so funny.

When Sara woke up in the middle of the night and remembered that she was in Most Important Man's home, not in the cold, away across the river, she felt deeply happy, more joyful than she had ever felt before. At that moment she would have stayed there forever, silently doing whatever was asked of her, just to stay in the bosom of that family and its small cookfire. She even said, "Warmth," out loud, and went back to sleep. But when she woke up in the morning, after sleeping almost twenty-four hours, her thoughts were about Broken Nose.

It had been many days now and Sara had heard nothing from him. She wondered if she had made up the scene between her and him, if she had made up what they had done together in the woods. And if they had groveled and panted together, then perhaps it was a thing that meant nothing to Broken Nose. Perhaps in his culture there was no attachment given to the thing done by man and wife. Sara felt some shame now.

Most Important Man stared at her and then pretended to show no interest as Little Bird gave her a hot broth of something in which dried elk meat had been put. It was so good, so warm.

"Do you speak our language?" Asks Questions asked. He looked much older since the last time Sara had seen him, though it had only been about a month. He had been on his four-day fast and it made him sit up straighter.

"Ow'," Sara said.

Walks Like A Buffalo gave her a sidelong glance not wanting to show how awestruck she was.

"Is it painful?" the boy asked now. He nodded his head toward the wound in her side.

"Ow',"

Little Bird squatted between Asks Questions and Sara and told Sara she must get something to wear, some proper blouse.

"I will make one if the first wife lets me have a piece of deerhide."

"Epun'—Deerhides!" Walks Like A Buffalo boomed. "I should skin you and let you sew your own hide into a blouse for the white woman."

Sara laughed. Then she remembered the knife and felt for it, but it was gone. She looked around the floor for it until Most Important Man said, "Forget about it."

The blouse was crude but sufficient—a wide piece of buckskin with a hole for her head, sewn up at the sides except for the armholes and tied around the waist with a strip of red cloth. Now Sara could sit outside in the sun. She caught sight of Broken Nose two times. He passed her and didn't look her way. He acted as though she was not there, or as if she was not of any significance to him.

Little Bird was rolling up the rest of the deerhide and saw Sara looking after Broken Nose.

"He is good to look at," she said and grinned.

Then Most Important Man came outside, and the two women said no more. He examined his arrows, touching the tips of them with his flat finger.

"The medicine man says that you flew here, like an

owl," Most Important Man said, still looking over his arrows.

"I cannot do that," Sara said.

"If you fly to the fort, I have a message for those soldiers." Most Important Man's voice was hard. "I wonder if you will give it to them. I wonder if you will tell them where we are and what we are planning to do."

"I have nothing to gain by doing so. They are not my people," Sara said.

"I am interested in knowing where you come from."

"It is far away to the east, beyond these mountains. In other mountains where there are lots of trees, and a great deal of rain."

Most Important Man nodded.

"Then you will go soon, for we have other things to tend to. And there is another good reason for you to go soon."

Sara stood up and turned to pick at the side of the dwelling, putting her crying face out of Most Important Man's view. He kept talking, and she felt like throwing herself at his feet. But she had seen no outbursts like this among these people; just then she did not want to expose her difference from everyone else, not at that moment when she needed to prove that she should not have to leave.

Most Important Man was explaining, "A healer who considers himself powerful does not like to have his knife taken from him. He will fight his fear for the sake of his pride."

"I just want to go home," Sara said. "I don't want to cause any trouble." She came nearer to him and squatted down. Her knees stuck out to either side.

Most Important Man nodded and chuckled a bit because of the irony of what she said. "You do not want to cause trouble," he repeated. "I will tell you that there is no trouble greater than what you and your people have caused."

He spread his hand out, following the course of a landscape in his own imagination. The veins in his hand stuck up like the bluish tunnels of animals who lived under his skin. His fingers bent downward a little though he made his hand straight.

"There was so much space once. The Superior People had time and space that seemed endless. And now there is an end to time and space that I can see. I do not hate all whites, though they are diseased. I want to tell you this because I may not be able to tell anyone anything anymore. I think that a white man and a Superior Man can be warriors together when the white man learns to look at himself in the dark. When he learns to go on a journey in the dark where he can hear nothing but his own heart and where he has no help but his own courage."

Most Important Man looked at this crazy woman and nodded.

"I'm sure there are white men who can do this. If a white woman can do such a thing, I am sure that there must be others. But I don't like to wait for things, especially things that will take a long time and may never happen. Especially when there are some Superior People who have lost their way in this new darkness. Some of us are beginning to look stupid, like animals who get confused when the forest is on fire and run the wrong way." He paused and then said, "At first I thought you were stupid."

"I have become one of the Superior People."

Most Important Man's eyes brightened so that Sara thought of a picture of Saint Nicholas in a book that her mother used to read to her.

"Ha, ha!" burst out of him, and Most Important Man shook his head and jammed one of his arrows deep into the ground.

XXIV

《《《

"I am as hot as fire, a sun-drinking lizard, a loose bird with orange wings. I am a tail feather broken off and fluttering across the desert with no soul. I have been let loose by hands; I am looking for hands."

Sara woke up, startled. It was raining again outside. She could hear it hit the hides on the top of the dwelling. It was totally dark inside, but she could have sworn that the person who was talking to her sat in there, had slipped back and forth between her dreams and was caught outside of them when she woke up. She felt for the doorway and poked her head out. It was almost as dark outside as inside.

"What do you see?" Little Bird's voice asked from behind her.

"I was dreaming," Sara said.

Still in the darkness she couldn't be sure that the masked man was gone.

"And when I'm awake I think of going home and I think also of something else." She rocked silently, thinking that she had come a long way. Her father would not recognize her as a traveler, though. He would only understand her as something familiar and irritating. And yet Broken Nose had said she must be an important person among her people. "I will never be important to him. Never," Sara said aloud. "When I was born,

226

a new life created by him, it meant nothing. I mean nothing to him and I never will."

Little Bird was quiet.

"I think of a man who is here in this settlement. He does not think of me, but he treated me as though I was his wife."

Little Bird came close to Sara's face, so that they could just barely feel the warmth of each other's cheeks.

"Go where he lives and he won't be able to turn you away."

"Is this the custom?"

"No, this is how men are. They have pride in front of many people, but when a woman is alone with one of them he is easy to handle."

Sara laughed a little. She was thinking that Little Bird was, after all, an Indian and didn't understand how things should be handled. A woman did not crawl into a man's bed, unless she was a whore. In this settlement there were no whores, no women leaning against boulders asking the men who walked by if they wanted to have a good time.

Sara couldn't go back to sleep. She stared up at the darkness, twitching, rolling from side to side, unable to stay still. Something was in the air, taunting her, teasing her to move, to roll over and pull her legs up, to bite her hand, to roll on her back, shake her feet. Death? Was it death she felt? She felt some doom coming, something big. Maybe Many Visions with a knife as big as his leg, maybe Broken Nose. Maybe she would wake up and be left alone, forced to go through everything all over again. Maybe she would go back to Roanoke and be locked up forever. Who was she in Roanoke, who had she ever been but something insignificant? And yet God was in her; she felt God in her and she always had, only she hadn't known what to call it other than restlessness. In Roanoke, people, her father, had tried to squash her will, to laugh at her, to cart her away to be locked up, and so they had done these things to God as well.

"This is too much," Sara said, sitting up and taking the blankets to wear around her as she went outside. "Too much."

She walked in the rain and dark, feeling a swelling desire to do something and she didn't know what it was. She got wet, the blankets got wet, and then she ended up standing in the dark rain outside of Broken Nose's dwelling. She sat down, leaning against one of the poles.

"I belong nowhere," she said. She started shaking the hides that covered Broken Nose's dwelling, making it rustle loudly. She shook the dwelling harder, muttering, angry at what her father had tried to do to God. Angry at what people did to God and the desires He put into her soul. Finally someone pushed the flap aside and said, "See if it's an animal. You go see." Sara shivered and held her knees, waiting and muttering curses.

"You son of a bitch," she kept saying over and over. "You son of a bitch."

Then Broken Nose came out, wearing only his pants and a blanket over his head.

Broken Nose looked down from inside his blanket. Then he reached out his hand and jerked Sara up. He pulled her into his dwelling.

"Go sleep with your sister," Broken Nose said toward his mother.

"You have broken your silence," the woman said. "And I think you are going to break another thing."

Sara felt embarrassed, but she was still harping on her anger and didn't want to care about anyone's mother. But it was good that there wasn't enough light to see the woman's face.

"You bring shame on me," the woman's voice said, but it was with patience and had in it a sense of useless affection. Sara felt sorry for the woman as she heard her shuffling about and then going out into the rain.

Broken Nose lay down and pulled Sara down beside him. He pulled her skirt up.

"No," Sara said in English. But Broken Nose persisted and Sara heard him take off his pants. Then she felt his amulets hit her chest and he was lying on her. His hand pulled at the knot in the cloth belt.

"No, what are you doing?"

He stopped. "There is one white woman who walked in the rain to my home, and another who has come in."

Sara got up. She was weeping with rage.

Dimly, Broken Nose could see this. He could hear her sniffling. He put his hand around her ankle and moved it up slowly.

"Who do you think that I am?" he asked her.

"I don't know," Sara answered.

Broken Nose got to his knees and undid the belt around her shirt. He stood up and lifted the shirt over her head. Sara stood shivering and holding herself. Broken Nose held her with her cheek against his shoulder and her arms still crossed over her breasts.

"This time you are like a child," he said. "Where are you hiding your power?"

They stood this way for a few minutes, both of them cold, until Sara unfolded her arms and put them around Broken Nose.

"And where is your power?" she asked him in Apache.

"At this moment my power is between your legs and I want to get it."

They were silent again.

"I am not your wife," Sara said.

"But the world is still beautiful," Broken Nose answered and he laughed, rubbing his nose in her ear.

"Do you feel that I have eleven fingers," he asked, "and that one is very large?"

He laughed when she didn't answer, and Sara tried to push him away. She was thinking to herself that only a whore would feel the feeling that she felt, that only a whore would let a man do what Broken Nose was doing. She saw herself as one of the women in the streets of Independence, Missouri, the ones with the shiny, scarlet dresses that showed black lace underskirts and showed their ankles. What did Broken Nose know of this? He knew that if a man's wife did it with another man she might have her nose cut off. But he didn't know about satin, shiny red dresses and black lace. Naked, she rubbed against him, calling herself a whore. The notion that Broken Nose had no reference for a whore's shame excited her and made her feel her will to be loved and powerful and free. Because there is nothing freer than a whore without shame and without need of money. A whore without shame or need is truly powerful. And only free and powerful men can give their love to a whore.

Sara rubbed her face against Broken Nose's chest, moving the amulets. They sank down to the ground together, making the bedding snap underneath the skins. Broken Nose covered them both with blankets. Sara pressed herself against him as hard as she could. They sighed and stroked each other. Broken Nose came inside her as they both lay on their sides, with her leg bent and resting on his hip. It was over too soon. Sara put her face against him and tried to calm herself. She could feel her shame coming back. She saw a picture of

Jesus in her black mind and she wondered what was going to happen to her when she got back to civilized people. She felt like a viper, like a woman of insane and insatiable hungers who would end up in hell. She turned away from him, turned her back toward him. But as a great shock to her, Sara felt him begin to have sex with her in that position. It had never occurred to her that such a thing could be done, or was done by anyone but barnyard animals, and yes, those shimmering, blue-green dragonflies down by the cow stream—the ones that flew together over the water and landed, still together, on the dogwood branches that hung over the stream.

"You are good," Broken Nose whispered. And then he pushed her down onto her stomach and moved her legs farther apart. He laid his head on her head, his cheek on hers, and took a long time, unhurried, slow, strong.

Sara took his hand and sucked on one of the fingers. Jesus still popped into her head and tormented her. She thought of the damned Last Supper with all that food, all that good food and wine and saw Jesus eating and drinking. And she laughed to suddenly see Jesus enjoying the hell out of himself. Jesus was at the table stuffing food in his mouth, laughing and wiping wine from his mouth. He was throwing pieces of bread at the disciples and toasting with the wine—his body, his blood. Enjoy! For God's sake, enjoy! Sit down at my table and eat good food, rip the meat off with your teeth, have a glass of good, red wine, put fresh butter all over your bread until it drips off of your lips, until it drips, all buttery and warm, from your sweet lips.

Sara moaned and said, "Oh, sweet Jesus."

Broken Nose was whispering over and over in her ear, "It is good, so good," until Sara could feel nothing but the heat they made together. And she laughed and laughed.

Broken Nose held her there, from behind, with one hand over one of her breasts. His other hand was busy at his neck. Sara could feel his movements. Then he rubbed something against her cheek. It was a small, smooth object with bumps on it and it was attached to a leather strip.

"A shell," Sara whispered. "A sea shell."

Broken Nose rolled off of her to lie with his hands behind his head.

"But the sea is so far from here," she said, feeling the ridges of the shell with her fingers.

"I am thinking, Sara," he said, teasing her with her own name that he had never spoken before, "that there is a time for a warrior to retrieve his power—to go back to where it was left and take it up again. A person can take such a spirit journey if he doesn't lie to himself and if he is brave."

When the darkness got fuzzy with grey light, Sara saw whom she was lying with—a dark man with black hair, a man who had a lightning bolt tattooed under his arm, a man who rattled with ornaments as he moved in sleep. Sara pulled the blankets off of Broken Nose to see him naked. He awoke to a chill that replaced the covers and felt the wind of Sara's hand passing over him like a hawk. He stopped her by grabbing her wrist and she crawled on him. Straddling him, she laid her ear over his heart. It is something women do, even some whores. She felt that she had sunk underground with Broken Nose and they had become earthen people.

Broken Nose pulled the covers over them both and it was as though he'd become pregnant with Sara, with this crazy woman rolled up on his belly.

XXV

Somebody set Coyote's tail on fire. He ran around in circles, blowing on it, yipping, whining. And some of the animals laughed. The owls didn't laugh. Owls don't laugh. But other birds fell out of the bushes laughing. Coyote ran all the way to the Rio Grande from some place to the west and he sat in it. The steam from his quenched tail rose up and covered the land with a strange fog. For a while Coyote made use of the steam, telling some of the less intelligent animals that the world was on fire and if they gave him all their belongings he would keep them safely for them in his stomach. He got a lot of food, but his tail was still singed. And he had a lot of fear about the thing coming eastward that had set him on fire.

Far, far to the east, in a world the Apaches didn't think about, bluecoats were fighting greycoats. It delighted the Indians who knew about this war between the white men. It gave them hope. They thought that Life Giver was still there after all. And as the faces of the dead, whiskerless boys stared up from the battlefields of the East, a motley crew of whites was marching from the west. Their fearless leader was General James H. Carleton, a man with a tick. He had a habit of stretching out his mouth in a thin line and then pursing it in a quick twitchy movement. He liked marmalade, and had it sent to him at posts and battlefields. Now he was in the part of New Mexico called Arizona. He was sweeping the Southwest of Rebels and Apaches. General James H. Carleton was marching eastward with three thousand whiskey-breathing, raggedy white men from California.

Carleton was a man who not only had military smarts, but, like all soldier-heros, had military obsessions, too. He had come up with the bold idea of killing two birds with one army. He would not only run the Rebels out of New Mexico, but also slaughter all the Apaches in his path. General James H. Carleton despised Apaches. They were arrogant, unruly animals who didn't show proper respect for the uniform of the United States Army. Other Indians could be controlled. They stayed in one place and became Christians. But the Apaches, the Apaches—it drove him crazy just thinking about them—those sneaky heathens.

He slaughtered a lot of Apaches, and he did it in a number of ways. The great Apache warrior Mangus Coloradus was shot in the side at close range in his cell. General Carleton invited several other Apaches to "treaty signings" at which they bled to death.

There was nowhere to hide now, not east or west, south or north. Smaller and smaller was Apache territory, smaller and smaller.

Sara went to the river in the afternoon when Broken Nose left to go to Three Fingers' sweat lodge. She needed to bathe. Little Bird and Long Skirt were at the river with Most Important Man's daughter, Strong Legs. Strong Legs' premature puberty was about to be honored in a ceremony. The two married women were washing her hair in the icy water when they saw Sara coming.

Sara squatted down near the river's edge, next to the

rock where she'd eaten a raw fish. The little bones were still on the ground. The others knew she was there but didn't look at her. They pretended not to notice her. Sara walked close to them to speak, but they turned their backs to her, Strong Legs looking confused as the women changed her position.

"I caught a fish with my hands," Sara said and no one answered. She sighed and looked up at the sky; it was a beautiful day, no clouds, and almost as warm as spring.

Finally Little Bird, with her eyes narrowed, pulling hard on poor Strong Legs' hair, said to Long Skirt, "It does not surprise me that a woman who is not one of the Superior People would eat fish."

Sara studied her face to see if Little Bird was intending this comment to be funny. Little Bird looked about to cry.

"If a woman sleeps with a man who is not her husband," Long Skirt said without the emotion that was in Little Bird's voice, "then she will also eat fish and build her dwelling so that the door faces west."

Sara didn't know what to say. She walked away and started bathing again. The noise of the river could not hide the mean laughter she heard. She stared at the water. When she stood up from washing, she did not know where to go, what to do. And as though Little Bird knew what she was thinking she walked up to Sara and told her, "You cannot come to our home. You are not welcome to pass through our door. For you, there are stones across the threshold."

"You told me to go to him. It was your voice I heard. I was not dreaming," Sara said. She looked pleadingly into Little Bird's face but then remembered that that was a rude thing to do, and she looked down.

"But you shamed his mother. You made her beg at

her sister's door for shelter, and you made it plain to all the people what you were doing."

Sara felt angry about being expected to have shame. Little Bird couldn't stop haranguing her.

"In the world of the white eyes does an unmarried woman throw out a man's mother so that she may fornicate with him? It is different with us. We have strong traditions and do not take such things lightly. This man you slept with has wanted me many times, but I have been a good wife."

She turned and left, and Sara's face burned. She was very tired as well and wanted some place to sleep, but now she was ashamed to go back to the settlement. She climbed the steep bank once more, crying angrily because she had thought she would never have to go sleep in the bushes again.

In the camp, Broken Nose's mother was wailing that her son had shamed her once again, that he should have stayed with the Hopis. She told her friends, who shook their heads in pity for her, that her son had not only been fornicating with a white woman, but that she knew for certain that they had been doing it all night and day.

Where was the medicine man, she asked, because she needed prayers and herbs. But everyone said that the medicine man had been scarce lately. Someone believed that he had gone out on the desert to fast.

Sara found the damp old bearskin she'd used before and lay down on it. She dozed, but could not sleep well because she had a terrible feeling of dread. She thought that this anxiety was personal and took her dreams about violence and bitter screams to be a reflection of her own turmoil. After sunset, she sat up and saw a lot of smoke coming from the settlement. She went down to see what was happening and hid behind a dwelling. What she saw there was a big fire around which ev-

eryone in the settlement sat. Everyone was quiet, even
the children. She saw Little Bird sitting with the women
and tried to stare her into knowing that she was hiding
there. The men sat at one side, in a group. They were
all focusing down at the ground, fiercely silent, holding
bows in their clenched fists. Some men had guns. The
fire made them orange and jumpy looking.

Then from the east of the fire four men came in.
They were in a line and they danced while holding
weapons. One of them was Most Important Man who
carried a gun. There were no bullets in it, but he danced
with it pretending to shoot. The four men danced
around the fire four times while someone in the shadows pounded a drum.

Sara looked hard and saw Broken Nose sitting next
to Eats Fish. He was scratching at the ground with one
of his arrows and his head was not straight like the others. He had it cocked as though he was not giving this
dance all his attention. Two of the dancers stopped on
the south side of the fire and two stopped on the north
side. The pairs faced each other and danced in place.
They were saying something under their breath, pushing themselves into concentration, saying, "Wah, wah,
wah, wah." They danced toward each other, changed
sides, turned around and went back. Some women
moaned. Men leapt up and danced while the drum beat
deeply and steadily. Sara had a reeling sensation that
she was in hell, watching demons dance around a fire.
She got onto her knees and shut her eyes. She put her
hands together and tried to pray. She thought of the
feeling of lying with Broken Nose and not wanting to
sleep—wanting always to be aware of him next to her.
She thought of seeing his face become clear as the sun
came up and they still were not finished with each
other, of feeling that there was an intimate understand-

ing between them that separated them from the rest of the world with its fears and limitations. They were safe inside each other; and even better, they were strong inside each other.

A woman screamed shrilly and Sara got up and stared, forgetting her prayers. More men jumped up and joined the dance. Eats Fish and Small Face got up and danced, and so did Kills Bucks and many others. But Broken Nose still sat, still looked at the ground, as though the noise wasn't great. Some men held as many arrows as they could in their teeth, some put them between their fingers and danced like animals with long claws. The men dancing made that soft sound under their breath that grew into a vibrating bass of "wah, wah, wah" as more and more joined. Sometimes men left the dance and went off to the side. They stayed to the side in huddles, and Sara strained to see what was going on. And then she saw that demon, that Many Visions. He was calling men out in groups and praying with them. They were praying about war, about killing and courage and blood and terror.

She cursed him. She could see his eyes glow brighter than anyone else's. He was making war sacred for them. He was firing them with a madness that would end in lots of killing. She put all her attention on Broken Nose. She stared at him. He was the most beautiful, alive human she had ever seen, and were it not for the other people, she would have squatted behind him and leaned against his back. Little Bird's anger could not have been free of envy, Sara thought. And she was more ashamed of betraying Broken Nose with her shame than she was of getting pleasure from him. She watched him with conviction. Broken Nose still sat. He had not joined the dance.

"Good for you," she whispered. "To hell with these

people and their scorn. Let them cast us out and have their wars. We will live together."

Then Many Visions, small and bent, stopped his praying and came into the firelight. The women looked nervous and some forgot to keep whooping and singing. Everyone was aware that Broken Nose had not danced. They didn't look at him; they were embarrassed for him. All day there had been jokes about his sore genitals. The drum kept beating and the crowd of men kept dancing, in a frenzy, bumping into each other. But Many Visions stood in the middle of them and when they noticed that he wasn't moving they got out of his way. Still they danced, in little steps, still they whispered, "Wah, wah, wah," but they made room for Many Visions to say something.

Many Visions started a song. He sang:

You, Broken Nose
Many times you have talked bravely
Now brave people of our tribe are calling to you.

The other men sang the song, still dancing. Broken Nose kept looking down. Then Small Face called out, "He is not one of us. He is Hopi and now he cannot fight when he is called. He thinks of his Hopi mother who carried him in her arms all day like a pup."

Broken Nose stopped scratching at the ground with his arrow. Small Face repeated what he had said, and the dancers moved in smaller steps. It was hard for Sara to see what was happening because the dancing had stirred up a cloud of dust in the firelight. But she heard Broken Nose's voice say, "You are stupid, Small Face. You are stupid to think that twenty hungry Apaches without bullets can wage war against the white eyes."

He was saying this to Small Face, but it was Most Important Man that the words hit.

"We will get more horses and bullets," the older man said. "But it is a fight of the heart, a fight for our people."

Many Visions held up both his arms like an evangelist and chanted, "We will get brave horses, brave horses to carry our warriors."

Some women whooped.

"Brave horses and killing bullets. Bullets that will put fire in the white soldiers. Bullets that go straight from the guns of brave warriors."

There was louder whooping. The men began to dance vigorously again.

Broken Nose stood up and threw his arrows to the ground. Sara stepped back as though he was coming to her, but he walked up to Small Face and held him by the throat.

"You speak from your sister's disgrace," he said. "You are a fool."

Small Face took Broken Nose's free arm and bent it backwards and then they wrestled. The drum didn't stop and dancers kept prancing in place, keeping an eye on the fight.

"Stop," Many Visions said. Then he squatted down and spit into Broken Nose's face when he said, "Are you a Hopi or not? Are you with us, or will you stay with the women so you can fornicate?"

Panting, Broken Nose said to the healer, "And you? You are going to fight the soldiers?"

Many Visions clenched his bony fists.

"I am a man of power, of spiritual power. I must stay here to say prayers and to protect the people."

"You are a coward. You are a small man who pretends to have power."

Sara laughed out loud, emitting a "Ha!" that some heard. She covered her mouth but was grinning hard, and she whispered to herself in English, "Oh, yes."

Walks Like A Buffalo glared so hard at her husband that he stumbled as he danced in place and knew that he had to say something.

"Give your anger to the white soldiers, Broken Nose. We need your strength. You are one of the Superior People. You are a brave man. Your brothers are calling to you. Your father was a brave man and now your brothers need your strength."

"You are a good warrior," Broken Nose said to Most Important Man. "You lead your people to war like a Superior Man, not like the whites whose leaders wait on the hilltop while the blood of their men is spilled on the battlefield. And you do not go into war to kill, as some do, but to give honor to your people."

Small Face squirmed to his feet and backed away. The dancing had died down. The women stopped whooping, but the drum kept beating. Broken Nose looked at everyone and spoke loudly.

"Then I will tell you what will happen. Before we go west to fight the soldiers we will gather at the big river. First four of us will go by horseback to the south and steal more horses and guns and then we will meet at the river again and go north where there are more of our people. We will bring them into our war dance. It is this way or I will not go."

Sara shook her head and whispered, "No, no. We will go away from here, you and I. No." She bit her knuckles and tears blurred her vision. The feeling of horrible things coming welled up in her again. "No, no. We must go away. We have to go home."

Someone came up behind her. She turned around quickly, afraid it was Small Face or someone like him who'd caught her. It startled her to see the familiar man behind her, the one who wore a mask that looked like the giant head of a horned toad. It was a frightening mask in the firelight and Sara shrunk away from it. He was very close to her, and she could see how tall he was, much taller than she. But the man didn't touch her. He looked at her through the mask. She could see the yellowed whites of the man's eyes inside the ceremonial head. The mask's eyes were shiny little pebbles above the eyes of the man. Leaves made the green scales of its skin and the sharp, menacing spikes on the top twinkled. The streamers of long grass that came from the sides of it were ablaze in orange flames.

When the man moved he jingled as usual, and yet Sara had not heard him approach. He looked down on her. He was very tall, maybe as tall as one of the dwellings.

"Crazy Woman," he said, "look to the west."

Sara looked. She saw an orange glow that she thought was the sunset, but the sun had gone down hours ago.

"What is it?" she said.

"Your people, playing with fire."

"But the whole horizon glows," Sara said.

"It is a big fire."

His voice was muffled by the mask. Sara could hear his breath and imagined that it was hot in the horned toad's head. The pieces of grass turned into black curls in the flames.

"Then we have to hide, run away. We have to go back home. Why do you tell me? Tell them. Soon all the women and children will be alone here."

Many people screamed. The screaming continued until the voices became hoarse and shrill; their moaning was pitiful. The drumbeat was heavy and cruel. Sara felt the heat of the fire make her skin tingle uncomfortably. The fire crackled, breaking people's bones in two. The drum beat harder and the wailing came over Sara like water, filling her own mouth.

"What does this mean?" she gasped.

"Don't be stupid, white woman," the mask said.

Sara took her hands off of her ears and whispered, "Who will die?"

But the dancer was gone.

Sara stood looking around, squinting and trying to see if anyone was running along the wall of the mesa.

Many Visions stood still in the midst of the fire, chanting, praying for bravery and extolling the virtues of the men who were going to fight. This is when Sara leapt in and pushed him down. A bunch of his hair touched the fire and got singed. The dancing stopped. Now even the drumming stopped. Sara was on top of Many Visions holding him by the throat and pounding his head into the ground.

Everyone screamed. The men stepped away.

"Get her off of me," Many Visions yelled.

The women looked from Broken Nose to the white woman who was now being pulled off of Many Visions by Small Face. He held her hard by clasping both arms behind her back.

"I tell you," Sara said, looking and sounding wilder than any Apache, "that this man is nothing. He has no power. He has no vision. I tell you that if the men go west and the women stay here there will be slaughter."

Many Visions' face was trembling with rage. When he spoke his mouth moved wildly.

"This woman is white. She is a white woman and means only harm to our people. She will lead us to slaughter."

"She has had relations with Broken Nose," Small Face said. "She shames us."

"I am telling you the truth," she said. "I have seen a vision."

Small Face squeezed her arms tighter behind her and said, "This time I will kill her."

Walks Like A Buffalo said something in a low voice. Most Important Man said, "Speak up, woman."

"Listen to what the woman has to say," she said.

"Yes," Little Bird said, standing up. "You'd better listen to her."

"Keep quiet," Many Visions said. "You women keep quiet."

"I'm telling you," Sara said, "that I have a bad, bad feeling. You must run into the hills and hide. . . ."

"See," Small Face said through gritted teeth, "she wants us to run and hide. She wants to make us whine and run like dogs."

"She wants to make us weak," Many Visions said. "But I too have had a vision. It was in my dreams that the white woman would come, that she would knock me down. I have seen this very thing in a dream. I have seen that she means to take away our courage and that she will make us weak and we will lose all our lands.'"

"You are wrong," Sara screamed. Small Face pulled one of her arms up sharply and she heard it snap. At first she felt no pain, just numbness and a floppiness in her arm.

"He has broken my arm," she said, addressing just Broken Nose.

Broken Nose stood still and said, "We are warriors. We will not run and hide."

"But he has broken my arm," Sara said. The pain was beginning to come on. It was a growing ache.

"I am a warrior of my people," Broken Nose said. "You are a white woman."

"It is broken," Sara said. "My arm. Broken."

Many Visions grinned and said to Small Face, "Break her other arm. Then break the bones in each of her fingers. Then break her legs."

But Little Bird jumped to grab a handful of ashes and ran over. She rubbed the ashes in Small Face's eyes and took Sara by her good arm. She ran, dragging Sara behind her. They didn't stop but ran all the way to the river. They didn't say anything, and almost out of breath they scurried up the bank. Little Bird kept pulling on Sara who wanted to stop and howl in pain. They got to some bushes and fell onto the ground. Little Bird clamped her hand over Sara's moaning mouth. She waited, cocking her head to hear if anyone had come after them.

XXVI

"I feel very bad."

Sara was lying with Little Bird. They were both wrapped up in blankets and the old bearskin. Sara was holding her arm that Little Bird had splinted. She'd made a splint out of cedar and strips of cloth from old, yellowed underwear that had been lying on the ground. The pain was bad.

"I feel a sickness in me, like a fever," Sara said.

"There's nothing we can do about that now," Little Bird told her. "Look, it is dawn." She crawled out of the covers and went to the edge of the river.

"Look, they are riding out. They are coming to the river."

"Who?" Sara said sitting up. "Who is coming to the river?"

"The four on horseback. There is Most Important Man and Small Face and Kills Bucks and . . . and Broken Nose."

Sara slowly got up. Her vision was dented and she felt very weak. She stood beside Little Bird, leaning on her.

"Look. See, down there."

"Yes," Sara said, "I see."

"Wait, look, he's looking up here. He raises his hand."

"He cannot see us."

"But he must know that you are here, that you see him."

Sara cradled her arm.

"Now they are moving away," Little Bird said.

"We must get something to eat," Sara said wearily, "or I will die."

"Listen, he is singing a song."

Sara sighed and stayed, still leaning against Little Bird. They stood there and listened to the song that Broken Nose sang. He repeated it over and over again until they could catch pieces of it between the rushing sound of the river.

I am going to war.
I am brave and will kill many people.
Keep my son warm.
Hold my child until I return.
I will tell my son about the brave things I have done
And he will be brave like his father.

"That is a strange song for a man to sing," Little Bird said.

Sara said, "Yes, it is."

"Part of it sounds like one of our songs and part of it sounds like something a Hopi would sing," Little Bird said.

"I think it is his own song," Sara said. "It belongs to him."

"He is singing this song to you," Little Bird said. "It is the kind of song a man sings to his wife before he goes to war." She looked at Sara.

"You are a strange white woman."

"Yes, I know," Sara said. She stumbled slowly back to their nest and fell into it.

"We should pray, Little Bird. To my god and to yours. To whatever gods there are."

"I will go get something for us to eat," Little Bird said and she was gone, down the bank.

After a few hours, Sara got worried. She crawled to the edge of the bank and looked down. There was no sound but water. She slept there until her eyes opened and she saw Little Bird coming back, running through the water with no thought to her moccasins. She came panting up the bank and, smiling, handed Sara a very large parcel of meat and corn cake.

"I took it from Walks Like A Buffalo. Her daughter prepared it and gave it to me." She giggled.

They ate, but Sara felt nauseated after she finished. She didn't get up and night came. Finally she was thoroughly weary of this adventure. It seemed that, after all, there was no point to it. She was sick of the discomfort, the cold, the hunger, the dirt and hard ground, sick of getting beaten up and thrown around, dragged, kicked, choked, knifed, broken . . . enough! And there was no shame in her resolution to live comfortably again. Comfort could no longer suggest that she cowered from hardship; it could now be seen as a reward for enduring and surviving hardship. Now a hot bath, a soft bed, and clean, rustling clothes seemed deliciously deserved.

She slept and heard Broken Nose singing to her.

The next morning Little Bird was sitting straight up, listening hard to something.

"What is it?" Sara said.

"Shhh, listen. It sounds like a war dance."

"A war dance? But the men are gone. Didn't those on foot leave as well?"

"Yes, but listen. I can hear the whoops of the women."

She stood up and looked toward the settlement as though she could see it through the trees.

"Come on. Let's go," she said. "Let's go and see what's happening."

"Wait," Sara said, putting out her hand. "I have a bad feeling."

Then they heard sharp cracks, many many sharp cracks that reverberated in the sky and multiplied like Fourth of July fireworks.

The two women looked at one another. Then at the same time their eyes widened.

"Dear Jesus," Sara said.

Little Bird leapt up and said, "Totah!" She slid down the bank. Sara got up and followed her. The world went white for a minute when she first got up, but she kept going, calling out to Little Bird to stop. She tackled her at the river.

"Let me go," Little Bird screamed. "Let me go to my people."

"You will be killed," Sara said.

Little Bird shoved her off and got up and ran again. Sara kept after her, dragging her down over and over again. But Little Bird kept getting up and running. They saw the dust of many horses riding away from the settlement. It was like a moving, brown cloud of horsemen from the spirit world. They were going away from the settlement, riding hard, so Sara let Little Bird go. The two women ran and came to what was left.

It was as quiet as snowfall in the camp, as quiet as the morning when Sara had awakened alone. The people were there, but they were all still. They were lying beside their pots and baskets. The children still had sticks in their hands. Babies were still lying on top of their mothers. There was blood everywhere, like red paint splattered across people's faces, poured on the ground, bursting from their chests. There was Long Skirt and her children, Long Skirt with blood running all through her hair. Little Bird came to Walks Like A Buffalo. She had fallen over something. Both of her arms were underneath her, and her legs were bent so that her backside was in the air as though she'd tried to get up. But there was a big red hole in her back. Little Bird squatted down and rolled her over. Her eyes were shut, squinched against the pain, and in her hands was a basket of cornmeal.

Little Bird fell on her and called out.

Sara found Many Visions. His eyes were still open. He was on his back and stared straight up at her. There was a stunned look on his face.

"I don't know why you're so surprised," Sara said to him in English.

Little Bird was screaming, standing in the middle of all those silenced people, her mouth wide open, screaming, but there was no sound.

"We have to take food and go away," Sara said.

Finally Little Bird spoke, staggering and saying in a low voice, "I want to find my husband. It will be hard for him to know that his first wife and his daughter. . . ." Then Little Bird howled and grabbed her hair in her fists, pulling it loose from the braids. Looking at her, Sara felt calm, filled with calmness. She had finally seen true evil, and it was easy to identify. She closed her eyes and prayed, putting in front of her a picture of the masked man, whose eyes, she now understood, were filled with compassion. She prayed without words, knowing that whatever she prayed to already knew what to do with the people before her. But the suffering, the thought of children suddenly forced into terror and chaos that they did not understand, seeing everything in their lives end, bleeding, dead. The children.

"Please," Sara said with her eyes closed, and then she followed Little Bird.

"We have to get enough food. Some of the men are walking to the big river. We can find them and wait for Broken Nose and your husband."

But Little Bird would not do it. She would not take any food from the houses of these ghosts. She would not walk past the bodies of children and see their hands and little fingers. They might grab her and pull her down into the pit of her sorrow.

"We have to go on," Sara said. "I will take care of you. We have to go."

It was time for the wild-haired woman from Roanoke to do what had to be done. God was keeping his mouth shut. And Little Bird had rolled up into a ball like a hard-shelled little bug who'd been exposed under a rock.

Seeing the children lying there with their little backs blown open Sara was finally certain that she knew wrong from right. There was no justification for such a thing, and now all the other justifications for wrongs she had seen tumbled down. What was revealed was an emptiness in which only actions existed. She had to act, without waiting for visions. Without caring about what her actions looked like from the outside. She saw her elementary school teacher, the woman who played the fiddle in Roanoke, who had played it like a man, with her eyes closed and her body moving.

Sara moved solemnly from dwelling to dwelling and wrapped as much food as she could in a blanket to take across the desert.

They left the dead place behind, but they were haunted by it for the rest of their lives. Its silence had gotten into them and as Little Bird cried her mouth was open and tears came down her face, but there was no sound.

XXVII

In walking through those next days her own strength was the thing most vivid to Sara. Days and nights passed by like big cloths blown by the wind. Little Bird did not speak and hardly ate. At night she huddled close to Sara like a child because she was afraid of the dark and the ghosts.

There was no sign of Broken Nose and the other men—no footprints, no horseprints, nothing in the sand and pebbles of the desert or by the cold, slow river. This confused Sara who, on the fifth night, had the impression that the men on horseback had shifted course and ridden an invisible road into the sky. She had a dream that four men rode up to the river and she ran to them. But their heads were covered in black sacks and she was afraid to call to them.

The two women walked and walked, finally crossing the river holding what was left of their food over their heads. The water was so cold they had to build a fire on the other side of the bank and sit by it for the rest of the day. Two soldiers, bluecoats on horseback, found them by means of the smoke. Little Bird had fallen asleep with her head in Sara's lap and Sara was leaning against a tree. Sara saw the soldiers coming and made no move to get up. Her main concern was that Little Bird not be disturbed in her peaceful sleep.

"Shhh," she whispered to them. One man had a greyish blond moustache that curled down his chin, and the other was a small man with silver-rimmed glasses.

The moustached man dismounted. Sara noticed right away that their horses were well fed and the chestnut coats shone. The soldier approached her cautiously, as though she and Little Bird were wild animals being studied in their natural habitat.

"This one's white," he said to his mounted companion.

"I'll be darned," the man said.

"You been livin' with Indians, ma'am?" he asked very politely, taking off his hat to reveal his matted-down hair that had obviously been cut along the lines of someone's mixing bowl.

Sara nodded her head. Little Bird woke up and sprang to an alert sitting position.

The moustache lifted Sara up gently by the elbow that was not splinted and said, "Well, you're all right now, ma'am. We'll take you on with us. You'll be all right."

He spoke as though she was very fragile. She rose calmly and brushed herself off. He kicked dirt into what was left of the fire and put Sara up on his horse. He meant for her to ride sidesaddle, but she put her leg over and waited. He exchanged a glance of conspiratorial pity with his cohort and got up in front of her. Little Bird stood at the side of the other horse until that man gave her a lift up. The horses shifted to get used to the new weight, and their leather paraphernalia squeaked.

"These horses smell good," Sara said in Apache to Little Bird.

"I'll be darned," the soldier with the glasses said again. And they rode off to Fort Union.

It took them five days to get there, and the two men

gave up asking questions. Sara and Little Bird just
talked between themselves, and Sara only gave yes or
no responses to the men, or she shrugged. The soldiers
exchanged glances to indicate that they both understood
something: the white woman had probably been driven
crazy by the savages and the terrible things they had
done to her, unspeakable things, things that the two soldiers wished they'd gotten to watch.

Fort Union was a long, low structure that made the
desert look ugly. It pointed out the worst aspects of bar-
renness and dirt.

"I have been with the Indians for about three
months," Sara told the commanding officer who
combed the back hairs on his head forward over his
bald spot and glued them there with hair oil. He had a
freckled face that made him seem more innocent than
he was.

He told his aide to get the doctor and then he offered
Sara a seat. He hid his emotions so thoroughly that he
couldn't lay his hands on any for the occasion. He acted
as he always did, professional and courteous with an air
of no nonsense.

"Are there family you wish to contact?"

"I would like to write to my parents in Virginia,"
Sara said.

The man looked at Little Bird.

The women were sent to the laundresses' quarters,
two mud rooms that faced the courtyard in which several tubs of laundry were soaking. Two Irish women
were sitting on the ground watching their children playing. A Mexican woman was hanging long johns out on
a line and a small cigar dangled out of her mouth.

Later on, a Dr. Robert Constantine looked in on Sara.
He asked her to come to his office and submit to a
physical exam. Little Bird followed. She went with Sara

like a shadow. When Sara spoke to her in Apache, the old doctor raised his sparse eyebrows at her.

"Now I don't mean any disrespect, Mrs. Willoughby," the doctor said, "but you've been through quite an ordeal and I want to make sure you're all right. That's all." He patted her knee and added, "Besides, I'm real tickled to have a patient who isn't inebriated or moldy." He went on speaking to her congenially as he tended to her arm, resplinting it under Little Bird's narrowed gaze. He listened to Sara's heart and looked at her skin and scalp. He had had many years of putting people at ease. He had a nice head of white, wavy hair and a directness of manner that showed he had no illusions about life or his status. He was an army doctor, after all, a man who should have been retired, but who couldn't stand the attention of widows. He had come out west where, in the company of soldiers, he could live like a monk and read poetry.

"I haven't had my monthly bleeding since before I was taken in with Little Bird's people," Sara told him.

The doctor was shocked by her bluntness and felt that he had to cover it up for her.

"You know," he said, looking up at the ceiling thoughtfully, "when I first came here, I thought I'd be patchin' up wounds all the time, seein' men comin' through that door with arrows stuck all through 'em. But you know what I treat most of the time? I treat diseases that come from nothin' more heroic than disreputable livin'. Why if I've treated one man wounded in battle, I've treated twenty with prostitutes' diseases and twenty more who can't get their hands off a liquor bottle." He looked toward Little Bird who sat stubbornly in the corner like a guard dog. "I don't mean to offend you, Mrs. Willoughby, and you've got nothin' to fear from these boys. They're just that—boys, away from home and scared. Why they're scared of Indians and at the same time crazy from just sittin' around."

"I think that I may be expecting," Sara said. "I can't say for certain, since I haven't had my monthly bleeding for so long and since I could only have been in such a condition for a short time. But I feel that I might be expecting."

"Oh, my," he said, "my, my, my. Could this be your poor husband's child, Mrs. Willoughby?"

"No. He's dead. He's been dead since the middle of fall."

"Well, you know, women often get all out of whack when they go through hardship. It could be that you've just shut down for a while, Mrs. Willoughby."

He shook his head. Then, washing his hands in a bowl of water he said to her in a whisper, "I can do something for you to make sure that there is no child."

At first Sara didn't know what he meant. Then she figured it out and shook her head.

"All right, all right," he said. "Could be you've got nothin' to worry about anyway. You goin' back to your family?"

"I don't know," Sara said. "I'm wanting to write to them."

"Mail's not too reliable what with the war goin' on." He patted her again and said, "But you'll be all right. You need anything, you come to me."

Outside, Sara told Little Bird that they were going to wait there for any sign of Broken Nose and Most Important Man. When the men came to attack the fort they would be waiting for them. Then they would ride away with them.

"I mean to take Broken Nose home with me," Sara said. "Back to Virginia, and you and Most Important Man can come, too."

But Little Bird didn't think that Broken Nose and Most Important Man would go somewhere where they weren't warriors. She didn't say this to Sara, though.

They worked with the laundresses, the two Irish women who had three children between them, and the Mexican woman married to the man who took care of the fort's sheep. The Irish women seemed to share the children and it wasn't clear whose were whose, or who, among the soldiers who hung around the washtubs, were the fathers. One of these laundresses was a red-headed woman named Sady, who had had all her front teeth broken in half in what she referred to as "The Calamity," an incident in her past that was never fully explained. The other Irish woman was named Mary and had blue eyes and black hair. She was very fat and religious. The Mexican woman told Sara to stay away from these girls whose morals, she said, were "akin to the morals of coyotes." This woman, whom everyone knew as Señora Martinez, had as her vice the constant smoking of dark cigarettes, the ashes of which dropped into the soapy water of the tubs.

The Irish women made fun of the way Sara was dressed and the way she talked to Little Bird. They called Little Bird Sara's shadow because she went everywhere Sara went. Little Bird went with Sara to get water from the springs, about a half mile away from the fort, where they left signs for Broken Nose and Most Important Man, signs in the broken branches of bushes and in marks scratched into rocks. Because of her respect for Sara, Little Bird didn't tell her that she knew all this was futile. She had also had the dream in which she saw the men wearing black cloths over their faces, and she knew what this meant.

The officers' wives, three women who liked to think of people as being less fortunate than themselves, donated a pair of black, lace-up shoes and a dark green dress to Sara. One of them offered Sara a silver hair clasp, but Sara laughed and said, "No, I don't think so."

Several of the soldiers wanted Sara to marry them, even after she started showing. Little Bird wanted to slit the throats of these soldiers. She wanted to kill them because they had liked killing her people. They didn't understand the terrible things that they had done.

Sara told Little Bird not to worry because soon they would be gone. At night, all Sara could think about was being gone because, in the dark, images crept up on her like thieves. She kept seeing people transformed into fallen things, sad pieces of expectations that broke off the world and dried up. She kept thinking about the people who'd made plans, who'd had notions about what baskets they were going to repair, who'd looked up and noticed the weather, who'd figured on some kind of weather coming toward them, and then had never felt it. Suddenly transformed, suddenly not there. It can happen so fast. Death is such a trick, such an incredible magic trick. It makes no sense; it does not operate according to logic.

They waited. They waited for Broken Nose, and when the waiting for him seemed foolish and sad, they waited for the child to be born. Sara sewed for the officers' wives whose seamstresses got married to soldiers as soon as possible and moved to Santa Fe. The officers' wives were always complaining that they couldn't keep good help. They found themselves at the mercy of women like Sady, Irish women and Hispanic women. It was a relief to them to have Sara there. She seemed like someone who could appreciate their superiority, who'd had just enough of it herself to appreciate it when she saw it.

Sara sewed quietly. She didn't say anything to dispel

anyone's notions about her—that she was snooty, that she was humble, that she was crazy.

When she was about to have her baby, Sara got a letter from her father. Just seeing his handwriting made her run to the outhouse. She sat there, fearing she'd drop the baby with everything else that came out, then she stepped out and read the letter.

> Sara,
> i was glad to git yer letter what said you were alive things have been terrible here and seein as how you dont have a husband to tend to I want you to come home where you belong your mother died of a bad coffin and your sisters run off to Richmond with a salesman who is near my age all the yankee soljers bot my animals and my crops for hardly nuthin and sum of the boys you no been killed
> > your father
> > Joseph Franklin

The letter was dated three months before. All Sara cared about was that her mother was dead. She sank down on the ground where Little Bird found her and thought that she had gone into labor. She took her back to their room and laid her on the cot where Sara stared up at a spider's web and wept with her mouth open and wailing. Little Bird went to work on hanging a rope from the center beam that Sara could hold on to while squatting on the ground to give birth. She was massaging Sara's back when Dr. Constantine came in and pushed her aside. They had quite a fight, Little Bird pushing back and telling him things in Apache, until Sara pulled herself together enough to tell her it was all right.

"Is it your time, Sara?" the old man asked gently.

"No," she said. "It's my mother. I've just learned that she's dead. She's dead. She's gone. My mother is gone forever."

Dr. Constantine helped Sara to his office where he put her on the cot. Little Bird insisted on coming. She was furious that her arrangements for the birth were being left behind. The doctor brought each woman a bowl of beans and bread. Little Bird sat with Sara all night, while the doctor snored in his chair. Sara told her about her mother, about what a good woman she'd been and how she'd pressed flowers in the pages of Sara's schoolbooks, because the mother had known that it was important to remind the little girl of beautiful things that anyone could see who looked for them. How her mother took her to see plays when Mr. Franklin was away on farm business. Little Bird nodded. She talked about her own disappointment in life. They both wondered together how people got so lost.

In the moments when she wasn't weeping, Sara fiddled with the shell that Broken Nose had given her. She still wore it around her neck.

"Are there women among your people who do it with men just to get food or horses?" she asked Little Bird, because there was no word for whore in Apache.

"A woman has sex with a man because it gives him pleasure," Little Bird said. "And then the man gives the woman a gift, to show that he is grateful. A good man also gives the woman pleasure. It is a source of pride to be able to give a woman pleasure."

This put thoughts into both of their heads that made Little Bird and Sara stop talking. Then they both got a few hours of sleep. But Sara woke up weeping to remember the amazing fact that her mother was dead. She went into labor when she tried to stand up and go behind the screen to use the chamber pot. It scared her to see the amount of liquid that poured out of her and she was mortified and apologetic to the doctor about it, not having any clue that this was a normal part of labor until Little Bird told her. Little Bird and the doctor had another tussle concerning the birthing process; Little Bird wanted Sara to squat on the floor while she massaged her belly. Finally, Constantine had the Indian woman fuming in a corner while Sara yelled out a nine-pound baby girl. She named the dark-skinned, black-haired girl Roberta, after the doctor.

"So much hair," was the first thing Sara cooed to her baby.

Even the officers' wives brought things for the baby who thrived as none of theirs had. No one mentioned the child's father.

"You are my little girl, my little Roberta," Sara said to the baby. She felt transformed, as though she would never be the same, as though this baby was a light that shone on her and changed the way everything looked. Sara stroked the underside of the baby's hand, stretching out the long, tan fingers and letting them curl again around her own finger. The child was strong.

"You don't belong in Roanoke," Sara said to her, smiling as though she'd made a good joke. "No, no, little Roberta does not belong in Roanoke, Virginia, does she? No, no, no."

Little Bird walked to the springs. It was how she got off alone to say her prayers, to think about dead people. The laundresses liked that she fetched their water. They didn't like to walk out into the desert. They wanted to sit around and tell stories about soldiers' kisses, soldiers getting venereal diseases, officers' wives' new clothes, the prospect of getting whiskey to drink on Sundays when they refused to do one lick of work. They liked to listen to Señora Martinez warn them about messing around with soldiers. The Irish women laughed at her and teased her about the things she did with her husband.

This way of life smelled bad to Little Bird. It was a terrible, unnatural punishment to be alone without one's people in this hell, with the enemies and their women. Sometimes she looked at the pale soldiers and wondered if they said any prayers when they killed Apaches, when they killed children. Where were their grandfathers? Where were their uncles? Why did they have to be alone like her? Why did so many white-eyes choose to be alone?

Little Bird told Life Giver that she had no grandfather, no father, no husband, no home to go to anymore. Didn't he know this? Had he known such a thing was going to happen? She might as well be a white-eye for all her aloneness. Little Bird leaned on the rock next to the spring and asked Life Giver why. She asked aloud, dropping the buckets and hitting herself on the chest, "Why am I alone? Where are my people? Where is my husband?" And then she called out the names of people; some of them she knew were dead, but she called their names out anyway, because nothing could be as ghoulish as this exile. She sank to the ground, calling out things, and twisting herself up in her own braids. Then she asked Life Giver to take her, too; she didn't want to live like these soldiers and these red-armed women who wandered like orphans on land they didn't love.

But Life Giver left Little Bird there. She waited, but she stayed alive. She could hear sounds under the ground where her ear was pressed. There was water gurgling under there, in a secret place where a whole other world existed, a world where voices that sounded like water laughed at the craziness that went on right over their heads. The voices kept speaking, consoling, chiding Little Bird, singing to her. The voices told Little Bird to think of something else to do besides dying.

XXVIII

When the supply wagon went to Santa Fe to take the mail and pick up some supplies, Sara and Little Bird rode in the back. Sara leaned up against the bag of letters and held Roberta all wrapped up in a yellow blanket that one of the officers' wives had given her. She had nineteen dollars and twenty cents in her pocket. Little Bird sat up straight, holding her knees and looking at what they were leaving behind. About two hours away from the fort, the quartermaster, a man named Curtis, stopped the wagon on the side of the road to eat his lunch. They were on the edge of the mountains and the three ate apples and bread while they looked at the waves of shimmering yellow that the wind made when it blew through the aspen trees. The sky was a solid blue.

Sara draped the white shawl she wore over her shoulder and nursed the baby. When Curtis went into the trees to relieve himself the women struck up a slow conversation.

"Men betray their hearts," Sara said to Little Bird. The Apache woman kept looking out at the trees, but Sara could feel how intently the woman listened, as she always did without looking at who was speaking.

"I think of him every day. And sometimes I am angry. Men give their hearts to women when they are naked together and then pretend that other things are more important. This is a form of lying, but I think they lie to themselves about this. A man, even the good one that I think of often, is afraid of his heart, though he considers what he does to be bravery."

Little Bird picked up one of her braids and combed through the end of it with her fingers. Sara noticed how clean Little Bird's hands were, clean and tan colored with smooth, white nails.

"The women among my people laugh about this. We laugh at men for saying they are the brave ones and then cowering in the face of their own thoughts. But we don't tell them why we laugh. They probably already know."

"Men are strange like this, both whites and Superior People," Sara said.

Little Bird flipped her braid behind her shoulder and sighed. "I am glad to be away from the soldiers. They are my enemies." Then she laughed at something she didn't share with Sara.

Sara buttoned up her dress. The two women watched Curtis coming back to the wagon. His big belly hung over his belt.

"White men are afraid of women," Little Bird said.

Sara stared at her. Curtis looked sternly at them. He didn't like to hear that Apache chattering. When he got in the wagon it dipped and creaked.

"White men don't want a woman to give them pleasure. They want to steal it from her. They want to steal a woman's power. I can see this. And so the women pretend that they have no power."

Curtis yelled at the horses to "hi-yon," and the two women were jerked roughly. Sara held Roberta tightly and Little Bird helped arrange the blanket around the baby. Then there was too much noise to talk.

When they got to where they were going, Curtis helped Sara get out of the wagon with Roberta in her arms. Little Bird jumped off by herself and dragged the big beige-and-pink carpet bag out of the wagon. They were in the plaza in Santa Fe and two dark men walked by them. These men had blankets over their shoulders and were speaking in Spanish. It occurred to Sara that these were the same two men who had walked by about a year ago when she and Reverend Willoughby had first come to Santa Fe. This thought made her stomach flutter. The men passed by her and Little Bird, smiling and nodding.

"It's this way," Sara said, leading Little Bird to a door on the plaza.

Little Bird followed, looking down so that she couldn't directly see the bulky women sitting along the plaza selling corn and squash—Pueblo women who didn't know a good horse when they saw one.

Sara adjusted Roberta in her arms. The baby was getting fussy. Undoubtedly her diapers were messy and she was hungry. Then Sara knocked on the door. She exchanged a look with Little Bird. It was a look that said they were going to have to be alert; they were going to have to go forward into this and keep their eyes open.

Maria, not Consuela, opened the door. Sara was not prepared to see Maria so soon. She thought she'd have Consuela first, as a way of easing into the Barkstones.

Maria rustled in her shiny brown dress and she still smelled like rose water. Her little heart-shaped mouth was slightly parted as she focused not on Sara but on the Indian woman standing in her doorway.

"Señora Barkstone," Sara said, "it is me, Sara Willoughby. Edmund Willoughby's wife."

"Oh. Oh, goodness yes!" Maria stepped backward as

though to view a controversial painting. "My goodness. Yes. And a baby! Is this your baby?"

"Yes," Sara said. Roberta started crying. "And this is my friend. May we come in? I have just gotten off the wagon and my little girl needs to be attended to."

"Oh, yes, yes." Maria stepped back more. She was very unsure of the situation, but let them in because graciousness was always her first response.

She led her visitors into the parlor. It looked the same as when Sara had last seen it, all European and delicate.

Roberta's crying gave them something to busy themselves about. Maria watched the two women with amazement as they spoke to each other in a language she had never heard before. Sara changed the baby there, kneeling on the floor with Roberta's behind exposed on the settee. She gave the soiled cloth to Maria who took it out somewhere and came back with three small glasses of sherry on a silver tray.

"I think we will need this," Maria said, her graciousness tinged with frankness now.

Little Bird took a taste of the stuff and put the glass down. The three sat down at the same time, Sara and Little Bird on the settee and Maria on a wing-backed, upholstered chair facing them. Maria and Sara sipped their drinks and looked at each other over the rims of their glasses. Little Bird sat like the white women with her knees together. She had gotten used to chairs at the fort.

"Many things have happened to you I am thinking," Maria said in a soft voice.

"Did you know that Reverend Willoughby was killed?" Sara said. She couldn't help getting red in the face from nervousness when she said it.

"Yes. Yes we heard that. My husband was called by the governor about some trouble at the Osuna church.

And then we heard a few months ago, I think, that your husband and your wagon had been found." She looked at the baby, and Sara could see her calculating. And then Maria added, "You poor thing."

In Apache Sara said to Little Bird, "She is wondering who has been making children with me."

"And so, you are alive. We had been wondering . . . and praying."

"Where is Reverend Barkstone?" Sara asked.

"He is in the study and I have told him that you are here and that we are to be alone for a while."

Sara put the shawl over her shoulder and undid the top of her dress. As she was nursing the baby, Maria leaned forward and said, "Are you going back to your family, in the East? Oh, but the war. It is not a good time, is it?"

"No," Sara said. "We are looking for somewhere to stay. I've been sewing for ladies at the fort. I do good work, and I have a letter from one of the officers' wives. I made the dress that I'm wearing." It was black and had a pleated bodice.

"It is beautiful. There are many women here from the East who will be wanting dresses such as that. And when the war is over there will be more people coming. That is what Señor Barkstone says. Business is not good for us now. The war is a bad thing. But when it is over, people will come here again. They are talking of building a railroad here."

"I have a little money. I have enough to stay in a boardinghouse for a while, and I thought you could tell me where there is a boardinghouse and rooms to let."

"There are two places that are good. There is a Mrs. Offenbach who lets rooms. She lives just a few houses behind the plaza. And, let me see. . . ."

"Where is your boy?" Sara asked.

Maria smiled widely. "Oh, my boy is with Consuela. They are out in the courtyard. Come, you must see him. He is a big boy! He is walking and he is so big and healthy. Well, we will go when the baby is done." There was still an awkwardness in her voice about the baby.

All three women looked at the veiled form of the infant at Sara's breast.

"It was very hot this summer, wasn't it?" Maria said, clucking her tongue and leaning farther forward, toward the baby. "Oh, you must have been so uncomfortable with being heavy and in such a hot summer."

Sara laughed a little and nodded. A mother will never lack for conversation with another mother.

"She was nine pounds when she was born. The doctor got the scales from the quartermaster to weigh her."

Little Bird stood up and walked around the room, looking closely at the portraits that hung on the wall.

"I am thinking," Maria said, "that there is a problem."

Sara looked up at her.

"Well, you see I am thinking that this Mrs. Offenbach does not let Indians stay in her rooms, and that . . . well, it will be difficult. . . ." Maria looked distraught.

"I am not looking to stay in your chicken house again, Señora Barkstone. I haven't come to ask anything of you but your advice. Perhaps this Mrs. Offenbach can be persuaded. . . ."

The baby had fallen asleep. Sara buttoned herself up.

"I want to speak to Reverend Barkstone before I go," Sara said.

Maria stood up.

"Yes, yes, of course. You can go into his study. It is all right."

Sara transferred the baby to Little Bird and said to

her in Apache, "Stay here. Don't let her think you are trying to steal anything."

"I don't need to steal anything from this place. What am I going to do, put one of those ugly pictures under my shirt?" She nodded toward the flat-looking portraits of men and women dressed in stiff, black-and-white clothing.

"I will be back soon," Sara said.

As it had happened a year before, Maria knocked on the study door and then left as Sara went in. And there was Reverend Barkstone, only this time he wasn't standing by the window. He had changed. Something mysterious had happened to him that made Sara feel uneasy about being in the same room. She didn't feel danger from him, but from whatever had gotten him, the way people feel when they visit a dying person in a stuffy room.

Barkstone was sitting behind his desk. This was in itself odd because there was nothing in front of him—no papers, no books, just the polished, brown wood. Yet he had a tired expression on his face as though he'd been working on something for a long time.

He was almost twice the size he had been before. He had gotten so obese that his face was wider than it was long, making him look like he was being slowly mashed down by an invisible hand. He didn't stand up when Sara came in. Sara had the impression that he couldn't stand up, that he always sat behind that desk. That he'd been sitting there when the sun went down and all through the night while the house was creaking.

"You have been through a great deal, Mrs. Willoughby," he said. "Will you be selling your story to some eastern newspaper?"

"I haven't considered that yet, Reverend Barkstone,"

Sara said, "but if I did I should warn you to keep that edition out of your house."

Reverend Barkstone didn't flinch. He didn't even sweat. He just sighed deeply. When he did, it seemed as if he might explode out of his clothes, spewing his soft flesh all over the room.

"I wanted to give you your money back. I believe I owe you three dollars."

Barkstone nodded and the folds of skin under his neck bobbed up and down. "All right. All right."

Sara's hand dove into her pocket and took out four bills, neatly folded. She straightened them out and pressed each one onto the smooth, empty desktop. Barkstone just stared at them and nodded, "All right," he said again.

"There's your three dollars and the interest owed."

He reached out his hand and Sara saw that one of his fingers was gone. He had only four fingers on his right hand. There was a nub between his thumb and middle finger.

Barkstone looked at his hand and then at Sara. He laughed in one syllable, like a hiccough.

"My wife cut my finger off. Cut it right off and it fell out of her onto the floor." He stared at Sara.

Maria and Little Bird were sitting next to each other on the settee. Maria was touching the baby's hair. She didn't look up when Sara came in. She didn't want to see the look in Sara's eyes after seeing her husband.

"I have a thing to tell you," Maria said. "It is silly for you to be renting a room when I know of a place you can use. You can go there without pay. There is a little house just half a mile from here, by the river. I know it because my brother and his wife were living there. There are only two rooms, you see, and an old stove, but there is no one there. I think you could stay there. I think that is a good plan."

"I can pay you. I have fifteen dollars," Sara said.

Maria said, "No, no. It will be good for you to be there. It is my father's land and we don't want bad people to stay there. You go, you and the Indian. It will be a good place for the baby. Sí?"

Sara spoke to Little Bird. "She is saying that there is a house we can stay in."

"I have written to my brother in Virginia," she said to Maria. "I have told him that when the war is over and when I have saved enough money I will send for him to come live with me. I told him to write to me here, to send the letter to you. I hope that I haven't taken liberties, but besides the fort there is no one else that I know."

"Of course, of course," Maria said. And she stood up, because she wanted Sara and her baby and the Indian woman to leave.

After they got directions to the house, Little Bird and Sara walked out onto the plaza. For a moment they stood there with the carpet bag and the baby and stared at the place that was now colored pink in the moments just before darkness. It was very quiet, and the Indian women and their wares were gone.

"This place has a bad feeling," Little Bird said. "This place is sad about what is coming and can't do anything about it."

"Those people are strange. They are very strange."

"I am hungry for a good piece of meat," Little Bird said.

"We need to go to a place to get food, to get supplies," Sara said and she pantomimed paying money and getting something back.

"I want some meat," Little Bird said. "Get me something to eat. That drink has made my mouth taste bad. I am hungry for good meat."

Then Little Bird put her hand into the waist of her skirt and brought out a piece of paper money. It was a ten-dollar bill.

"Here," she said, trying not to laugh at the look on Sara's face. "Get me something good to eat. Get some good meat." Then she burst out laughing and her laughter made the sun finally go down.

XXIX

Naked, Sara stood in the small river. In Roanoke it would have been called a creek. Little Bird watched her and hung white sheets on the line. When the spring wind blew, it twirled the sheets around Little Bird and Sara thought of her mother, hanging up sheets in Roanoke, Virginia, in another time. But Little Bird wasn't like anyone in Roanoke, Virginia. She was like a woman on a spirit journey, tangled in the clouds, played with by the wind.

Sara was holding Roberta, who laughed and laughed every time her mother dipped down into the water. Sometimes she took her mother's nipple, now so tantalizingly bare and unimpeded, and gave it a good squeeze in her little fist.

"Hey!" Sara said, and smacked the baby's hand softly. But Roberta laughed.

Sara placed her mouth right on the baby's cheek to tell her things, to say phrases over and over the way mothers do.

"Such a good baby. Roberta's such a good baby. Yes you are a good baby."

When she was dressed again, Sara went into the house. Little Bird wasn't around. The sheets flapped and snapped in the wind and Sara wondered if she had finally gotten swallowed by them. Every time Little

Bird was not around, Sara wondered. They had a horse now, a white-and-grey mare who stood switching her tail and stamping her foot. She was called Boobah because that was exactly what Roberta said when she first saw the big animal. Sara always checked to see if the horse was still there when Little Bird wasn't around. Boobah was still tied to the fence in the back. It was one part of a fence, actually. Two of the sides had been blown over long ago. Now it just served as a hitching post.

Sara put Roberta down on a small rug that covered the dirt floor. There was a horseshoe there that Roberta liked to try to drop on lizards that skittered by her. It was a game she and the lizards understood. So far, no one had gotten hurt. Roberta could hardly lift the horseshoe and her coordination was still infantile. The lizards understood this; it was their intention to motivate the child to become skilled and then duck out just at the time when her aim was good. Neither Sara nor Little Bird realized the private deals that were already being made with the world by Roberta. The baby also had an old leather shoe that she chewed on. This was one of the many discarded items that Sara and Little Bird had found in the house when they first got there. Sara remembered how Little Bird's people gave their babies pieces of leather to chew when they were teething, so she boiled the shoe and let Roberta clamp her gums on it. The baby couldn't pick the shoe up; she had to bend over to it and gum the edges.

Sara sat down on the bench by the table to do some sewing in the last of the daylight. She picked up a piece of red velvet out of which she was making a little jacket for Maria. Then she heard some people walking around outside. She looked out the back window and saw four Indians, long-haired men in shirts and trousers with high moccasins on. Their dark faces were still as they looked around and pointed with their heads at things. They stopped and examined the horse.

Like a white woman, Sara was afraid. She picked Roberta up and went into the other room where there was a bed, a cradle, and a pile of blanket-covered leaves where Little Bird slept. Sara stood there holding Roberta, wondering what to do. Maybe the men would just steal the horse and leave.

Then Little Bird came in, suddenly appeared as though she'd always been there, as part of the wall or something, and just stepped up.

"It's them," she said.

The men walked into the house, through the black doorway, and Little Bird casually got some bread and made some coffee. Sara still stood in the doorway between rooms, holding Roberta and staring at them. There weren't any chairs for them all to sit on, so they sat against the wall on the dirt floor. Finally Sara started doing something. She made up some hot mush while holding Roberta on her hip. Roberta sat in her mother's lap at the table and had the mush spooned into her mouth. The four men laughed because the stuff slid down Roberta's face. When they laughed, Roberta grinned and more mush seeped out of her mouth. But no one said anything. They sat and they ate.

In all this heavy silence Roberta fell asleep and Little Bird put her in her cradle in the next room. It got dark, and the fire in the stove threw a quiet light over everything. In that light Sara looked at their faces. Broken Nose was not there, and though she'd felt that this was so, knowing it made her sigh and look back at the fire. One of the men was Eats Fish, another Kills Bucks. There was also Asks Questions, Most Important Man's son. Little Bird hardly recognized him because half of his nose was missing and he had a scar that ran from between his eyes to his upper lip. The fourth man was a stranger, someone from another settlement. Sara wanted to ask questions, but she didn't want to know the answers, so she kept quiet. They all sat together, not saying a word, looking into the fire. In the dark, when the fire went out, someone lit a cigarette. It was made of store-bought tobacco and white, store-bought rolling paper. Sara could see this when the match was struck. Following the little orange light and its trails, Sara fell asleep with her head on the table. When she woke up it was morning and there was no one but her in the room.

Sara clutched the throat of her dress. She ran into the bedroom and saw Roberta still sleeping, but no Little Bird. She ran outside, her wild hair flying all around her crazy head. The sun was coming up over the mountains and the ground was freshly yellow. Chickens tiptoed jerkily around under the big cottonwoods.

Back in the house, Sara saw the money on the table. There were at least fifteen ten dollar bills, enough to send for Timothy, enough for that and more. The money sat there on the table, and Sara knew that it was all that Little Bird had had, that where Little Bird was going she wouldn't need it, wouldn't want it. Little Bird had relieved herself of a burden and intended never to touch white man's money again.

Sara left the money there and got on her bed. She heard Roberta stirring in the cradle.

"The railroad is coming," was all that she could think. That phrase she'd heard from Maria just went around and around in her head. "The railroad is coming." Then she said aloud, "They're gone, all gone. They've gone back under the earth, and the railroad will rumble over their heads."

She saw it all happening. She saw the desert change;

she saw the First Presbyterian Church of Roanoke sitting in the middle of the desert with trees and vines popping up around it, choking the mesas, hiding the sky. She saw herself putting her ear to the ground, listening for them under there and hearing the train coming, shaking the earth like a drunk man shaking the shoulders of his wife.

"They're gone," she said again and she saw that Cheyenne woman on her horse, the one she'd seen somewhere in the flat, grassy middle of the country when she was a part of that snaky wagon train. Sara could see that Cheyenne woman sitting on the horse staring at her with all the dignity and arrogance of a queen. And Sara wondered why whites pretended that these people aren't here, haven't always been here.

Now, maybe that woman was dead, like Walks Like A Buffalo and Many Visions and Long Skirt and all those flush-cheeked boys in grey and blue woolen uniforms, all those boys lying dead in Virginia meadows.

There were dead people lying all over the land.

Roberta rustled around and then burped and dozed again.

The sun made a carpet of yellow just outside the bedroom doorway. Sara stared at it and then saw a man's feet step into that light. They were big feet, covered in doehide, high moccasins. Sara propped herself up on her elbow and looked at him.

He wasn't wearing the mask. But his face was painted black and white. He had long black hair that reached all the way to his waist. His eyes, in the midst of the black paint, were very white.

"Are you going to take me with you?" Sara asked.

When he walked he rattled softly. He sat down on the edge of the bed and touched Sara's face.

Sara sank back down, closing her eyes.

"It's time to rest now," he said. "Do you want me to stay with you?"

"Yes," she said, "yes."